Breaking Bailey

Breaking Bailey

Anonymous

Simon Pulse
New York London Toronto Sydney New Delhi

WW SIMON PULSE

An imprint of Simon & Schuster Children's Publishing Division

1230 Avenue of the Americas, New York, New York 10020

First Simon Pulse hardcover edition June 2019

Text copyright © 2019 by Simon & Schuster, Inc.

Jacket photographs copyright © 2019 by Thinkstock/Yasinemir

Also available in a Simon Pulse paperback edition

All rights reserved, including the right of reproduction in whole or in part in any form.

SIMON PULSE and colophon are registered trademarks of Simon & Schuster, Inc.

For information about special discounts for bulk purchases, please contact

Simon & Schuster Special Sales at 1-866-506-1949 or business@simonandschuster.com.

The Simon & Schuster Speakers Bureau can bring authors to your live event.

For more information or to book an event contact the Simon & Schuster Speakers Bureau

at 1-866-248-3049 or visit our website at www.simonspeakers.com.

Jacket designed by Tiara Iandiorio

The text of this book was set in Adobe Caslon Pro.

Manufactured in the United States of America

10 9 8 7 6 5 4 3 2 1

Library of Congress Cataloging-in-Publication Data

Title: Breaking Bailey / by Anonymous.

Description: First Simon Pulse paperback edition. | New York : Simon Pulse, 2019. |

Summary: Sent to a fancy boarding school by her stepmother, a prominent attorney, Bailey keeps a journal chronicling her involvement in a "Science Club" that makes and sells crystal meth.

Identifiers: LCCN 2018039720 (print) | LCCN 2018046846 (eBook) |

ISBN 9781534433083 (hardcover) | ISBN 9781534433090 (pbk) |

ISBN 9781534433106 (eBook)

Subjects: | CYAC: Drug traffic—Fiction. | Substance abuse—Fiction. |

Boarding schools—Fiction. | Schools—Fiction. | Diaries—Fiction.

Classification: LCC PZ7.1 (eBook) | LCC PZ7.1 .B751547 2019 (print) |

DDC [Fic]—dc23

LC record available at https://lccn.loc.gov/2018039720

September 3

Dear Diary,

Does anyone actually say that anymore? Maybe some fifth-grade girls. The type who have unicorn-and-rainbow diaries with easily picked locks and "I heart Billy" drawn on every page. This one doesn't have unicorns, which is surprising since it's from Dad. He probably thinks I still play with Barbies. It's not that he doesn't care about me. Just more like he doesn't notice me anymore. He hasn't since he started dating Isa. Truthfully, he hasn't really noticed me since Mom died, but I can't blame him for that. The past couple of years have been a giant blob of suck. At least Dad has Isa, though. I guess one of us should have someone.

Isa. That stupid name makes me want to scream. I almost poked through the page with my pen writing it. Any normal person would shorten Isabelle to Belle, or even Isy, if they wanted to be cute. But Isa? EEEESUHHHH. God. Most Pretentious Nicknames for a thousand, Alex.

But she's the reason I'm here, at Prescott Academy, where graduation nearly guarantees you a spot in an Ivy League. And she's the reason Bex gets to go to the Campbell School, which means she'll get into Prescott, too, when she's old enough. Dad can't afford fancy private schools, but Isa the Bulldog Lawyer can. So I guess I can put up with a stepmother when I'm required to come home. Holidays already suck without Mom, and the same fake smile hides both grief and irritation.

Bex hugged me so tight before they left. She's scared to go to a new school, and she's never been away from home before. She's never been away from *me*. That's going to be hard. As cool as it's going to be on my own here, what am I gonna do without Bex's hugs? Her nonstop chatter? Her—

Sorry. My roommate showed up. Her name is Emily. She seems cool, and she didn't bring anything annoying like wind chimes or beaded curtains, but she did bring chocolate. :) Off to the dining hall for dinner.

September 4

Okay, so I think I'll try to write in this thing every night before I go to sleep. I don't know why. I've never really kept a diary before, but . . . I don't know. I guess it's nice that Dad got something for me. And it will be fun to document what it's like to go to Prescott Academy. Maybe years from now, when I'm a famous chemist, I'll use it for reference when I write my memoirs. But anyway . . . about that documentation. Here I go. . . .

Today was just so weird. Prescott isn't just a different school, it's a different planet. I got to my first class, English, and sat at an empty desk. Everyone around me was talking because they all know one another, but it wasn't like home. At home, if someone asked how your summer was, you'd say it was lame or talk about a summer job or something. These Prescott kids . . . It was all "Oh, Paris is just so lovely in the summertime!" and "Daddy's new yacht couldn't even fit at the dock in the Hamptons" and "I tried amazing caviar on solid gold plates!"

Okay, it wasn't that bad, but it wasn't much better. These are the kinds of kids who clearly never had to wonder IF they'd ever get a car, just when. Oh, and also, since we all have to wear the same uniform, apparently the trend is to show off the only things that we can individualize: makeup, jewelry, and what brand of flats you wear. Seriously. I'm guessing my Payless fake leather won't get me into the upper echelon at Prescott. I suppose I could ask Isa for better flats, but . . . honestly, I'd rather die than feel like I owe Isa anything.

Thank God Emily and I had calculus and civics together, and we found each other at lunch so I didn't have to eat by myself. She told me last night that she's a scholarship student. That's the only way her parents can afford this place. She begged me not to tell anyone, but she didn't have to. I get it. I told her about my dad and Isa. I didn't mention Mom.

Emily wants to be a writer. Like movie scripts and stuff. She's pretty quiet, but if you get her talking about movies, she could go for days.

That's another thing that's different about the kids here.

They're really focused on the future. Everyone seems super smart and ambitious, and they take classes seriously. Back home, classes were just sort of a necessary evil until summer. And they certainly weren't supposed to be interesting. Here, even my least favorite classes are going to be interesting and challenging.

Speaking of favorite classes . . . There's a guy in my chemistry class. His name is Drew. Definitely not a scholarship student. His dad owns a restaurant chain or something—at least that's what Emily said. Anyway, he's kind of cute. Preppy, but his hair does this floppy thing that's truly adorable. I saw him later at lunch, too, sitting with a very serious-looking bunch of people. Serious but glamorous. They were just sitting at a dining hall table together, but they might as well have been posing for a *Vanity Fair* cover. The girl had the prettiest, thickest black hair and dark red lipstick. She had large black rhinestones on her flats. At least I think they were rhinestones. For all I know they could have been real gems from Tiffany. It wouldn't surprise me in this place.

I'm going to have to buy some better shoes.

September 5

Day two at Prescott was just as weird as the first, made even weirder when Drew actually spoke to me about halfway through chemistry.

Drew: Bailey, right?

(I nodded dumbly, like I'd forgotten the
English language.)

Drew: You seem like you really know this stuff.

Me: Um. Yeah. There was a really good
chemistry teacher at my old school. I used to
do extra assignments for her. For fun.

Drew, looking amused: For fun?

Me: Well, um, yeah. I was kind of good at it,
so she let me work ahead of the class.

Then he just nodded, sat back in his desk, and locked eyes
with Dark Lipstick Girl. They looked away from each other
at the same time. He said nothing else to me, after class and
all day. But when I walked by his table of glamorous people at
lunch, he and Dark Lipstick Girl stared at me in this sort of
predatory way.

What is this? Am I the girl who accidentally stumbles upon
a group of vampires and werewolves at her school?

I asked Emily about Drew. She warned me to stay away from him while also drooling over the way his Prescott uniform sweater tightens over his chest, so . . .

September 7

Tomorrow is the first Friday here at Prescott. In other words, it's the first Friday night I've ever had without parents around. Prescott has a curfew. We have to be back in our dorms by eleven, but that doesn't mean we have to sleep. I've heard a few people talking about parties in the dorms, but no one's invited me. It's okay. Emily and I have decided we're going to stay up all night and watch movies and pig out on chocolate. I guess she wasn't invited to any parties either.

September 8

The plot thickens.

Mr. Callahan asked me to stay after chemistry class today, so the whole class I was sick to my stomach with nerves. Turns out he wanted to know about my old school back home. He said he noticed I seem to be ahead of what he's teaching at Prescott.

Ahead of a class at Prescott!

So I told him about Miss Beverly at my old school and how I'd spend a lot of days after school in the lab, doing special stuff that no one else got to do. I also told him that I want to be a chemical engineer. He laughed when I told him I hadn't even known that was a thing until Miss Beverly told me about all the jobs that use chemistry, but now it's the only thing I can see myself doing. He asked if I'd thought about college, like I haven't been dreaming about Harvard since I was three. He said he'd help all he could.

I thanked him and walked out the door, and that's when Dark Lipstick Girl grabbed my arm and dragged me into the ladies' restroom.

DLG: Bailey, right?

Huh. The same way Drew greeted me the first time. Weird. Definitely vampires.

Me: Yeah. Were you listening to me talk to Mr. Callahan?

DLG, shrugging: Not on purpose. You're pretty good at chemistry, then?

Me: I guess. I'm sorry. I didn't catch your name.

DLG: Katy. Katy Ashton. Your last name is Wells, isn't it? Are you on scholarship?

I got super uncomfortable with our conversation at that point. The assumption felt awful. Maybe it was my cheap flats? Or maybe it's just that my family doesn't summer at the same vacation spot as everyone else? Whatever. She sort of backtracked after that. She put her arm around my shoulders and started walking with me toward my next class.

Then she invited me to Science Club. Seriously? This gorgeous girl is part of something like the Science Club? Prescott isn't like my old school AT ALL.

> Katy, formerly known as DLG: It's Saturday night. Herschell Hall. That's the upperclassmen boys' dorm. Seven o'clock.

> Me: The Science Club meets in a dorm on Saturday nights?

Katy just smiled at me, all secretive and glamorous, and told me she'd see me there. Seriously. If Science Club is code for Vampire Club, I will be not be surprised. Pissed at how clichéd it would be, but not surprised.

~~September 8~~ Sorry! It's actually September 9 now!

Emily is fast asleep. I'm about to pass out too. I know it's probably lame that we stayed in and watched movies, but I had a lot of fun. She's really down-to-earth. Honestly, she seems like she could be from back home. We watched *Notting Hill*. Emily had never seen it before and seemed to love it, so maybe she won't mind watching it again sometime. It was Mom's favorite. We used to pop popcorn and put on fleece pajamas and watch romantic comedies all the time. We'd both cry at all the sad parts and some of the happy parts and tease each other about being saps. When Bex got a little older, she'd stay up late with us too. She'd always have a box of tissues ready for when Mom and I would start sobbing.

I wonder how Bex is doing. I miss her.

I really miss Mom.

September 9, later

Walking over to Herschell Hall was the most I'd really seen campus since orientation day over the summer. So far I've kept to the class buildings and Baker Hall, my own dorm. Herschell, though, is on the other side of campus, and there's a pretty pond and park in between. The leaves are starting to turn and I can tell it's going to be gorgeous here in the fall. Maybe I should start studying outside.

Katy met me at the entrance, holding the door open for me so it wouldn't lock us both out. When she told me we were going to meet in Drew's room, my stomach did a massive somersault. How is he in Science Club? I've never heard him answer a single question in chemistry. Of course, everyone here at Prescott is a genius, or at least that's what their glossy brochures try to tell you.

We walked up three flights of stairs and into a dorm room that looked a bit like mine, only it had window seats and a slanted ceiling on account of the room being on the top floor. I guess I expected the room to be gross and smelly, like frat houses in movies or something, but Drew's room was tidy and, maybe I'm mistaken, but I think it had been professionally decorated. It kind of looked like the reading room at the New York Public Library. Soft lighting, dark wood furniture, everything just a little gilded.

Drew was smoking a cigarette on one of the window seats, the window wide open, no screen. He took a big puff and then handed what was left of it to a boy who sat on the floor by his feet. And while Drew looked like he'd stepped out of a Burberry ad, the other boy was every bit the geeky kind of person I'd been hoping to meet since I got here. Like a lankier but more rugged Harry Potter, the boy took the cigarette, braced it between his lips, and stood, extending his hand to me.

He introduced himself like James Bond. "Clark, Warren Clark," he said. Crystal blue eyes locked onto mine and didn't look away, even when I did. Drew started talking about me, about how I really knew my stuff in chemistry class. He said Warren was just like me that way. That, and Warren is a scholarship student too. I told them I'm not on scholarship and they acted totally surprised until I told them that my stepmother is Isabelle Marlowe, which made Drew chuckle, and Katy said her own father had been up against Isa and lost on more than one occasion. Then Drew started talking about how Katy's father had represented his in some sort of embezzlement charge and got him out of it with just community service, and then everyone was talking about people I didn't know, places I'd never been to, and stories I wasn't a part of. Weekend trips to sunny beaches, cabins in the Berkshires, wrecking a Porsche and getting a replacement the next day. And they were funny but I felt even more out of place than ever. Even Warren has history at Prescott. It sounds like he spends a lot of time with Drew, and spends just as much money. He didn't mention having a job, but maybe he does. How else does he have that kind of money?

But at some point I noticed he was looking at me again, his blue eyes kind but intense. I met his gaze and did my best to smile back.

At no point did we talk about chemistry, or even science.

When Katy walked me back to my dorm, she hooked her arm through mine and tossed her gorgeous hair over her shoulder and told me I was welcome at the next meeting. I feel like I passed some sort of test I didn't even know I was taking. Of course I told her I'd go.

September 11

I guess I thought Katy would invite me to sit with them at lunch, but she didn't. They only nodded slightly as I passed by their table on the way to sit with Emily. Warren was wearing a beanie, which is against the uniform code, but I get the feeling that the so-called Science Club can get away with anything. I've asked a few other people about Drew. Turns out his family owns most of the neighboring town of Wiltshire, so I bet the headmaster is afraid to touch him. He flat-out put his head down and slept during chemistry today, and Mr. Callahan didn't do anything about it. And I looked out the window during civics this morning and Warren was sitting in a tree, feet and overcoat dangling, smoking a cigarette. Smoking on campus, sleeping during class, skipping classes . . . All of those things are against the rules at Prescott, but I haven't seen Drew or his friends face any consequences.

Oh, and Warren is in English with me. Or he's supposed to be, when he bothers to come. I didn't realize that because I guess he always sits in the back, and I always sit in the front and don't turn around much because I'm trying so hard to focus on the merits of Shakespeare. (Okay, I actually hate Shakespeare. I know it's a necessary evil in school, like eating four servings of vegetables every day, but really. So stuffy. No wonder I have to focus so hard. Everything else I can ace in my sleep, but not Shakespeare. Oh no. He demands undivided attention.)

I asked Emily about Warren. She told me he was a scholarship student, which I already knew, and that he's from her hometown. She said nothing about his personality, and I could be wrong, but I think maybe she doesn't like him. There was something kind of cold in her eyes when she talked about him. When I pressed her further, all she said was that he spent last summer at Princeton in some sort of science program, so he'll probably go there when he graduates.

Well, at least one person in the Science Club seems to like science.

September 13

I feel like maybe I'm getting the hang of Prescott. I mean, I still wear my Payless shoes, but I'm getting used to everyone being so rich. And I feel like I can kind of fake it, or at least play along when I have to.

The classes aren't as hard as I expected, either. It's a lot more work than my old school, and I feel like all I do at night is homework, but it's not harder, really. It's just like they expect more. It's kind of weird not having parents around. You'd think everyone would slack off with no one telling them what to do. But everyone seems to try harder because of it. I even keep my side of the room clean. Well, sometimes.

Mr. Callahan had me stay after school and balance some really challenging chemical equations today. He didn't tell me I did well—I think compliments are going to be hard to come by with him—but he was smiling ear to ear when he checked my work. I asked him about the Science Club. He just chuckled like I'd said something funny and told me I didn't need a club. Then he told me I didn't have to do the chemistry homework tonight. I might have some free time!

September 14

I don't even know where to start today.

Emily and I were about to go to dinner when Katy showed up and told me it was time for the meeting. I felt really bad leaving Emily to eat alone, but I had a feeling that if I turned Katy down, I'd never get a chance to hang out with her again. I'd be out of the club, so to speak, and I just can't give up this chance. It will be so nice to have a group again. Somewhere I belong. I hope Emily isn't too mad.

So we get outside and I start walking in the direction of

Herschell Hall, and Katy grabs my arm and turns me in the opposite direction, almost off campus, to a building that looks like it hasn't been used in years. It's creepy as hell. The old walls kind of sag in places, several of the windows are busted out, and there are no streetlights in sight. It looks sort of like a big, yawning stone monster.

> Me: Here? Is this even Prescott's building?

> Katy: Of course. We use the old science building for our meetings. Come on. I promise there are no ghosts.

> Me: Not my main concern. More scared of rats, live wires, dead bodies . . .

Katy just laughed and pulled me through the doors. We went down some stairs and a beautiful smell hit me. Chemicals! It was GORGEOUS down there. There's a fully equipped lab. Something simmered and steamed and hissed pleasantly on a burner. Tubes and beakers and vials and jars and all kinds of equipment lined the shelves and was scattered on old lab tables.

Okay, and I admit it. An even prettier sight was Drew and Warren, both of them in lab coats, hair pulled back by the goggles they'd pushed above their foreheads. They were leaning over the simmering brew, looking like they knew exactly what the hell they were doing. To a girl who loves chemistry, there's nothing hotter.

Drew smiled at me, but it was Warren who met my gaze and, with a slight jerk of his head, beckoned me over. I don't know why, maybe it was because I finally felt like I wasn't so out of my element, but I walked right up to him and asked him what he was working on.

When he answered, the room spun. I can't believe I'm going to write this. I should definitely get a lock for this thing.

Drugs. Warren was working on making crystal meth. That's what he said.

And I laughed because I was sure he was joking, but he wasn't. Katy started explaining what they do, how they sell to local dealers, and how the area around Prescott is kind of depressed and has a lot of addicts, so it's easy money. Warren said he needed the cash to get by, and it sounds like he's the real talent. Katy and Drew make the sales and manage distribution. They explained it to me like it was no big deal. Like it's completely normal to do something so illegal. Like it's just a little side business like making decorative wreaths for Etsy.

It was so surreal. The more they talked, the more I felt like I was dreaming or I was the butt of a terrible joke. As they explained, my ears started ringing and I couldn't breathe. And I didn't say good-bye or anything. I just ran out of the building and all the way back to my dorm.

Diary, I need to hide you now.

September 14 again, later

I could be imagining it, but I swear Emily knows. I keep catching her looking at me like she's suspicious or something. And again she warned me to stay away from Drew. This time she threw Katy's name in there too. Do you think she knows what the Science Club is up to? I wonder if I should tell her? I mean, of course I shouldn't. I don't want to get Warren or any of the Science Club in trouble, but this is just . . . too much. Telling her would be a relief. Someone to share the load, so to speak.

I guess I'm telling this diary, though. It can be the secret keeper for me, since obviously telling someone is out of the question. And I'll definitely have a lot to tell if these first few weeks here are any indication. Sheesh. What a strange place Prescott is.

September 15

I tried to avoid Warren when I saw him in the hallway but he wouldn't let me. He asked if we could talk and then pulled me into an empty classroom.

Warren: Are you okay?

Me: How could I be?

Warren: Look, I know it's a lot to handle, but it's not what you're thinking. It's really not that bad at all.

Me: Oh really? What's not bad about making drugs to sell to the poor addicts in town?

Warren, looking at me like I'm adorable for having a conscience: They'd do it anyway, Bailey. At least if they get it from us, it's safe. We're not like those guys that throw poisonous fillers in to make more money and end up getting their clients killed.

Me: Clients? Is that what you call them?

Warren: It's business, so yes. But not like you see on TV, okay? No cartels, no one who's going to shoot your kneecaps or something for breaking a deal. No one is dissolving dead bodies in bathtubs. We just provide a product and make a sale.

Me: With people buying who are slowly killing themselves.

Warren, with a huge, impatient sigh: If someone wants to eat burgers and fries for every meal and they die of a heart attack, it's not the manager at McDonald's who is to blame, is it?

I still felt uneasy, but I had to concede that point. Then Warren started talking about how much he can use the money. I get the impression his parents aren't in the picture anymore, but he didn't seem to want to explain why, just that they don't help him financially. And Princeton is going to be incredibly expensive. But he hopes he can eventually become a scientist who could find a cure for addiction. I'm not sure if it's hypocritical or just poetic that that's what he wants to work for, but I assured him I won't tell anyone about the Club.

He asked me if I'd come by the lab again. Apparently they're short one chemist after a Science Club member graduated last year, and Warren can't do it all.

I told him I'd think about it, but how can I even consider this?

September 16

I got to talk to Bex! Turns out Isa got her a phone so that she can call home, and she called me, too! She sounds super happy at Campbell. It also sounds like she's popular. She rambled on about all the kids she's friends with. Doesn't surprise me. Bex is the opposite of me in a lot of ways. She's really extroverted, athletic (she's going to be playing soccer for Campbell's junior girls team), and even though she's ten and should be kind of awkward, she's not at all. I got all the awkwardness, I guess. But Bex never makes straight As like me, so I'm fine with the way the current flowed in the gene pool.

She asked how I'm doing, and I told her about Emily, and I told her there are some cute boys in my class. Of course I didn't mention the Science Club. There are some things that even Bex can't know about me, and I wouldn't want her to know this. She'd be disappointed. Or worried. Or both. That's the last thing either of us needs.

Before we hung up, Bex told me she wishes she could tell Mom about Campbell. I told her to tell Mom anyway. Is it silly to think she listens? Probably. Probably clichéd, too. I don't think there's anything about Prescott I want to tell Mom yet, but I did put her picture in this journal. There's a little pocket in the inside of the back cover where I can keep it safe and sound.

Maybe, in a way, I'm *am* telling her things.

September 17

Warren came to my room. I opened the door and he was smiling in that reserved way of his, and he asked if he could show me something. Super weird—Emily, who was doing homework, barely even looked at Warren. He didn't say anything to her, either. It was like they were trying really hard not to notice the other. What is up with that?

I went with him, even though I still had homework to do. The members of the Science Club have been a little cold to me since I ran out of their lab the other night, and I wanted to at least prove to them that I'm not going to rat them out, even if I didn't join them.

Neither of us was in uniform, since classes were over. I was in jeans and a comfy tee. Warren was wearing his long overcoat, even though it wasn't that chilly out. I asked him why he always wears it. He said it belonged to his brother but didn't say any more. I didn't press. I barely know him but I can tell talking about his family is off-limits.

It didn't take me long to figure out that Warren was leading me to the lab. When I hesitated, it was as if he read my mind. Not breaking eye contact once, he told me there was nothing to be afraid of. The rest of the Science Club wouldn't even know I was there. That the decision was completely up to me and there was no harm in just coming in and learning.

Going with him wasn't a commitment. It was just . . . learning. And I thought that maybe it could help me decide.

In the lab there's a station for every step of the process, so that they can have multiple batches cooking at once. He said he makes it a point to stop by every few hours during the day, and that for the most part, nothing is running at night. Apparently the old building has most of the equipment they needed. It's the ingredients they get elsewhere. Whatever money is left after reinvesting in ingredients, that's what the Science Club gets to keep, and apparently there's generally a lot left over. He explained a bit about the group dynamics, how they absolutely trust each other, always, 100 percent, and are completely loyal and dedicated to each other. Warren gets the biggest cut, since he's the brains of the operation and has the biggest job. Drew and Katy make the deals, handle the logistics, things like that. That Warren makes a lot of money became evident the more he talked. Underneath that dingy overcoat, everything he wears is designer. He doesn't seem like the type of person who actually cares about brand names, but then, if he's making as much as he intimated, I can't blame him for buying the best. Goodness knows my first purchase would be better clothes.

As Warren explained the chemicals, the reactions, and the methods to what he was doing at each station, I realized something: This is just chemistry. All of it. I could almost forget what we were making, and what it was meant to do, when we were talking about formulas and ratios. It's actually fascinating. The things I'd done for Miss Beverly were like this, but making meth is even more involved. More nuanced, even. Warren talked about how he's constantly coming up with new ways to produce it more efficiently or more cleanly, and I could feel myself getting excited too. His passion was contagious, and it was the same passion as mine. This is what I like to do. It's what I want to do with my life, really. I want to make the world a better place, one ion at a time.

I started asking questions, and Warren was really eager to talk about everything. And he actually wanted my opinions. We started bouncing ideas off each other. Warren almost became a different person. Instead of reserved and stoic, he became animated and witty. We joked, and laughed, and it felt so good to have someone who had the same type of brain that I do. I honestly forgot about the final product until I was back here, in my room.

As I'm writing I'm realizing something, though . . . Warren never pressured me to join the Science Club. Not once the whole night. In fact, he didn't even bring up me joining. I have to admit, the money would be nice, but more importantly, the group itself would welcome me in. It's not just that the Science Club is so mysterious and glamourous, it's that they clearly look out for one another. Their loyalty is fierce.

Loyalty is something I need, I think. After Mom's death, some friends fled from my grief, some stuck around for a while but ultimately couldn't handle it; even my own father abandoned me. Knowing that this group wouldn't do that, even if the reason has to be kept a secret, is so tempting.

Maybe it wouldn't have to be permanent, either. Maybe I can do this, just for a while, just until they find someone else. Long enough to get to know Warren some more, and maybe earn a spot in their tight-knit circle. Maybe I can even give Warren some advice on how to perfect the product, without actually doing it myself. Maybe this might work.

September 20
At breakfast, I asked Emily about Warren. Why she doesn't seem to like him. She shrugged and said he was just kind of a jerk. I don't know what's up with this school and everyone acting like everything's a big secret.

I had lunch with Emily, but Katy brought over a wrapped brownie for me. It had a note attached:

(Katy's note, taped to the diary page, in Katy's girly handwriting):

> *Drew's driving into Wiltshire tonight. Want to go*
> *with and shop? I need new shoes. Herschell Hall, 6 p.m.*
> *Shh, don't tell.*

I doubt Katy needs new shoes. Not in the same way I need new shoes. And I have no money to spend, but this isn't about shopping. And it's a secret.

Looks like I've got secrets too.

September 20, again.

I'm back from shopping with Katy and Drew, and oh my God, you should see the shopping bags sitting here. I can't even believe how many there are and what stores they're from. I feel like I'm a movie star or something.

At Prescott there are specific rules to going off campus. Only upperclassmen are allowed to, and you have to be back before curfew. You can't spend the night elsewhere, and you cannot go to what our rule book calls "unsavory establishments." I'm assuming that means bars. It could mean brothels and strip clubs too. Ha. I guess it's kind of a catch-all rule for that purpose. Very clever.

So Drew's car. I mean, I have to say something about it. I don't like to think of myself as a shallow, materialistic person, but maybe that's just because I've never had a car like this. It's nicer than Isa's, even. Drew said his dad bought it for him for his birthday last year. That's just amazing. I think I got a gift card to Bath & Body Works. Anyway, it's this dark silver sporty thing. Hardly a backseat, but I didn't mind. It seriously sounded like a race car as we roared down the country roads we had to take to get into town.

Drew dropped us off at the mall. When I asked Katy if he didn't want to shop with us girls, she said that he had business to take care of. I know, of course, what that meant. Drew was going to check in with the dealers, maybe even drop off the, um, product. I hadn't thought of that. If he'd been pulled over for speeding and the car had been searched . . . I got kind of sick thinking about it, but . . . I felt a bit thrilled at the idea. Like we'd gotten away with something. I asked Katy if they are afraid of getting into trouble. She obviously didn't want to talk about it in public. She whispered and looked around nervously as she answered, but she said they aren't. That between her father being a lawyer and Drew's dad owning a good chunk of the town, they figure they'd get a slap on the wrist at most.

Then she bought me a pair of flats like hers. When I protested, she held up her hand and said she likes to buy her friends things. She also noted, somehow not unkindly, that I could use a better pair. And she wouldn't hear of me trying to pay her back. She repeated that at four different stores, big department stores that I usually don't even go into. I have a new wool coat, a makeup palette specifically matched to me from a glitzy-looking makeup counter, some hair products that Katy promised would make my frizzy hair smooth, and some new sweaters for our days out of uniform. Every time, Katy took out a credit card that had her name on it. She never minds paying for quality, she said. But I'm not sure if she really meant herself or her father. Who pays the credit card bill?

We met Drew outside one of the department stores. Katy asked if he'd been successful, which he answered by showing her a huge wad of cash. He said we should go eat somewhere fancy, so we did.

He chose a place with a French name, which turns out is owned by his family. The staff called him "Mr. Richmond" the whole time and kept bringing us complimentary appetizers and glasses of wine. *Real* wine, not like the sugary cheap stuff my friends from home would get if their older siblings were in a good enough mood to buy for us. I find it kind of hilarious that they were complimentary, since the whole meal was on the house, or on Drew's house, I guess. I had thought his father owned only a few fast-food chains, but Drew explained that they'd bought some nice restaurants all around the state as well.

They did ask me to join the Science Club again. In a way. Katy and Drew talked about the advantages to having disposable income and not ever having to ask their parents for money. And of course it's good to have nice things: brand names, high-end makeup, trendy clothes. I had to agree. If I do this with them, I'd never have to ask Dad (or worse, Isa) for anything. I might even be able to buy stuff for Bex. And if what Katy said is true, I won't have to worry about getting into trouble. I can't afford to have a record if I want into Harvard.

It's no problem, Drew said when I asked about getting into trouble again. There's no way their families would ever let them get a record. Drew and Katy both have their eyes on Yale. They can't afford trouble either, and with Warren wanting to get into Princeton, it has to be the same with him.

By the time we got back to Prescott, I was feeling much better about the Science Club. I asked them when the next meeting is. Katy and Drew seemed incredibly happy that I was interested.

Emily looked at my (Katy's) purchases and seemed curious. I told her I'd gone shopping with Katy Ashton and her eyes almost bugged out of her head. She told me to be careful around Katy. She said Katy only *seems* nice. I think Emily's just jealous, honestly. The more I hang out with Katy, the more I like her. But I have to admit, I'm afraid she won't like me back. I know she bought me all this stuff, but I feel like I have to impress her somehow, if that makes sense. Drew, too, although now that I've talked to Warren more, I think Warren is definitely the cuter one. Maybe not as classically handsome, but definitely smarter and more intriguing. There seem to be a lot of Drews around here, but there's clearly only one Warren.

September 22

Another Friday night with no invite to a party, but that's okay. I know it's just because there aren't any parties, at least any I'd want to go to. I heard Drew tell Katy in chemistry that they need to do a lot of work this weekend, so I know they're at the lab. I could probably join them, but I'm still not sure I want to. Plus I kind of feel like I haven't fully been accepted yet. I don't know how or when I will be, but I'm almost 100 percent sure I'll have to prove myself. Like an initiation or blood oath or something. Or maybe I've seen one too many mob films. Still, I have no doubt that they are serious about secrecy and loyalty, so with all I know, they have to make sure I'm not going to rat.

Emily and I skipped the dining hall and ordered a pizza and did our movie thing again. She has a whole collection of DVDs. She keeps them in one of those old-school flip albums like my dad has to store his CDs. She organizes them by director, not alphabetically or even by genre. I let her choose tonight. She decided on a movie called *High Fidelity*, which I'd never seen before, but I can see why she likes it. The main character reminded me of her a little because he was so into music, but in this cool way, like he could recall the history of the songs he liked and random trivia about musicians. Emily is like that with movies.

After the movie we sat around talking. She asked me about my mom and I told her a few things. Then she asked me what happened to her. And it's okay. I mean, I'm used to getting asked, I guess, and it's nice that she cares. I told her about how Mom was driving me to get some school supplies. Luckily, Bex was home with Dad. We had a green light. Mom even looked both ways before she started to go through the intersection. She was always cautious like that. It was just that this other car was so fast. And the driver was texting, not paying any attention. She hit Mom's side of the car and we spun so hard that I hit my head on my window. I passed out. At the hospital I was told I had a concussion. I was also told Mom didn't make it, but they didn't have to tell me. I remembered—still remember—every detail of the last time I saw her alive. The side of the car was folded in over her. She was covered in sticky red. It smelled like metal and burning. Her mouth was open, frozen in a scream. She didn't answer me when I called out to her, before I lost consciousness.

I didn't actually tell Emily the gruesome parts and I don't know why I wrote it down just now. I guess it feels good to write it, like something I needed to get off my chest. The girl who was texting walked away with hardly more than a scratch, like she hadn't irrevocably changed anyone's life. That girl is still alive. I am too. At least, mostly alive. I've heard people say that a part of themselves died when they lost someone they loved. I'm not sure any of me died with her. But I am sure that I'll never be the same. It's been two years now and I still don't really feel like myself. I managed to keep my grades up, and I went through the motions at school, but I didn't make any friends. The ones I had got tired of me being not much more than a zombie who did homework. I never went out with them anymore. Pretty soon I just wasn't invited. I'd like to say it hurt, but it didn't. Not really. I was kind of relieved that I didn't have to act normal around anyone.

Dad was kind of like me, too. He'd be better around Bex, because Bex needed both of us to show her that we were okay, that we were all okay, or we were going to be. But when it was just us, Dad and I were the same. Until Isa came around. Then Dad wasn't just pretending that things were fine, he actually was fine. He pulled himself out of the hole we'd made for ourselves and cleaned up the house, bought new furniture, got rid of Mom's clothes, and, I noticed, he took down the pictures of Mom in his room. Meanwhile, I kept her picture by my bed and slept with her pillowcase on my pillow, still deep in the grieving hole. And I guess that's what I'm mad about most. Not that Dad found someone new or even that he's over Mom. Just that he left me behind, and now it feels like I'm the only one still grieving.

I didn't tell Emily any of that, either. She started talking about movies where moms die, like they could be some kind of therapy for me. It's sweet of her, in her own nerdy film-buff way, but I don't need therapy. I don't need movies. I just need Mom back. Failing that, because of course I can't have her back, not being alone would be nice. And now that I think about it, having new friends who know nothing about my mom . . . Honestly, it would be kind of a relief. A fresh start. I could eliminate the sad elephant in the room and just try to be Bailey again.

I think maybe I should just flat-out ask Katy what I need to do to become an official member of the Science Club. It would be amazing to be part of a group again. I had a decent-sized group of friends back home. Two of them, Jess and Anna, had been my friends since first grade. Evan, Cat, P.J., and Chelsea were added in middle school, and we oddly stuck together through high school. I thought they were going to be there through thick and thin, but I realized that wasn't going to happen after Mom died.

I can't really blame them for not understanding, and they were just amazing before then. Very accepting of my know-it-all-ness and Ivy League ambitions, even if they would have rather spent their nights driving around aimlessly in the country and hardly ever read books unless they were for school. As fun as they were, though, it would be great to have a group of friends with ambition like mine, and of course the chemistry part of it would be fun. Plus, well, Warren. Maybe it's too soon to say this, but I think there's a connection there. I can already see how great it would be to have a boyfriend who wants to go to Princeton and loves learning and chemistry. Back home, I think it intimidated most of the guys I knew, how focused I was on college. And let's face it, if I join, I'd certainly never have to be lonely, because it's clear the Science Club takes care of their own. And if my mom's death taught me anything, it's that being lonely and not understood is the worst thing in the world.

I guess I've made up my mind.

September 24

I found out what the Science Club initiation is.

I went to the lab again. It was Sunday afternoon and I was bored. Emily was elsewhere—she didn't tell me where she was going. I assume the library, or Prescott's AV room. I'd finished all my homework, even the extra set of formulas Mr. Callahan had me work through. There was nothing to do except watch sitcom reruns or read, and the rest of the dorm was too quiet. I threw on one of my new sweaters and went to the old science building.

The doors outside were locked, but I could see lights on through the frosted glass of the basement windows. I knocked as loud as I could. Katy laughed when she opened the door and saw me there.

Katy: Password?

Me: Um, *labor omnia improba vincit?*

Katy: You honestly think Prescott's motto is going to be our password?

Me, stuttering: Um, okay. Etlay emay inyay, easeplay.

Katy, smiling: Glad to see you here, Bailey. We were hoping you'd join us. You do want to join us, right? (I nodded.) There's something we need from you before you do, though.

Me: Is this the initiation?

Katy laughed, like I was such a kidder, but she got serious really quickly. Then she explained what they needed from me.

Collateral. They need something to make sure that I won't rat them out. Something to make the consequences horrific for me if I did.

And as Katy explained exactly what I needed to do, I started to realize exactly how horrific.

She must have been able to see my thoughts on my face because she told me to think it over and to come back when I was sure.

I don't know how I could ever be sure of this.

September 25

Something truly weird just happened. Emily and I were doing homework after dinner when there was a knock at the door. She went to open it, and there was a package sitting in the hallway. No one was there. Pretty handwriting on the top announced that the package was for me.

It was wrapped in simple brown paper and tied with twine, like an old-fashioned Christmas present. I opened it immediately. Inside there were two chemistry textbooks. Textbooks I know plain well are used at Harvard. Both are written by professors there.

Emily asked me if they were from Mr. Callahan, but they're not. I know exactly who they're from.

September 27

This has been, by far, my best day at Prescott, and I owe it to the Science Club. It was like they planned a wooing coup (God, that sounds ridiculous, but I don't know what else to call it). I don't have much time because Katy's going to be here in about twenty minutes to go get coffee and study for our civics quiz, but here are the highlights:

Warren showed up after my first class with a cup of coffee for me. He walked me to my next class, looked me straight in the eye and told me it was great to see me again, then walked away. Swoon. For such a chemistry geek, he has swagger for DAYS.

At lunch I walked by the Glamorous Table like usual, but this time they waved me over to them. And then they slid over and made room. Just like that. It was SO COOL.

Katy taught me how to use lip liner between third and fourth period. Then she gave me one of her dark lipsticks. It was Chanel. I told her I couldn't possibly accept it, since they're so expensive, and she just shrugged and said, "Please. That's pocket change compared to what we make in a week in the Club." And then she asked me to get coffee with her tonight.

Drew announced to the whole class that I am brilliant with chemistry. He actually called me the Chemistry Queen. It was embarrassing and also amazing and I think some of the girls wanted to kill me.

Emily is gone again. No idea where she goes, but I'm okay with that for now. She isn't happy that I ditched her at lunch, I don't think. But I did ask everyone if she could join us. Warren said no, absolutely not. I feel really terrible about that. Emily doesn't seem to have many friends here at Prescott. She's not exactly a pariah, but I don't think she MEANS to be a loner either. Maybe something happened with her before . . . like maybe she used to have a lot of friends but they don't talk to her anymore for some reason. Which leads me to the next point:

I'm beginning to feel like maybe Emily and Warren used to date or something? I can't help but wonder . . . Why does Warren seem to dislike her so much, and vice versa? Must ask Katy later.

I promise I'll write more tomorrow, but for now, all I can say is I feel like I'm "in." And it's wonderful. The best I've felt in ages. And I can't be out again. I just can't.

I know what I have to do.

September 30

This time when I showed up at the old science building, it felt like everything had changed. Everyone was a lot more serious, but I also felt a lot more welcome. Like I belonged.

Drew helped me give them what they needed for collateral. I feel this weird sense of trust with him now. And I know he will use it only if absolutely necessary. But I also feel like he was completely understanding about how hard it was and how scary. I feel like he truly cares.

Katy and Warren hugged me, and we all promised to protect one another. Then they gave me a new lab coat and a pair of goggles. Warren took my hand (!!!!) and led me over to the first station, and my first official lesson in making meth began.

Over the next three hours, I was on a different planet. It was just us and the reactions of chemicals, the only real magic there is. But to be honest, it wasn't even about the chemistry. Or that what we were doing was going to make us rich. It was that I felt like a part of something, and not just any part, but a truly integral part. I felt needed and wanted.

And when we were done, Warren walked me back to my dorm. :)

October 3

I managed to do two steps of the process completely by myself tonight. Warren stood there watching me, like a proud parent or something. And I was proud of myself too. In a way this is some of the hardest chemistry I've ever done. It's not that I can't understand it. No, it makes perfect sense the way the chemicals mix and break down and react. It's just that everything has to be perfect and precise; otherwise it won't be Science Club–worthy. Apparently there's some competition that isn't so careful and doesn't produce excellent results every time, but the Science Club prides itself on being consistently superior. That's our gimmick, if it can be called that and if our specific type of product can have gimmicks.

Warren handled the rest himself, but I could tell he was happy and maybe a little bit surprised at how well I did. He said he'd be back tomorrow, same time, and would love it if I could help. Of course I agreed. He walked me home again.

Emily asked me if I'd been with Warren and I told her yes. She didn't say anything else, but she seemed so judgmental about it. Maybe even angry. She told me she had to run to the AV building and left, but I think she was just trying to get away from me for a while.

I'm going to have to talk to her about it. I like Emily and I want to get along, especially since she seems so lonely, but Warren is a part of my life now. Hopefully he will be an even bigger part. I need to figure out why she dislikes him so much. I hope it's not something that will be a Big Deal or anything. I'd like to be her friend, but I can't be as isolated as she is. I can't go back to that, and I can't let whatever happened to her dictate my friends here at Prescott. I need people.

Oh, also, Drew told me tonight how much of a cut I'm getting.

Yeah. I'm going to be able to buy all the flats I want.

October 5

Mr. Callahan had me stay after class again today. He wants me to apply for a chemistry program for high school students that would mean spending most of my summer at Princeton. Of course I was flattered and I said yes, but I have to admit, part of me is super excited about possibly spending the summer with Warren. Or near him, if he's still doing the science program there. Perhaps it's even the same program?

Mr. Callahan said I'd have to keep my grades up in all subjects because entry is determined by GPA and a few other things, like an essay about your career goals and recommendations from teachers. I'll be fine in everything but English, so I'm going to have to work extra hard in that. I know, I know. I write all the time in this thing, but give me a literary metaphor to explain or a story's theme to dissect and I cannot put a proper sentence together to save my life. I'd much rather deal with numbers and formulas. Even the guesswork with those is logical. English makes no sense!

I've been in the Science Club lab almost every night this week. It's mostly just me and Warren who cook, but Drew sometimes pulls out some rubber gloves and helps. Katy, for the most part, is just there to keep us company and to talk to our customers. Last night she quizzed me on *Macbeth* while I worked. When I got the answer wrong, Drew would make this annoying buzzer sound and shout out the right one. Apparently his talents lie in the written word. It was funny and made studying tolerable, but I got too many wrong. I'm going to have to study hard for the midterm.

When Drew and Katy left, I asked Warren if they were together. They seem to be a little . . . overfamiliar sometimes. Warren laughed and rolled his eyes and said that they weren't together, in spite of themselves. I told him I was sure most of the girls at Prescott would be relieved to hear that.

Warren, quietly: Yeah. Drew never lacks attention from the girls. Hell, some of the boys.

Me: Well, he's cute and smart and charismatic. That's everyone's type, right?

Warren, even more quietly: And is it your type?

Me, with a shy but hopefully suggestive glance in his direction: No. I prefer stoic over charismatic, actually.

Warren, smiling and looking down at his hands: Noted.

We were quiet and kind of awkward after that, but when he walked me back to my dorm, he put his arm around me. He was warm, and I fit so well, and he smelled great, like subtle spices and ocean waves. Probably a very expensive cologne. I have to admit, I've never had a boyfriend before, just a few flirtations that amounted to nothing in the end, so I didn't know what to expect. Would he try to kiss me? Would he go for the mouth or just the cheek? Or should I kiss him? I was super nervous and even more nervous since I didn't know what to do. In the end, he didn't try to kiss me, he didn't even hug me, but it's okay. Honestly, just his arm around me was the sexiest thing I've ever experienced in my life.

October 6

Well, I officially feel terrible. I think Emily assumed we'd be spending another Friday night watching movies and eating popcorn. She started talking to me this morning at breakfast about possible themes for tonight and I had to break it to her that I actually have plans with Katy. I mean, she took it okay, but I could see she was disappointed. She just kind of sat there drinking her orange juice quietly.

Then she said: So are you part of their group now?

Me, trying to keep my face neutral: What
group?

Emily: You know. Katy and those guys. Drew
and Warren.

I noticed she didn't call them the Science Club, but she
could have just been keeping that a secret, like I'm supposed to.
I told her that yeah, I guess I'm part of their group now, and she
asked me why I'd want to be.

Me: Why not? They're fun. And smart.

Emily: And snobby. They're only friends with
themselves. They don't hang out with anyone
else. I'm really surprised they let you in, no
offense.

I defended them, of course, which only made Emily double
down. Again, I had to wonder if Emily had been cast out of a
social group, maybe even the Science Club itself, by the way
she was acting. The weird thing was, I realized she's right:
I'd never seen any of them associate with anyone outside the
Science Club. They talk to other people here at Prescott, but

it's not like they'd ever invite them anywhere with us. Half the time we're in the lab.

I wonder how much of it is really snobbery and how much is just secret keeping?

I do feel bad, though. Emily reminds me a lot of me at my old school, without any real friends. What I could STILL be if I hadn't decided to join the Science Club, I guess. At least I have them now, and thank goodness for that, but Emily doesn't seem to have anyone.

I think I smoothed things over by offering to spend most of Sunday watching movies with her, but I'm not sure. I didn't sit with her at lunch. I didn't see her at lunchtime at all, actually, and I probably wouldn't have sat with her anyway. Warren patted the seat next to him when he saw me walking through with my tray, and draped his arm over the back of my chair. Katy raised a brow and gave me a look, so I guess we'll be talking about *that* tonight.

October 7

I feel awful, but I think last night was so worth it. We met at the lab, me and Katy. Drew and Warren were already there. Warren looked AH-mazing. He was wearing this dusty-blue turtleneck sweater, all studious and preppy and sexy. How does anyone manage to make a turtleneck look hot? And it was super soft.

Cashmere, he said. Some brand name he told me that I don't remember. All I know is that when I leaned against him, it felt so wonderful on my cheek.

Drew passed out our shares. My first "paycheck." I can't even believe how much money I have right now. New shoes are definitely a must, and maybe something for Bex. Maybe I can even get Drew to drive me over to Campbell and give it to her in person.

Then Drew brought out a bottle of champagne and we toasted the "new" Science Club and our first payday together. Warren and I checked on the progress of our latest batch and it was good to go, so we went to Drew's room and he had even more champagne there waiting for us. It was so classy. Honestly, just being around them makes me feel cool by proxy. And considering what Emily said yesterday, I kind of feel lucky to call them friends. They don't let just anybody in, after all, and they chose *me* for some reason. And I don't think it's just for my chemistry skills because Katy asks me to hang out, no chemistry involved, and Warren . . .

I don't know. Sometimes he looks at me in this way that makes me tingle all over. I'm rolling my eyes at writing this because I can't stand puns, but really, with him it's all a different kind of chemistry.

I had a lot of champagne. I swear, the bottles just kept

appearing, and I clearly don't have the experience with alcohol that they do. They acted like it was nothing, like they do this every day, so I kept the slight scandalized feeling I had to myself. I felt light-headed after my second, and we were all laughing like idiots. I don't even remember most of what we talked about. Okay, I do remember doing a pretty nasty impression of Isa once, and they gave me a standing ovation for it. And I *definitely* remember sort of settling against Warren at some point, his arm around me again, his soft sweater and his warmth. The next thing I knew, he was gently waking me up, telling me I should probably get back to my dorm before we all got caught. He was smiling so sweetly at me as I struggled to keep my eyes open, and I was so grateful that he was looking out for me.

I didn't really want to leave Warren there all snuggly and warm, but getting caught would be ugly. So Katy and I left. I somehow managed to get in without waking Emily and fell asleep. Now my head is pounding and the thought of eating breakfast is horrifying. But . . . I have money, I have friends, I have (maybe only kinda sorta) Warren. I have found my place, and it's probably the coolest place at Prescott. I will deal with a hangover every day if I get to have nights like that.

And now back to bed I go.

October 7, later

Drew picked up pizza tonight, so we took a break from chemicals and chowed down. A batch was nearly done, so he'd been out taking orders, so to speak, and it looked like our next paycheck was going to be pretty great as well.

We were sitting there, no sounds but chewing and bubbling chemicals, when a thought occurred to me.

> Me: So, how do we *know* this is quality? I mean, Warren and I have been making some subtle changes, but how do we know it's working? That it's making our, um, recipe better?

> Drew, around a mouthful of pizza: A couple of the sellers are also users. Not badly enough that we should be worried about them holding up their end of the bargain, but enough to dip in every now and then. They give us feedback.

Seemed like a decent system, with no danger of any of us getting hooked or anything, but I was curious about what we'd been busy making. What was it like? What did it make you feel? What did it DO?

Me, looking at all of them: But have any of you ever tried it?

Katy, laughing: Not me, but these two idiots have.

Warren, with a shrug: We thought we'd better know, is all.

Me: And . . . ? What's it like?

Drew and Warren exchange a glance. Then, Warren: I felt like it gave me superpowers. I felt smarter and faster and stronger.

Drew, nodding: Totally like superpowers. The comedown sucked, though. You instantly miss feeling powerful. Did you want to try it, Bailey?

Of course I said no. I know I'm the world's biggest hypocrite here, but anything that could make you addicted terrifies me. I don't even understand how someone could inhale something or stick a needle in their arm knowing they might not ever want to stop. It scares me a little that the boys have tried it, that they've risked addiction or even flirted with the idea of it. They seem so rational and in control, and they certainly don't seem like the type to do drugs. Just make them.

How does that even make sense in my head? But it does. Drew and Warren are too smart to be addicts, I'm sure of it, and maybe that's why they felt like they could try it. I wanted to ask them more, but I also . . . didn't want to know more. I don't like thinking of either of them like that.

We worked until about one in the morning and crept home. I promised Emily the movie day tomorrow, and I'm glad I did. I could use a day to just relax.

October 8

Emily and I had a really good time watching movies, and we went to dinner together. She talked to me about her parents (both are teachers, both pretty strict, but both encourage her to write). She's an only child, so her parents are her entire family. I can't imagine that. I love Bex so much, it almost makes me feel sorry for Emily even more, that she doesn't have a little sister to share with. Maybe I'm just lucky that Bex is so awesome and we're far enough apart that we hardly ever fight.

Afterward, we helped each other with homework. There was a chemistry question I got stuck on and nearly texted Warren for help, but thought better of it. He hasn't texted or even mentioned how I fell asleep on him the other night, but maybe he's trying not to embarrass me. Maybe he's trying to gently show me he's not interested? I don't know. It's just that I thought for sure he was thinking what I was thinking, but he hasn't really made a move, other than putting his arm around me. Maybe he moves slowly? Maybe since I have no idea how this works, I'm expecting too much?

Or maybe . . . and I hate to even list this as a possibility, but . . . maybe he's just not that into me.

I didn't ask Emily about him again. I think, whatever it is that makes them uncomfortable around each other, I'd rather hear it from him. She seems angry or at least cold whenever we talk about him, but Warren just seems . . . I don't know. Indifferent? I think his perspective might be better. At least I think I'd rather deal with indifference than anger when asking about a possible past relationship with a guy I would like to have a possible relationship with in the future. Ugh.

October 11

I had a ton of homework tonight, so even though I was "helping" at the lab, Warren did most of the work and I sat there studying and writing civics notes. I swear, I could feel every time he looked at me like it was a physical thing. And he seemed to look at me a lot. Maybe he's trying to figure out if he likes me? I don't know. But I could actually hear my heartbeat in my ears at one point, it was so nerve-racking to be so close to him and not know what he was thinking. I kept my eyes on my homework, mostly, and didn't talk much. I was too afraid I'd say something stupid. Warren, on the other hand, seemed to want to fill every silence. He talked about all of his classes.

> Me: How do you keep up? You're always here,
> and I hardly ever see you in class.

> Warren, smiling slowly: I go to class.

> Me: Not . . . enough. How do you do it?

> Warren, still smiling, though it's cockier now:
> I don't sleep much and I have a really high IQ.

> Me: Must be nice. Jerk.

He laughed and had me come over to help him transfer a particularly heavy container of chemicals into the first station tub. Then he let me run the first part of the process, which I'm getting super good at, while he quizzed me about civics and wrote my answers down for me.

Me: I think Mrs. Goodman might be a bit suspicious about the change in handwriting.

Warren: Then tell her you were dictating to your personal secretary, Warren Clark.

Me: Secretary? That sounds so . . . mid-century. How about "assistant"?

Warren: Personal slave?

Me, giggling: Deal. (Pause in which I work up the courage to ask him the hard questions.) So . . . why do you hate my roommate?

Warren, looking up from my notebook with surprise: Emily? I don't hate Emily.

Me: You wouldn't let her sit with us.

Warren: We don't let anyone sit with us. We might need to discuss business.

At least that explains the elitism.

Me: Well, when I asked her about you she got pissy. So I guess I thought . . . I don't know. Maybe you two had something going on, and now you don't? Bad breakup?

Warren takes a long moment, seeming to collect himself, then: You're not wrong, exactly. Emily and I had a thing last year, I guess you could say. It wasn't long, but it was really intense. Not healthy. I had to end it.

Healthy or not, I am not sure I love the idea of Warren having any sort of intensity for anything outside of me and Science Club, but I put my jealousy in check. He hasn't even wanted to hold my hand yet, after all.

Me: I guess some people just don't click, huh?

Warren, looking at me, intense but sweet: Right. But some people click. They really, really click. Perhaps right from the start.

Me, blushing as I picked up on his meaning: Really? I thought maybe I'd misread you. I mean, you haven't been very . . .

Warren: Forward? Pushy? Those kind of guys are the worst, Bailey. I'm not one of them. Not my style. There's an art to waiting for the right moment. Don't want to mess anything up. Don't you agree?

I very much agree.

And I don't think I'm going to be able to handle it if he ever feels it's the "right moment."

October 12

I didn't do as well on the civics test as I'd hoped. It isn't a terrible grade, but it isn't Princeton Summer Program/Getting Into Harvard good. I'm going to have to study harder. Prescott is more challenging than I thought it would be. At my old school I would hardly study and still get As. Trying to slide by like that at Prescott means my grades will slide too. I'm just going to have to spend more time with the books. Warren seems open to me studying in the lab while we work, so that will help.

Dad called. I realized it was the first time he'd called me since I got here. I've called a few times, but this was his first. He wanted to talk about holiday plans. Prescott has two weeks off at the end of the year and most of the students go home or travel somewhere fun with their families. But Dad told me Bex wanted to go to New York with a new friend for skiing and shopping, so she wouldn't be home much, if at all.

I'm not 100 percent sure, but I kind of got the impression he was hoping I'm not coming home, either. He and Isa probably want to go somewhere by themselves and not have a teenaged third wheel tagging along. Especially one who is still in the grieving hole, missing her mother and being a total downer and all.

That hurt, but it also made me angry. So I sucked up my pride and made up a lie about possibly going with Katy instead of coming home, and I definitely heard relief in my dad's voice then. I know I talk about Mom all the time, mostly just because I want to remember her and know that someone else misses her too. But it's got to make Dad feel super awkward and probably irritates the hell out of Isa (which I count as a bonus).

I might actually check with Katy to see if I can tag along, wherever she's going. Even if Dad was happy about me coming home, I'm not sure I'd want to go. It hasn't been the same without Mom. She'd always insist on letting us open one present on Christmas Eve, usually something she'd picked out herself, especially for us. The year before she died, she got us matching pajamas. The year before that, glass ornaments we could paint. But of course it was never about the gift. It was just that we did something together, just us girls.

I'm a little sad that Bex wants to be anywhere else for Christmas. I really wanted to see her. Maybe she doesn't want to be home without Mom, either.

Does it make me a horrible person to hope that's the reason why?

October 13

Turns out I didn't even have to ask. An opportunity presented itself in an awesome way. At lunch today, Drew announced that his family would be spending Christmas in Vermont at a resort. He said his mother has some sort of fantasy-land hope that it will be just like *White Christmas*, and somehow they'll all miraculously get along and sing carols and sip hot chocolate and stuff like that.

That's exactly the kind of Christmas I'd like, but I kept my mouth shut, since everyone else thought it was ridiculous.

Katy said she's going to St. Lucia with her family, which sounded fun and warm but not like anything I'd probably get invited to. I turned to Warren, who had his arm around me again, and asked him where he was going.

The whole group got quiet, so I knew I'd stepped in something. It was Drew who answered for him.

Drew: Warren stays at Prescott.

Warren: Someone has to be here, making the product. Supply doesn't go down because of the holidays.

Drew, smiling: Nope, it goes way up. The holiday season makes everyone tense. Our clients especially.

Drew was basically saying that we needed to sell more of our product because addicts might be especially upset or depressed or lonely this time of year. And for the first time in weeks, I remembered that there is someone on the other end of all this work. There is someone on the other end of the money I'm handed once a week. I lost my appetite.

Katy must have noticed, because she smiled really big and reassuringly at me.

Katy: Are you going home, Bailey? What does your family do for Christmas?

Me, shrugging: I don't know. I think my dad and Isa really want to be alone. My sister is going skiing with a friend, so if I didn't come home, he and Isa could have a few weeks to do whatever they want.

Warren: Then stay here. With me. I certainly wouldn't mind the help. Or the company.

Me, my heart thundering in my ears: Really? The school doesn't mind?

Warren: There's hardly anyone here. It's nice, actually.

Me: It's not . . . lonely and sad?

Warren, his blue eyes staring straight into my soul: It wouldn't be if you stayed with me.

It was so intense I could have sworn the rest of the dining hall disappeared and it was just me and Warren and him basically asking me to stay with him, alone, for two weeks.

But then Katy let out the type of squeal I was kind of mentally doing inside and told us we were beyond cute. Which made me blush and Warren laughed. Then it was time for class and Warren walked me there, apologizing for Katy being so Katy about it. I told him I was happy that perhaps someone else thought we had potential. His blue eyes danced with laughter at that, and I spent all afternoon thinking about holiday break and being alone with Warren instead of listening to my teachers.

October 13, later

I called Dad and told him I also had holiday plans and not to expect me home.

I'm not sure what I hate more: the relief in his voice or that he didn't even ask what I was doing.

October 16

Mr. Callahan gave me the application for the Princeton chemistry program. It doesn't look too bad, just a bit longer than I expected. They want two teacher recommendations. I think I'll steer clear of my English teacher. Ha! The second page asks for transcripts of science-related courses. I'll have to go to the guidance office (always a bit awkward and scary) to get that, I guess, and maybe call my old school. Twice as awkward.

Midterms are coming up, so I'm really going to have to buckle down. I have a routine, at least. After classes, I catch dinner with Emily or sometimes the Science Club, depending. Emily seems to shut herself in the AV room quite a bit, so a lot of the time she's not around. Sometimes Katy and I go for coffee and study together (i.e., gossip), or I just go straight to the lab. Depending on where Warren and I are in the process and how many batches we have going, sometimes it takes only an hour. Sometimes, though, we're in there until midnight or one a.m. After the long days, I feel like I could sleep for a week. I wish I could be like Warren and get by doing the bare minimum in class, but it just doesn't come that naturally to me. I hate admitting that, but there it is. He's got to be amazingly smart. I mean, I don't think I'm dumb or anything, but I'm nowhere near his level. It's incredible the way his brain works. Just as sexy as his blue eyes or his slow smile.

Sexy, sexy, sexy.

ANYWAY.

As hard as the long nights are (and the mornings after), at least I'm spending time with Warren, getting to know him more, and he's helping me study. For the most part. Also, Drew dispensed cash again. Katy's promised me she'll shop with me this weekend.

I'm thinking new ski boots for Bex.

October 21

Drew didn't have any business in town on this fine Saturday afternoon, so he let Katy borrow the car. I couldn't believe it. And I couldn't believe it even more when we got in and Katy revealed she was actually terrible at driving a stick. It was hilarious. She accidentally killed it about four times before we even got off campus. I'm pretty good at it (Dad insisted on teaching me how to drive a stick when I had my permit because he's one of those Boy Scout types and didn't want me to ever be stranded somewhere with only a manual transmission and not be able to drive). So . . . Katy let me drive! With the caveats that we did not tell Drew, that I did not wreck, and that we switched back once we were on campus again.

I got us safely to the mall, where there was a sporting goods store that would have everything Bex needed.

We lingered by the cute workout clothes before we made it to the ski section, naturally.

Katy: Sooooo Warren . . .

Me, grinning like an idiot: Yes?

Katy, taking pointed interest in yoga pants: Is it, like, official yet?

Me: I don't know? He hasn't kissed me or anything. We just . . . hang out. Talk a lot. He makes me laugh. But he's not in a hurry. At all. Like, frustratingly.

Katy: No, that's not Warren's way. But he's
soooo into you.

Me: How can you tell?

Katy: The way he looks at you! Oh my God.
It's like . . . so intense, you know? Like he's
seeing your soul or something.

Me: . . . So did he look at Emily like that?

Okay, so at that point, Katy got really quiet and wasn't
laughing anymore. She told me Emily was selfish and kind of
weird and blamed Warren for a lot of things that weren't his
fault. Serious issues. That's what she said Emily had. Serious
issues. Then she said after it ended between them, the Science
Club decided without really talking about it that they were
pretty much going to pretend she didn't exist. Loyalty, and all
that.

I suppose Emily could be seen as weird, since she doesn't
really have friends. But didn't the Science Club basically create
that situation? Seems kind of harsh to punish someone for
being an outcast when you're the one who did the casting out.
But I didn't say that to Katy. I don't want to seem disloyal either.

Me: She is kind of weird, I guess. And she's not around much. It's like I can't find her some days, and sometimes she's even later than me getting home. She's super into her films and stuff.

Katy: Yeah. She gets kind of obsessive about things. Anyway, now you're with Warren, or you will be, and none of that matters anymore. Trust me, he may take his time, but that's only because he wants it to be *perfect*.

That made me grin from ear to ear, then we went and picked out new ski boots and a matching coat for Bex. She'll be the best-dressed girl on the slopes, even among the other Campbell students. And all thanks to Big Sis's new "job."

October 22

I was beginning to wonder exactly what criteria Warren was using to measure the perfect moment. I guess I know now: anticipation, a beautiful fall night, and fire extinguishers.

We were in the lab, just me and Warren. Katy and Drew had been there but had already left, claiming studying and homework. I'm not even sure how it happened, really. I mean, chemically, I know. Ammonia and heat don't mix well. But I'm not sure how either of us was so distracted that we didn't catch our mistake.

Okay, well, I guess I know the answer to that, too.

It really was a beautiful night. The air was cool with a crisp promise that winter was on its way. All of the trees seemed to change color at the same time here on campus, and they're all bold oranges and bright yellows and deep reds. The breeze picked up just enough that while I was walking to the lab, I had a magical moment where the leaves were swirling around me. I felt like I was in a movie, and I was smiling and practically giddy by the time I got to the lab.

Drew and Katy were soon off, and Warren and I were deep into a groove with the process.

I've done a little research online about making meth, just to learn, and only when I was certain I could erase the browser history. Most makers have a two-day process. Warren likes to spread it out over four days, just to guarantee perfection and quality. He likes to examine it between each step and let the finished product breathe a little before handing it over to our sellers.

My research let me learn not only how to make it but how to do it well. Each step is nicely drawn out and meticulous, and now that I have some experience under my belt, Warren and I circle around each other to different stations like a well-choreographed musical scene.

And I guess that's why it was probably easy for him to predict where I was going to move next and . . . suddenly I was in his arms.

I laughed and blushed and immediately felt like it was all a little too much. I had the basic shape of him mapped out in my head, thanks to his well-fitting clothes and the occasional falling asleep on his shoulder. But when he pulled me close I started to understand how swooning was a thing.

He's lanky, sure, but he's *fit*. Maybe it's all that time he spends climbing trees around campus. I didn't expect his strength, and I really didn't expect how assured he was. He turned me, leading me into an ungraceful spin, and then pulled me back to him again. And he leaned close like he was going to kiss me, and there was fire.

A literal one, unfortunately.

I'd set down a beaker of ammonia too close to the burner and it went up in flames.

I panicked, but a different kind of self-assurance kicked in with Warren, and he spun for the nearest fire extinguisher. It wasn't a big blaze, luckily. It didn't even set off any alarms (although I'm not honestly sure the old building has any working ones). Basically once the liquid dispersed onto the floor and everywhere else, the fire didn't have much life in it, and what it did have, Warren easily put out.

> Me, hands over my mouth: Oh shit, I am so sorry.

> Warren: Okay, new rule—no dancing while we work?

Then we both broke out into hysterical laughter, fueled by adrenaline and relief.

Then Warren set the fire extinguisher aside, took a moment to make sure we were safe, and pulled me into his arms again. He kissed me then, and it was like another fire started, this one much more welcome but just as sudden and hot. And he is just as much an expert at kissing as he is at everything else. His arms encircled me, lifting me up slightly, and his lips were soft and tempting and gave and took. When he pulled away, those dazzling eyes stared straight into mine.

> Me: You're right. Timing is everything.

> Warren, laughing: Worth the wait, I hope?

Me: Yes, but I'm not going to let you make me
wait that long again. In fact . . .

This time I was the one to kiss him. And we kissed and
kissed, so much that I was light-headed by the time we were
done, and I don't think it had anything to do with the lab's toxic
fumes.

October 24

Another perfect day at Prescott. Warren walked with me to all of
my classes (holding my hand or with his arm around me always,
like he can't resist me or something). Mr. Callahan was super
impressed with the extra assignment I'd turned in for fun. Neither
me nor Katy had a lot of homework, so we got to spend extra
time obsessing over the kissing with Warren. Then Warren and
I had the lab to ourselves, so there was chemistry and *chemistry*
happening (last time I'll let myself make that joke, I promise). He
asked if he could call me his girlfriend, and of course I said yes!!!!

And . . . I got to talk to Bex!

She is SO excited about her ski trip, and she's going to go
wild when she sees what I got her. We made plans to see each
other Saturday, contingent on Drew letting me (or Katy) borrow
his car, of course. Campbell isn't that far away, really, so I'm
banking on him saying yes.

I asked if she was at all sad that she wasn't going to get to see Dad, and she said she was but that she was more afraid of going home and missing Mom the whole time. That made me think, and I've come to the conclusion that I'm the same way. I might miss Dad this Christmas, but the void Mom left is so much bigger. Plus it would have been so weird to sit there with Dad and Isa and pretend I was happy, or even comfortable with this new arrangement. All in all, I think I made the right decision not to go home.

I told Bex a little about Warren. Not that we are official or anything. I'll save that news for in person. But just about him and what he's like. She's starting to pay attention to boys now, so she was pretty curious, and I loved being able to share some girl stuff with her.

I'm headed to bed relatively early and all my homework is done. Feels like it's been weeks since both of those things happened at one time.

Like I said: perfect day at Prescott.

October 25

Okay, so a really weird thing happened just now. Warren walked me home tonight after we finished up at the lab, and we were at the gate to my dorm and Emily was returning from wherever she goes. If she didn't already know Warren and I are a thing, she does now. No way she could have missed him kissing me.

But it was like she didn't even see me standing there with him. She got super close to him, almost pushing me away in the process, and told him they needed to talk.

Emily seemed so different from when we were just sitting around watching movies. It was like total tunnel vision, and Warren was at the end of that tunnel and nothing else existed. I can see what Katy meant by "intense." It almost seemed stalkerish.

Warren was cool as could be and smiled at her. Sweetly, even. Then he said he'd talk to her and looked at me with an expression that was apologetic and also calm, like he was trying to tell me it was okay and he would be okay. He told me he'd see me tomorrow and to sleep well, and they walked off.

I don't even know how to feel about this. It's been two hours and Emily still isn't home. I could text Warren or something but I don't want to seem just as intense and possessive as Emily, so I'm not going to. Where could they be? What on earth did she want to talk about? And Warren didn't seem surprised or even nervous that she asked, or that she was in his personal space bubble. It was almost like he was . . . used to it or something.

I won't text Katy, either. I'm just going to try to go to sleep. Failing that, I'll pretend I am, so Emily won't think I've been freaking out all night long.

October 26

Okay, I guess my freak-out last night was over nothing, at least as far as Warren is concerned. He was waiting for me outside of English, cup of coffee in hand. He smiled and handed me the coffee and told me it was very cool of me to be okay with him talking to Emily last night. He thanked me for being supportive and understanding. I asked if they got everything sorted out, and he shrugged.

> Warren: I'm not sure. She will have to sort out a lot on her own, you know? She's got some issues that go far beyond me and our whole thing, and she's got to learn how to get those under control. I can't hold her hand through that. That's not my job. It wasn't really even my job when we were together.

I nodded like I totally understood what he was saying, but I didn't get it at all. I wanted to ask about a billion more questions, but after he'd thanked me for being so chill about it, I didn't feel like I could.

> Warren: Did she come home last night? After we talked?

Me: I don't know. When did you finish talking?

Warren: We only talked for about an hour.

Me: She must have gone somewhere else, then. She wasn't there when I woke up this morning, either. Maybe she went to a friend's? Or to the AV room? I guess I can understand if she didn't want to be around me. If I'd known . . .

I stopped there, shook my head, and smiled at Warren.

Me: Okay, if I'd known, I probably wouldn't have done anything differently. Am I a horrible person?

Warren, laughing: No! I liked you from the moment I first saw you. I probably would have been relentless if you'd turned me down, especially if it was because of something silly like your roommate.

Me: Well, hopefully she'll get over it. I have to live with her until summer.

Warren: She'll have to. You didn't do anything wrong. Our breakup was mutual, really. Just do me a favor?

Me: Sure. Anything.

Warren: She'll probably try to convince you that *I'm* a horrible person. Don't believe her.

Me, leaning up to kiss him in spite of the harsh penalties at Prescott for PDA: I could never believe that about you.

The rest of the day was fine. I sat with the Science Club at lunch, I went to the lab after classes, and Warren and I quizzed each other about chemistry as we worked, because we have a test coming up.

I stayed pretty late at the lab. We didn't even have that much work to do, but I really didn't feel like dealing with Emily yet. I'm not afraid she'll be angry, more like I'm afraid of that weird kind of intensity that she had with Warren last night. I don't think I could handle that if it was focused on me. Also, I'm really curious about her and Warren. Oddly obsessed. I don't really want to know, but I also *really* want to know. And I guess

I'm kind of scared too that maybe he'll make me as nuts as Emily. I'm already scared of losing him, and I think about him nonstop. I mean, it's not out of the realm of possibility that I'd take it pretty badly if he broke up with me. Maybe not stalkerish and trying to talk to him in the middle of the night months later, but . . . it would really hurt.

But I didn't have anything to worry about. Even though it's really late, Emily still isn't back in the room.

October 30

Not much to report today. I thought Halloween would be interesting here at Prescott, but it turns out they have strict rules against dressing up and celebrations because of a couple of pranks that went south a few years ago. So lame. I feel like these rich kids could really do Halloween right, but I guess it's not worth the risk of punishment. The teachers, to their credit, have largely ignored that and passed out candy in every class I've been in. I thought about asking Emily if she'd want to watch a scary movie or something, kind of an olive branch, but I haven't seen her at all since the whole thing with Warren, mostly because she's been elsewhere. I feel like I should be there for her. She's obviously not dealing well with everything, and I think I might be her only friend, but I have no idea how to navigate this now that I know about her and Warren. Added to that, school is getting increasingly difficult. Maybe the teachers are just piling on the work because it will be winter break soon, and then we'll only have a few weeks before midterms. I don't know, but between homework, Emily, the Club, and break, I have a lot to juggle.

And UGH. I have to write an essay about *Macbeth*. I really do not want to write an essay about *Macbeth*. Please, God, anything but *Macbeth*. Katy said she'd help me, which might be the only reason I'll get a good grade. I've decided to write about the prophecy and how it influenced Macbeth's actions. I personally don't think he and Lady Macbeth would have acted the way they did if they hadn't been convinced that the witches had predicted their future. But then, maybe the witches knew that telling him would lead to that, so they were right anyway? Either way, I think they felt justified and maybe even absolved sometimes because they believed so strongly that ruling was their destiny. I don't know. It's all so confusing. Maybe I'll just do what everyone else is doing and write about how Lady Macbeth manipulated her husband into doing awful things. I only have a little over two weeks to get it done.

Drew actually wants to come to Campbell with me, so he's going to drive. I guess he has a little brother there. Katy is going too, so naturally Warren is coming along. I can't wait to see Bex. I wonder what she'll think of Warren???

I wonder what Mom would think of Warren too. And would she be happy for me that I finally have a boyfriend? And about how happy I am?

And is it . . . is it okay to be this happy? I mean, this is what I've often wondered about Dad and Isa. I know Mom would be happy that I'm happy, but I don't know. It feels somehow disloyal to Mom to be smiling when she's gone.

November 1

I finally talked to Emily. It was sort of hard to read her, really, because I got the feeling she was being overly . . . well, overly enthusiastic about me and Warren, actually.

I basically told her I hoped it wouldn't be a problem that I was seeing Warren now, and she assured me it was fine. She said the other night was just about some stuff she had to get off her chest but that she is completely, 100 percent over him. Then she rambled for a while about how she realizes now how unsupportive he was and how he never really understood her. She also said it was pretty much all lust between them, which made me a little angry and jealous if I'm being honest. It was like she wanted to remind me that she'd also kissed him and she was there first. But really, she's over him and I shouldn't be worried about anything.

Oh, and she threw in this comment about how she hopes I

won't believe everything he says about her, which is exactly what he said about her.

I told her that if it made her uncomfortable, I'd never bring him around her, and she snapped at me and said it was all fine and she didn't care at all. I left it alone after that and we both did our homework in silence. Then about twenty minutes later, unprompted:

> Emily: Warren can't just ignore me all the time, you know.

> Me: I don't think he would do that. Maybe he's just nervous that you're still upset with him.

> Emily: That's totally something he would do, Bailey. But you don't know him that well, do you? Not like I do.

At that point I put my headphones in and listened to music until I was done with homework. I'd have given anything to go to the lab and stay there instead or something, but it was late and I would have been busted for curfew. Luckily, Emily turned off her light and went to sleep and I didn't have to deal with her anymore.

I think she's just trying to get in my head, but she's definitely managed it. I wish I'd seen Warren tonight, even just a little, but with all the studying and homework I had to do, I'd told him earlier there was no chance of helping him tonight. It will be all right, I know it will. I just haven't had a relationship before, especially not with someone as amazing as Warren. So I'm paranoid that he's not as into me as I am him, and I think that's only natural, right?

And of course I realized as I was writing this that I didn't work on my *Macbeth* paper. I'm in no frame of mind for that tonight. I'll have to start tomorrow. I can't stop thinking about what Emily said.

Like, I am trying SO HARD to be there for Emily and to make her feel like she's got someone to talk to. So why would she pick at me like this? I hate to say it, but maybe the Science Club has the right idea about her. Who would blame me for ditching her with her acting like this?

November 4

Bex! Oh my God. When I saw her, we hugged and hugged and laughed and then hugged some more. I've been so busy and distracted (a good thing, I guess), I hadn't realized how much I've been missing her until I saw her. I feel like this is something only an old person would say, but she looked like she'd grown about five inches. And she's learned how to fix her hair, a necessity at boarding school. She's clearly rocking a straightener.

And everyone at Campbell loves her. That's clear. I swear everyone we walked by said hello to her by name, even some of the older kids. Of course. Who wouldn't love Bex? She's funny and caring and pretty and tough.

The drive didn't take too long, and Warren and I snuggled in the backseat the whole way there. We split up when we pulled into Campbell's visitor parking lot. Drew and Katy went to go find Drew's little brother, and Warren and I headed to Bex's dorm. Her face when she saw Warren was with me and I introduced him as my boyfriend! Priceless. I thought she was going to fall over dead of shock. We took her to lunch. She requested a restaurant off campus, naturally, and a kind of funky one that wasn't a chain. A gastropub, she said, like she knows all about gastropubs or something. So sophisticated now. Ha. Warren, sweetly, picked up the check. And when Warren went to the bathroom and we had a moment alone, she told me she liked him. She said he was funny, and cute in a geeky way, which is Bex speak for "not my style but I can see why you like him."

We met up with Drew and Katy and Drew's little brother Matt. Matt and Bex know each other, even though Matt is a year older. Bex got a little quiet around him, and I will definitely be teasing her later about that. How funny would it be if Bex's first crush was Drew's little brother? He's like a miniature version of Drew, but maybe a little sweeter, so why not?

Bex loved her boots and coat! She couldn't believe I got them for her, and she was super impressed that I'd picked that particular brand. She asked how in the world I could afford it, and Warren answered her by saying that since I'm not going home for the holidays I could give her Christmas now. Bex accepted that pretty easily, and I was grateful to Warren for covering for me. I feel stupid for not thinking about how to answer that question before.

It was kind of weird (and awesome, really) to see how much Bex looks up to me. She clearly had heard my friends' names before, so now I'm the coolest ever in her eyes. But I could see it even more when I told her I was thinking of doing a summer program at Princeton. I always think of her as naturally so much cooler and social than me, so it never occurred to me that she would admire me for anything other than just being older.

Now I'm sitting here wondering what Bex would do if she found out about Science Club. She's too young to understand, really. She would just see it in black and white; one mention of drugs and she'd be mad, disappointed, and probably scared for me. How could I possibly make her understand how I see it? Would she get how much I need loyal friends? Or that I've been so lonely? Or that it's helping me get out of the grieving hole?

November 6

The high of a carefree day with Bex wore off, and I was slammed back into the reality of unrelenting work at Prescott.

At least, thank goodness, Emily seems to be back to her old self. No more mention of Warren. No more snarly, jealous comments. She actually suggested we go to dinner together, and we did, but I had to bail on watching movies tonight. I'm just too panicked about all the classwork piling up.

That *Macbeth* paper is like a rain cloud looming over me constantly. Mr. Callahan continues to give me extra work on the side in chemistry, and it's challenging but also fun, so I never dread it and do it first. Calculus is the same way. Civics is tougher. With everything going on, I feel like it's hard to keep all the civics stuff straight, and since I certainly have no aspirations to be a politician or lawyer, there's no reason TO keep it all straight.

I did my calculus and started on my *Macbeth* paper, even though everything I wrote sounds stupid and I'll probably have to redo it. I finished most of calculus and then packed up and headed to the lab.

I actually beat Warren there, and he was startled when he walked in. He seemed a little frazzled, but then he just seemed grateful to see me. He kissed me so hard we almost tumbled into some chemical bottles.

Me: Rough day?

Warren: Much better now. What is with everyone demanding everything all at once?

Me: I think our teachers are all freaking out that they still have so much to cover before the end of the semester and are taking it out on us. Did you get all your work done?

Warren: Yeah. You?

Me, pushing my chemistry book toward him: Go over these with me? I just want to make sure I'm right.

Warren, taking the book and a kiss as well: You usually are. You're the most gifted chemist I've met. At Prescott, anyway. Genius.

Me: Ha! I'm not the one who manages to
gets straight As while also running a full-time
business. How do you do it?

Warren: I've made a clone of myself so I can
be in two places at once. Which Warren is the
real Warren? Maybe I'm the clone. What if
I'm the clone, Bailey?

Me, swatting at him playfully: Seriously!
How?

Warren, suddenly sobering: Magic, I guess.
And luck. And I never get much sleep.

I laughed, but . . . I don't know. It was like I suddenly
NOTICED. I looked at him and didn't just see my adorable
boyfriend; I saw the dark circles under his eyes, the slight droop
of his shoulders, and how thin he really is.

I'm going to help more. I told him I could be at the lab
more to check in on our work and do more of the process than
I usually do. He told me not to worry about it, but I saw relief
flash in his eyes, so I insisted.

I don't know how exactly I'll put in more time at the lab, but

I have to. I'll just work on homework here more often or get less sleep myself. But I do know I can't let Warren take on all of this by himself.

It will be fine. That's what I keep telling myself, anyway.

November 8

Had the scare of my life tonight. I legitimately believe it took a few years off my life.

I was in the lab alone, just me and my civics book and the quiet bubbling of all the tubes and pots around me, when I heard the doors open and shut above me. I called out, thinking I'd hear Katy or Drew answer back, or even Warren if he decided to come in after all. But instead a superdeep male voice answered, and an imposing shadow appeared in the doorway.

My heart nearly stopped.

Not only was I alone, I was also surrounded by evidence of a highly illegal business.

The figure stepped down into the basement's fluorescent lights and it was a police officer. Campus security, I guessed. He had a badge but also a hat that had Prescott's crest on it. In the light, I could see that he was just as surprised to see me as I was to see him. I stepped in front of the largest vat of chemicals, futilely.

Officer: You're not Katy.

Me: No, sir. I can, um, call her if you need her.

Officer: No, it's okay. Are you the newest member?

Me: Oh. Um . . . I . . .

Officer, smiling: I'll take that as a yes. I'm Mark. Campus security.

Me: I gathered. Um, what can I help you with, Mark? I'm just here doing homework.

Officer: You can drop the pretense. Apparently they haven't explained how things work.

He walked toward me, hand extended to shake. I shook it, in shock.

Me: Hi . . . Mark. I'm Bailey. I'm sorry, but what exactly have they not explained to me?

Mark: Oh! Right. It would be better if they explained. Plausible deniability and all that. But Drew or Katy was supposed to meet me here tonight.

Speak of the devil, Drew appeared, thundering down the stairs in a rush. He and Mark greeted each other, smiling, with a macho hug like guys are prone to doing, while I'm standing in the background with all my blood in my feet and not breathing well. They chatted like old friends for a few minutes, catching up on each other's lives. Apparently Mark's wife is expecting another child in May. Then Drew took out a thick envelope from his back pocket and slipped it into Mark's breast pocket. Mark thanked him, said he'd keep in touch, and was on his way.

I sat down on a metal stool and tried to breathe.

Me: What the hell was that?

Drew, sheepish: I'm sorry, Bailey. I should have told you this before. Mark is a security guard.

Me: I can at least follow that, thank you. Why the hell didn't he arrest me? Or you? And obviously he knows about what we do?

So Drew told me. For as long as they've had Science Club, which has been three years now, they've had Mark. Drew discovered he was easily swayed by money, and so they made an arrangement: Mark gets paid a tidy sum monthly in exchange for his silence to Prescott and the police about us, he makes sure his reports about this building always say it's secure and untouched, and he gives us any info that may be valuable, like if the janitors decide to come in and clean or if the admin gets suspicious.

It all makes total sense, of course, but I feel like I'm in a movie or something. A mob movie. This can't possibly be my life, that I'm doing something a crooked cop covers up for a price, right? But I am. This is reality. I am making drugs that are sold. And if Mark cracks or something goes wrong, I could go to prison.

> Drew, his hand on mine comfortingly: We
> have to involve others. It's just the nature
> of the game. But I make sure we can trust
> them. Don't worry, okay? I have this covered.
> Trust ME.

And the strange thing is, I do. I trust him, and Katy, and Warren. They really know what they're doing.

I guess you could say I trust them with my life.

November 13

Another night that I just cannot concentrate enough to work on that damned *Macbeth* paper. I got everything else done, though, and I still have a few days for the paper, so it will be okay. I worked at the lab with Warren (and okay, there was some pretty heavy making out in addition to work, but nothing blew up this time) for a few hours and came back to the dorm. Emily was here working, and she asked me if I'm ready for the civics test, and I think I am. Then ...

> Emily: Did he ask you to stay with him over holiday break?

> Me, awkwardly: Warren? Um, not like WITH him. Just that we will both be here. Are you going home?

> Emily, totally ignoring my question: I thought he'd come home.

> Me: Right. You're from the same town. I kind of forgot that. It's right outside of Wiltshire, right?

> Emily: Kingsley. It's not far from here. I can come back if I need to.

Me: Um, sure. I'm sure I'll be fine, though.
I mean, it will be nice to have free rein of
campus with almost everyone gone.

Emily: Yeah. Have fun.

She threw her headphones in and started watching a movie on her laptop, jotting notes in a little notepad she always carries around with her. It shook me a bit, that she just basically wanted to know about Warren. A little of that weird tunnel vision. I don't feel like she's abnormal in any way except for that, this obsession with him, and when she slips into it it's really uncomfortable. He told me she has a lot to sort out, and I can be patient while she does, but this part of it, with Warren, is going to get old soon. I may have to confront her about that, and that's really the last thing I want to do. She needs to understand that it's over between them, and he's with me now. Undoubtedly with me.

What could Warren have seen in her? I don't consider myself pretty, really. I'm certainly no Katy Ashton, but I'm not plain. Emily . . . is. She's got kind of rounded, soft features and big eyes, but her hair is medium length and stuck in a weird in-between shade of brown and blond, she's not too tall and not too short, and she's not thin but she's not curvy, either. There's just nothing that really stands out.

I shouldn't say that. She's super smart. Probably smarter than me in a lot of ways. And goodness knows Warren isn't in it for looks with me. I guess I'm just curious and a little . . . Wait. Am I jealous? Is this what jealousy feels like? Ugh. I suppose I could talk to Katy about it, maybe get her advice about how to talk to Emily, but I have a feeling Katy would tell me to go full nuclear on her, and I don't want to do that. It wouldn't go over well with us being roommates, not to mention her issues, but I also just don't want to do that to Emily. Everyone else has deserted her, and I know all too well how that feels.

Mom would know how to handle this. She was always so patient with everyone, always gave people the benefit of the doubt, and always looked for the best in people. She'd help me with Emily. But I guess I'll never know what advice she would have given me.

November 15

Yeah. You know how I've had some really good days at Prescott and it's been amazing?

This was the worst day I've had at Prescott.

I stayed up all night to do that stupid *Macbeth* paper, and it still turned out like actual crap. And I should have spent more time studying for civics, or at least getting some sleep last night. The teacher handed the graded tests back and I got a B-. I've never gotten a B- on anything in all my life. That's only a small step up from a C! And a C is as good as failing.

The Club tried to comfort me by taking me for a burger and fries at a little diner not far off campus, but I felt guilty spending that time away from my books. Warren asked me if I wanted to stay the night with him. Just sleeping, he clarified, and I'm glad because I'm not quite sure I'm ready for anything else yet. He's amazing but . . . I never have, so . . . yeah, nervous and I feel sort of embarrassed, I guess, that I'm so inexperienced. BUT ANYWAY. That said, I'm not sure "just sleeping" would be a thing that could happen if I was allowed to be next to him all night. But God, his arms around me all night after the day I've had? Hard to turn down.

We said good-bye to Katy and Drew and he walked me home. He kissed me really sweetly and hugged me close and told me all we had to do was make it until the holiday break. Then we could be alone and not have to worry about classes or homework or anyone else but the two of us. And sure, all that time alone with Warren is a little scary, too, but in a good way. A really good way.

He's right. One step at a time. And there's so much to look forward to.

November 20

C.

That's what I got on the *Macbeth* paper.

I don't know what I'm going to do. I have a few more small assignments and the exam, but basically, this paper is such a huge part of my grade that I'd need to be perfect on all of those things to average a B.

I didn't tell Warren or Katy or Drew. As a matter of fact, I didn't even go to the lab tonight. I asked Warren if he could handle doing it all on his own and he said of course. He looked concerned and I could tell he wanted to ask, but I quickly made an excuse and came back to my room as fast as I could. I suppose if he texts tonight I'll tell him, but I'm so embarrassed. Especially since he has it together so well.

Emily, however, was amazing tonight. She was here when I got home from classes and immediately knew something was wrong and I . . . I just broke down. I told her I was afraid that I couldn't keep up with Prescott's classes and that with everything else going on (I did not say what, but I'm sure she thought I meant Warren and nothing else), I was falling behind.

She handed me a box of tissues and talked me through it, but first she picked up her laptop and ordered pizza for us.

By the time the pizza arrived, she'd talked me safely out of the panic attack zone. She also admitted to me that she has a hard time keeping up too. I should have realized that. Of course that's why she's always gone. She's working on her writing or her films in addition to all the classes we're taking. She puts in as many hours as I do. Probably more. She never seems to sleep.

Then she told me she'd help me with English if I wanted, and suggested asking the teacher for some extra credit. Apparently this teacher gives it out like candy if you ask.

I thanked her, and confessed that I kind of thought maybe she hated me. Just a little.

> Emily: I don't hate you. I mean, I kind of
> think we're friends? At least I'd like to be.

I didn't realize what a relief it would be to hear that. Because that meant maybe living with her while dating Warren wouldn't have to be so hard. But also because . . . well, if I'm honest, if Emily can still want to be friends with me even if she's still not over my boyfriend, she's going to be there through thick and thin, right? And I could use a friend like that.

> Me: We're friends. I just thought that maybe
> things had changed. Because of Warren.

> Emily: I was upset, I guess. Kind of mad,
> actually. I was just so into him. He's so
> confident and smart and . . . all of those good
> things, you know? He's perfect. Or at least I

92

thought he was. But he's soooo not. And I can see that now. You know what I mean. I'm sure you've seen it by now too.

Me, not at all sure I "know" what she's talking about in the slightest: Sure.

Emily: Thought so. Just be careful. He'll get you hooked.

Me: I'll be careful.

When I was stuffed with pizza and feeling much better about things, Emily said she was going to go to the AV room for a while, and I was truthfully a little happy to have some time to myself. I took a long shower and sulked and I'm going to take advantage of Warren working for me tonight and get to bed early

November 22

So tonight, Warren and I were alone in the lab, which isn't unusual. Katy and Drew stop in a lot but are rarely part of the process. Things are going so well with the product. He and I have found such a great rhythm together that we practically communicate with our own language. With a glance or hum or slight shake of our

heads, we tell each other everything we need to know.

And, uh, there are times when those things communicate another type of message entirely, and we tug off our gloves and goggles and his mouth meets mine without a single word ever having been exchanged.

Tonight we were probably fifteen minutes into a heavy make-out session when Warren pulled back and looked at me with those gorgeous eyes of his.

> Warren: So, holiday break . . . Drew is going home.

> Me: So is Emily.

> Warren: So, we'll both be alone. In our dorms. With no one there to interfere.

> Me: Or miss us if we're gone. But what about the dorm advisers? Won't they be patrolling?

> Warren, shaking his head: Not as often, and they really don't care.

> Me, cocking my head at him: Have you paid them off too?

Warren, laughing: No, although I think they'd
be easy to bribe. So . . . does that mean you'd
want to stay with me?

I do, I really do. But I'm nervous. I tried to explain my
nervousness to him, telling him how I have no experience
whatsoever (so embarrassing) and how I'm not sure if I'm
ready. But as usual, words and I do not mix, and it all sort
of tumbled out like incoherent nonsense. And I must have
went on and on because suddenly he stepped close to me,
took my hands in his, and silenced me with a short, sweet
kiss.

Warren: Bailey, we will take all the time you
need. You know how I am about finding the
perfect moment. And . . . (he ran his fingers
through my hair soothingly) don't worry
about any of that. I mean, everything we've
done together so far has turned out pretty
great, hasn't it?

He was right, of course. And this is Warren, after all. He'll
make everything perfect. So it's settled. I'll stay with Warren
overnight when I'm ready.

I'm already so nervous I could puke.

December 7

Last night a snowstorm passed through and the entire campus was covered in a foot of snow. It was gorgeous, but of course, the drawback to being at a boarding school is that no one has any excuse to miss class. Even in a foot of snow, classes are happening, and you're walking. But they do allow boots in the snow, so at least my feet weren't blocks of ice by the time I reached my first class.

This isn't the first time it's snowed on campus, but it's the first time it's snowed enough to do anything with it. Everyone was antsy to get classes over with and get outside, even the teachers. It was like, for the day, we were all little kids again.

Warren met me before first period with a coffee, and it felt so warm and cheery in my hands. He seemed to be in a really good mood, just like everyone else. I swear the whole campus got quieter. Even some of the teachers took a day off, so to speak. In English we were allowed to read all period. Mr. Callahan had us do our work individually and silently at our desks, and in civics the teacher showed us a video about John F. Kennedy instead of actually teaching anything.

Let's be honest, they were just as excited as us and wanted to get home and enjoy the snow or hibernate or whatever teachers do in this kind of weather.

The day seemed to fly by, and as soon as I got out of class,

I ran home to change into something warmer and snugglier. Emily was home, doing the exact same thing. She said she was going with some of the AV kids to sled behind the arts building. She said it was pretty much Prescott tradition. I told her I hoped I'd see her there, and I was going to check in with Katy and the gang first.

I didn't have to wait long. Katy, Drew, and Warren showed up at my door (literally, my door. The dorm mom let them up). Drew had a plastic sled.

Me: Behind the arts building?

Katy, winking: For a while, then we have even better plans.

Emily wasn't wrong. All of Prescott, freshmen to seniors, was behind the arts building, where the steepest and biggest hill on campus was. It was already getting a little dark, but there were some lights coming from the arts building and beside it from the parking lot.

Katy and I sledded down together the first time and came to a crashing halt at the bottom, flipping over a few times before landing hard in the snow. We both lay there giggling like idiots until Drew and Warren came over and practically carried us back up the hill, we were laughing so hard. Everyone was going down so fast and it was so crowded, it was pretty dangerous.

Some of the kids even got creative and were using things like trash can lids and cafeteria trays as sleds. So hysterical. As Drew and Katy went down together, I looked around for Emily and saw her with a whole group of people I recognized but hadn't spoken to much. AV kids. She looked happy. They were laughing just as hard as me and Katy, and I don't know why, but it made me so happy to see her smiling. I don't see her with other people much. She disappears all the time, sure, but she never really talks about anyone else, so maybe she does have friends and it's just that they're all as busy as she is.

Then Drew and Katy were back, and it was me and Warren's turn. He sat behind me on the plastic sled and wrapped his arms around me as we coasted down. We glided easily all the way to the bottom until another sled rammed into us and we had to help each other up. We kept slipping and grabbing for each other all the way back up the hill, absolutely cracking up at how clumsy we were.

I'm not sure how long we stayed out, but it was cold enough that my toes and fingers were completely numb. And that's when Drew and Warren signaled to each other and grabbed me and Katy and pulled us off the hill.

We went down through the courtyard area and then back behind the freshman boys' dorm, which is famously the farthest dorm away from the school. Then, without a word, we slipped into the woods behind the dorm and walked until we could no longer see any of Prescott's lights.

To my surprise, we were not the only ones there. There was a fire pit in the center of a small clearing, and it was blazing brightly. (I later learned that a senior had stolen it from a local hardware place years ago, and the delinquents of Prescott have been using it ever since.) There were people everywhere, mostly upperclassmen from what I could tell. They were gathered around the fire, talking in small groups. Some stood a little farther away, talking in hushed tones, and then there were couples at the very fringes of the fire's light, taking advantage of some time away from the watchful eyes of teachers and dorm parents. First Snow Bonfire: the other Prescott tradition, my friends explained.

Warren and Drew had disappeared somewhere, and when they came back they had cups of hot chocolate for us. I sipped it, then turned with surprise to Warren, who winked. Someone had definitely spiked the hot chocolate. It was a little minty, and it was good. Katy and I settled onto a fallen tree branch and talked to some people around us, and with each other, as Drew and Warren worked the crowd. I noticed that Katy mostly watched Drew but thought better of pointing out that fact.

Katy introduced me to people I already knew from classes, it's just that I'd never seen them in this particular context, and if Katy was taking the time to introduce them, they were probably somebodies in the Prescott world. I nodded my head and drank as she did most of the talking.

I looked over at Warren at some point. He and Drew were with a group of boys I knew were sort of jocks. Prescott didn't have a football team or even a basketball team. We were too small for that. But we had lacrosse and crew. And those boys were athletes. Warren and Drew were doing their silent communication thing—I could tell even from the distance—and when one of the jock boys gestured in question, Warren and Drew nodded at each other before reaching out and shaking the jock's hand in turn. Then the whole group, Warren and Drew included, went off into the woods for a while.

The alcohol hit me all at once and I started giggling out of nervousness. Katy thought it was terribly amusing and went to get us refills. By the time Warren and Drew were back, I was sufficiently warm and tipsy.

The boys got us yet another refill and I sort of just slumped against Warren, letting him hold me and keep me warm, and I felt incredibly happy to be here, at Prescott, with Warren and my friends, who were obviously amazing, in the snow.

I heard Katy ask Drew about the boys, and their voices got quiet but I could tell from their tones they were excited about whatever they were discussing. I mumbled something to Warren about it and he chuckled, all low and sexy, and told me that yeah, things were good, and things were going to get better if we played our cards right.

I'm not sure what cards we are playing, and I'm not sure how anything could get any better, but I'm up for it, whatever it is.

December 8

Emily and I both slept until lunch today. Whoops.

Apparently, most of the school did, or at least the upperclassmen. Emily followed the proper Prescott procedure and called the school secretary for both of us, thank goodness, and the secretary sarcastically said something about a sudden illness raging on campus.

She and I went to lunch together and headed off to class. I do wonder why Emily slept in, though. I didn't see her at the bonfire at all, but I didn't ask. Maybe she did something with the AV kids, and that's a good thing, right? I'm certainly paying the price for all my fun. My head is STILL killing me.

Warren was just fine. As a matter of fact, he seemed to be in a great mood. Perhaps it was because things were going to get better, like he said last night. I didn't ask, honestly. I just tried to absorb some of his good mood. He was so calm and lovey tonight at the lab, exactly what I needed as I recovered. He even did most of the work tonight since I was still nauseated. I swear he's the perfect boyfriend.

The countdown until break is creeping by. I can't stand it! I'm soooo nervous, but also, the anticipation is KILLING me. I want everyone to go away so it's just me and Warren. I think I'll fill the time with more shopping with Katy and, of course, some extra time at the lab. ;)

December 19

Today is the last day before the holiday break, and even though the teachers assigned homework for the next two weeks, everyone seems to be in a great mood.

To my surprise, Emily gave me a present this morning, explaining she'd be leaving for home right after classes are over, so we probably won't see each other again. It was a copy of *Notting Hill*, the director's cut with all these extra features on it. It was amazing of her, really, to get me something that kind of bridged our worlds, with her love of films and . . . Mom. She knew it reminded me of Mom. I'd gotten her something too, though my gift was nowhere near as cool. Just passes to the movie theater in Wiltshire, which I knew were useful if not creative. She seemed really happy to get them. Maybe she and I can go together sometime, if things are still going okay between us.

I gave Katy a scarf-and-gloves set I'd seen her admiring on our last shopping trip. Katy got me an adorable travel bag for makeup and toiletries, perfect for spending the night in the boys' dorm, she added with a wink. She also gave me some, um, pointers for my first night with Warren, and it was honestly the sweetest thing anyone's done for me so far here at Prescott. It wasn't just stuff about how to make Warren feel good but a few tidbits for me, too, to make sure it wouldn't hurt much the first time. She told me about losing her virginity last year and it was sort of a cautionary tale, I suppose. Some older guy she wanted to impress who broke her heart after, so she told me to be absolutely sure I wanted to be with Warren. We kind of bonded over it all, and that was truly the best gift she gave me.

Drew and I exchanged nothing except an awkward hug and he gave me a very pointed and knowing "Have a great time here alone over break." I guess Warren told him, which is fine. I can't really expect Warren not to tell his best friend, and it's not like he told the whole world. It's just kind of embarrassing, and . . . I don't know. It's like it adds to some of the buildup or something.

Like the more we talk about it, the more I can't possibly compare to whatever people are thinking.

I didn't have any idea what to get Warren. Not one thing seemed good enough, so in the end I got him a few things to make up for it: a Princeton hoodie, a fur-lined hat that I thought would look Russian chic and perfect with his ever-present coat, and a metal paperweight for his dorm desk that was made to look like a molecule.

We aren't exchanging presents yet, though. We're going to wait until Christmas.

Drew isn't gone yet, but Emily and Katy are. I've got the room all to myself tonight, which I kind of feel like I need. Honestly, I had myself a good cry about Mom while no one was around to see. It's the second Christmas without her. Last year everyone was down and missing her so much. Now Dad has moved on. How is he okay with not decorating the tree with her or making her ooey-gooey fudge? I used to complain about having to stir that chocolate for so long on the stove; now I wish I could get every minute back.

December 21

It's day two of holiday break and everyone is gone except for me and Warren. There are probably some other people here, but honestly, it feels like he and I are the last two people on earth.

In a really, really good way. I'm not sure I'd even notice other people on campus anyway. It's just us and the lab and the work.

We pretty much spend most of our time in the lab. We go straight there after breakfast and work until lunch, then we walk to the coffee shop and grab a sandwich. Yesterday we had to go back to the lab right away because of where we were in the making process, but today we spent the afternoon watching movies curled up in his bed, dozing or kissing or both. We had to go back and work late afterward, but it was worth it. We are absolutely swamped right now with orders or whatever you want to call them. Drew was right about that: The holidays have driven demand right up. He'll be here tomorrow to get the product and make deliveries. Mark stopped by and I watched, kind of awestruck, as Warren handed him a thick stack of bills. I didn't ask how much it cost us. I don't want to know some things. Also, I'm more than satisfied with my own cut, so it really doesn't matter to me.

Speaking of my own cut, Warren and I have gone to a nice restaurant for dinner every night, once in Wiltshire, and we went to Kingsley tonight, and we're thinking of heading to Covington tomorrow for a seafood place, if there's time. For the first time ever, I don't even glance at prices. Warren drives. Warren bought the car by himself. I get the feeling his parents don't buy him much of anything. I haven't asked him outright, but he's said as much. Maybe I'll ask him tonight at dinner. I don't know much about his family, and that's part of being a girlfriend, right? I could bring up my family first. Even Mom.

It would be really nice to talk to someone about Mom. Especially Warren.

Okay, I need to get ready for that dinner. We'll probably have to go back to the lab when we get back, just to check on things. Then I'll go to his place.

So far I haven't been ready, exactly. But Warren is super sweet about everything and there's been no pressure. I don't know how I got so lucky, with him and Science Club in general. They may not be a secret coven of vampires, but it feels just as cool.

December 22

Wow. Just wow. I asked Warren about his family and I am still kind of reeling from everything he told me. We'd had some wine with dinner (it was one of Drew's family's restaurants, so they knew Warren and it was on the house, no questions asked), so I'm not really sure if he'd have been so honest without it, but I'd like to believe he just trusts me that much.

Really, I only asked because I told him about Mom tonight. He asked me about her, and I don't know, it was like a dam broke, and a rush of emotions spilled out. I told him how she died, how I tried to be so strong for Dad and Bex, how Dad found Isa, how sometimes Bex seems to not remember as much about Mom as I do, and how I feel like sometimes I'm the only one still grieving.

He reached across the table and took my hand, and he was a little teary as he listened. And that's when I worked up the courage to ask him about the family he never mentions.

He started telling me about his parents and what happened with them in a rush, just like I had, and I am certain he needed to tell someone. I think this might be eating him up inside, and he can't afford to keep it in anymore. I'm not sure he even talks to Drew about this, although I'm sure Drew knows. I don't know. I just feel very, very honored that he opened up to me about it. And knowing what I know now, it's no surprise he felt he could: We actually have a lot in common.

Warren had an older brother named Mitchell. Mitch was a lot older, meant to be an only child, but Warren was an "oops" for his parents eight years later (we both had a good laugh when he said that). When Warren was in middle school and his brother was in college, though, things went really sour. His parents kept it from him for a while but he figured it out soon enough: Mitch was an addict. What had started off as an addiction to pills—something to soothe the pain of a baseball injury from high school—had become more. Unable to get enough pills to satisfy him through a prescription, he'd turned to getting them on the street. When that became too hard and too expensive, he'd found something cheaper and easier to get: heroin.

Warren said all he really remembered about that year was his mother crying a lot, his dad constantly leaving, looking for Mitch, who had disappeared again. There was a stint in a good rehab, an even longer visit to a great rehab, and a period of sobriety. Then a setback, then again, days of not hearing from him, not knowing where he was. It was his father who discovered Mitch after a long disappearance, blue and swollen and alone, a needle still in his arm.

Though that hadn't been easy for him to tell me, the next part seemed even harder for Warren to speak out loud.

It was like a light went out in his mother. It wasn't just grief or even depression, it was . . . more. She lost her job, wouldn't leave the house; she barely responded when spoken to. Warren's father tried to help her. He had all sorts of therapists and doctors come to work with her, but nothing worked. He even sent her away for a while, to a facility in Florida, thinking some warmth and like-minded people would do her some good, but she came back virtually unchanged. After a while, Warren's father gave up, or at least he accepted that nothing was going to change. He started to stay late at work, went away for long business trips, anything he could do to avoid home. They never officially divorced; his father still takes care of his mother in most ways, but he no longer lives there.

And meanwhile, Warren was growing up, and they didn't notice. The only way they seemed to acknowledge his existence at all was when he would do something truly extraordinary, like getting into Prescott, being accepted into Princeton's summer program, getting the Headmaster's Award for chemistry. Sometimes they would be sad about it, saying it was something Mitchell should have done, but it was still attention. It was still some kind of recognition. So that's what he tried to do, all the time. Excel in everything. To make them see, to be seen. To make up for Mitchell's loss. To do the things Mitchell would never do.

So when I ask him how it's possible that he does all that he does, I guess I know how. He doesn't really see any other choice.

We were quiet for a while on the way home. I kept replaying the things he'd said over and over in my head, trying to grasp the scope of it all, how shaped Warren was by his brother's choices and by his family. But as I was sitting there, trying to comprehend everything Warren had to go through and everything he's still dealing with, Warren

109

started asking me about Mom. Not asking me about her death or how much I missed her or anything, but just MOM in general. What she was like. What was my favorite thing about her. And I found myself smiling, remembering things I hadn't let myself think about in a while and telling Warren all about them. He was smiling too, laughing along with me at my stories, and I realized: I'd never felt so close to him. Our pasts tied us together somehow, two scarred people just trying to keep going. I admire him so much for that ability to go on, and my heart breaks for him, for how hard he works to be noticed. He's really amazing, and I think . . . I think I'm in love with him.

At that moment I decided I didn't want to wait any longer. I squeezed his hand and told him so.

Warren: You mean . . . ?

Me: Yes.

Warren: You're sure?

Me: I'm sure.

Warren: Because if you're not . . .

Me: Warren. I'm sure. I know you're all about
finding that perfect moment. I think this is it.

So we went back to his dorm.

That's all I can write right now. I'm finally back in my room,
and . . . well, I need to get some sleep. More to come . . .

December 23

Okay, back to it. I'm not supposed to meet Warren at the lab
for a half hour, so I have time to write. It's sort of embarrassing
to write all this down, but I want to remember, later. I want to
remember everything about last night. Honestly, I might veer
into a sappy romance-novel kind of thing, but that's what it felt
like, so it's just the truth. Last night could not have been any
more perfect. Warren was perfect.

After I told him I was ready, we both kind of sat there in
dumb silence for a moment and I almost started to panic, like
maybe he was going to change his mind, then I looked over at
him and he was grinning like an absolute idiot and I started to
giggle. Then he started to laugh and it was like we couldn't stop
laughing. I think it was just nerves or something but whatever it
was, it totally relaxed me.

We parked and checked for the dorm mom when we
sneaked in the front door. She was nowhere in sight, and it was

late enough that maybe she wouldn't do rounds again. When we got to Warren's room . . .

Okay, so I won't lie. At first it was like this totally intense making out. Greedy and needy and hot. The kind of thing you see on TV where it's out of control and clothes get torn. But it was like Warren came to his senses at some point, or at least had the decency to step back and, like he promised, be patient enough to make it right.

So he lit some candles and everything got a lot gentler and slower and he was so sweet. Intense, but focused on me totally, and it was amazing to feel like the center of his universe.

I can't even believe I'm going to write this down but here it is: It didn't hurt like I thought it would, just kind of foreign feeling and new. And . . . good. Very good. He looked in my eyes and kept mumbling my name in my ear and afterward he made sure I was okay and held me like I was something really precious to him. Then we talked all night, getting to know each other even more. Things we remembered from our childhoods, before things got hard, dreams for the future, the pressures we're facing now at Prescott. We just . . . we just click. He's wonderful in so many ways.

I am seriously the luckiest girl in the whole world that I got to lose my virginity to Warren Clark.

We have a full day ahead of us at the lab, and we're going to try to get homework done today.

You know, if we don't lose our focus. ;)

January 2

I feel bad that I haven't written in a while, but I'm not really sure why. I guess because Dad got this diary for me, so I feel like it's an obligation to him, even though he'll never read it. It's not like he feels any obligation to me.

I shouldn't have written that. It's just that I've barely heard from him at all. I spoke to him on Christmas, but I have to wonder if it's only because I called him. If I hadn't picked up the phone to call, would he have?

He said he and Isa had a wonderful Christmas. They visited her parents and spent a weekend at a cozy bed-and-breakfast. He inquired about my Christmas and I told him it had been great (it had, even if it was just me and Warren and Chinese takeout, which I did not mention), and he asked how school was. I kept that brief too. He asked if I'd received his presents and told me he enjoyed the ones I'd sent to him and Isa (gold cuff links for him, now that he has to attend fancy events with her all the time, and emerald earrings for her. No one seemed to notice that emerald was Mom's birthstone). He did not ask how I'd afforded them. I hung up the phone feeling like we hadn't really spoken at all.

I don't know what I'd expected or hoped for. Maybe an "I missed you so much, Bailey!" or an "I feel terrible that we didn't get to spend Christmas together." And of course he made no mention of Mom.

And I don't really know why I'm complaining. I did talk to Bex on Christmas and she has decided she was basically meant to ski. She said she was a natural on the slopes, which I don't doubt. And it *was* a great Christmas. Warren loved his presents. He got me a cashmere sweater in forest green (to match my eyes, he said), a sapphire necklace (his birthstone), and a pair of really good safety goggles, which we both had a good laugh over. He told me they were for Princeton, not our "work," and I was touched.

He got a little fake tree with lights on it and we sat in the glow of the lights and ate the takeout and laughed and he held me all night again.

I don't know what I'm going to do when everyone else gets back tomorrow, and the dorm mothers are going to be patrolling regularly again. For a while it was just me and Warren, and no stress or worries other than making sure the process was still going smoothly. I wish we could go on forever like this.

January 3

Well, I think Emily is back to hating me, or whatever it is she called it. She came in and dumped her suitcase on her bed and asked how break was. I told her it was fine. Quiet. Hardly anyone around. I guess from there she must have deduced that I spent most of the time with Warren and went silent. When I asked about her break she was completely bitchy. Like me talking to her was irritating. Thank God I got a text from Katy that she was back and so I ran out the door to meet her.

Katy got her hair cut! I can't believe it. There's no way, if I had her hair, I'd have chopped it off, but of course, this haircut just makes her look more sophisticated and fashionable. It's a shoulder-length bob now. I swear she needs a beret or a cigarette holder or something and the look would be complete. Très chic.

Drew and Warren met us for dinner but afterward we sneaked off again for girl time. Warren promised he'd handle the lab, so Katy and I got ice cream and I dished about my break with Warren. She faked tears and put her hand over her heart and said she was a proud mama. I swear, we went over every detail, and she properly reacted to it all, giving me more advice when necessary and beaming proudly at other times. I also told her about Emily being kind of awful.

> Katy: Yeah, well, that's Emily. I'm surprised
> she hasn't made a voodoo doll of you or drawn
> some kind of curse symbol under your bed.
> Even now she still follows Warren around.

Me: Wait, what? She follows him around?

Katy, licking her spoon: Yeah. Sometimes she
talks to him. Sometimes she just trails him.
It's creepy.

Me: So Warren knows?

Katy: Yeah, of course, but Warren's too nice of
a person to do anything about it. Every time he
talks to her I can tell he just feels sorry for her.

Like, I don't know why it bothers me that Warren hasn't
told me about Emily, but it does. It's not like I suspect there's
anything going on between them, but that seems like something
I should know. What if she's watching us? Following us around?
It's creepy. I feel like I should start carrying Mace but . . . I live
with her. It's not like I can protect myself too much. Thank
goodness she's not there most of the time.

Katy had continued talking but I only noticed when I heard
her say:

Katy: . . . but Warren's a fantastic kisser, so I'm
sure he's good at everything else, too, right?

Me: How do you know he's a fantastic
kisser???

Katy, laughing: Don't worry! It was a long
time ago. Eighth grade. We made out at a
party at Campbell. I think we were dared
to, actually. But I had braces so he probably
thought I sucked. I don't know. I've never had
the courage to ask him.

I laughed, amazed and surprised that Katy Ashton, of all
people, didn't have the courage to ask Warren about a kiss three
years ago. And that she'd had braces! I assumed her straight
teeth were a result of great genes, just like her hair and high
cheekbones and body, magically toned even though I know she
never sets foot in the gym.

There is a weird part of me that is super glad Katy Ashton
had flaws at some point. It makes me feel way more hopeful
about the future.

January 8

Ugh. I don't know what's gotten into me, but I totally forgot
that I should have been working on the Princeton science
program application over break too, because it's due next week.

Luckily, Mr. Callahan already had a letter of recommendation drafted for me, so all I have to do is find another teacher to have my two. But there's an essay due as well, plus my transcripts. So now I'm going to have to get those expedited to Prescott in some way. Maybe my old school can fax them? Are faxes still a thing?

And don't even get me started on the essay. Macbeth was bad enough. I should have been working on this for weeks. At least it's only five pages, but I'm supposed to talk about how I want to use chemistry to achieve my goals. It SHOULD be easy but it's not because, honestly, I don't really know what my goals are. I just know I'm good at this, so I want to keep being good at this and get into a great school for it, but it's not like Warren. He wants to find a way to cure addiction. Of course he does, after what he's gone through with his brother. What can I say? I want to cure cancer? Embrace a cliché? Maybe I can say, "Hey, Princeton. I don't really have any original goals on my own so I'm just going to say I want to help my boyfriend do all these amazing things," because really, what else have I got?

Ugh. I've got to get my shit together.

January 9

So, after thinking about it all through classes today, I think I'm going to write my essay about making drugs that will help people who are in pain but aren't addictive. So it's LIKE Warren's idea, kind of piggybacking on it, but a different way to think about it. I'm happy with that, and it's a good goal. Maybe I'll actually adopt that as a goal.

I was writing the essay tonight at the lab, thinking about Warren and his brother, and for some reason, I just couldn't keep my mouth shut.

Me: Warren? Can I ask you something?

Warren, looking up from mixing a compound in a beaker, his goggles making him look like an owl: Anything, Bailey.

Me: Does it ever bother you that you're doing this? Making meth and selling it?

Warren, pushing his goggles up on his head: Haven't we talked about this before? I thought you were okay with this?

Me: I am. I think. I was mainly trying to ask about you. Since . . . since your brother and everything.

Warren set aside the chemicals and leaned on a stool, looking at me all seriously. Then he started talking, and although he seemed just as sincere as he had the other night when he told me about Mitchell dying, there was something almost robotic about it. Like he'd given this speech a hundred times before. So much that it was memorized.

I had to wonder if it's because it's something he has to constantly tell himself.

He said his brother is the whole reason why he does it. He went into more detail about Mitchell's death, saying that the heroin he'd used the night he died was laced with fentanyl, which is a thousand times stronger than heroin. And that even though his brother was an addict, he'd still be here if he hadn't gotten a product that was bad. If the product had been reliable and safe. So he wants to make sure that what's available is good and pure.

But he also told me that meth is different. He said a meth overdose is really rare and that usually, if it happens, it's because the person was sick in some other way, in addition to being an addict. Not that I'd imagined people dying because of what we were doing (don't get me wrong, I knew it was a possibility, but I keep that far from my mind because I know we make something safe), but I do feel better knowing it's rare. Like Warren said, people are going to do drugs. We just need to make it safer for them.

Maybe I can put something like that in my essay.

January 15

Okay, is it just me, or did the teachers literally double up the amount of homework now that everyone's back from break? I have to read two chapters of *Canterbury Tales* tonight, solve about a bajillion calculus problems, and answer all the chapter review questions for three chapters in civics. Just tonight! Even Mr. Callahan assigned twice the equations to balance that he usually does. I don't even know why I'm bothering to write in this diary right now. I have too much other stuff to do. I'm beginning to think maybe it's my way of telling Dad what's going on with me, even if he could just ask.

Or maybe it's my way of telling Mom. . . . I don't know. I don't have time to psychoanalyze myself tonight.

I talked to Mr. Callahan a little after class about maybe backing off on the extra work for a little while. He said that adjusting to Prescott's expectations can be difficult for a first-time student because the work definitely gets harder as you go, and there's more of it. He said in a few weeks I'll get the hang of it and know how to balance my time, and we could resume then. He didn't seem angry or even disappointed, so I was relieved. He asked about the essay for the Princeton application and I told him it was done.

It's not. It's not anywhere close. I have two more days. But I DID call my old school and they said they could scan and e-mail my transcripts to my adviser here. Thank goodness. I feel so behind and so unorganized, which is totally UN-Bailey, really, but . . . let's be honest. A lot about this year has been pretty un-Bailey. I'm part of a pretty elite group, I have extra money to spend, I have a sexy boyfriend, not to mention my "side job." It's no wonder I'm a little behind, but who could blame me? And honestly, it's worth it. I DO need to get more organized, though. I can do everything if I just focus and schedule myself better.

I didn't feel like I could skip out on Warren at the lab tonight, even though he said he'd be fine without my help. We're still trying to meet a high demand. Almost everyone who, um, distributes for Drew is out of product, so we're trying to build up a supply again.

Warren was super sweet, though, and mostly handled everything while I did my civics and calculus. He looked over my calculus homework and I only missed one. He takes that class as well, just a different period than I do, so I told him just to copy my work and get a different question wrong. Hey, at least one of us won't have to do it all tonight, and it was the least I could do since he handled the lab work. He said he'd do the work tomorrow, and that sounds like a good deal to me.

By the time I got back, Emily was asleep, which is just fine because I'm in no mood to deal with another human being, even if she decided to be Nice Emily. Ha. Maybe that's how

I should refer to her from now on. She's either Nice Emily or Scary Emily.

Just a few more chemistry formulas to balance and I can go to bed. I swear I could sleep for days, that's how tired I am. But there's no way I can slack off now. In fact, I need to do more than usual to keep on top of things. If I don't, I swear all this work is just going to pile up and suffocate me, like a big giant stress monster swallowing me whole. Okay, that's the weirdest sentence I've ever written, but also so true. I feel like I'm barely ahead of all of this, and if I don't keep up or I falter in any way, it's going to get me.

January 16

I wrote part of my essay in chemistry today. If there is any class I can afford to not pay attention in, it's chemistry. Plus, it's chemistry related, so I think it counts. It's too bad Mr. Callahan can't give me extra credit for all I do with Science Club. Ha! He didn't notice that I wasn't working on his stuff, I don't think. We weren't doing a lab today at all. He was lecturing about acids, stuff I know pretty well from my old school. I got the notes from Katy later anyway.

Everyone was at the lab tonight, and it was funny because I guess Warren and I are kind of used to having it alone now. We were doing our dance, mind-meld thing as we worked and Katy and Drew thought it was sickeningly cute. And once, after we finished an incredible-looking batch, Warren picked me up and spun me and kissed me like no one was around. Drew started whistling and clapping. Honestly, it's really cool that they're so happy that we're happy. And I really miss alone time with Warren. . . . I wonder when Drew will go home next. Ha.

The only downside to having everyone there was that I didn't get nearly as much homework done, so I had a lot to do when I got back to my room. Emily was still up, doing her own homework, and she smiled at me and we commiserated about how much we had to do before settling back into it. She finished before I did and crawled into bed. I should have worked on my essay more before writing in here, but I'm just too tired. Katy's notes were good. Maybe I can write more in chemistry again tomorrow. I have another day. All I really have to do is type it up. The rest of the application is done.

January 17

Okay, well, I have GOT to get ahold of myself.

I overslept this morning. I hit snooze, only it wasn't snooze; I turned my alarm off. Luckily, Emily shook me awake and asked me if I was sick. While she was trying to inform me about sick day procedures at Prescott, I jumped up in a panic and pulled on my uniform. I barely had time to comb my hair.

I went to class without makeup and without a shower. I wanted to disappear all day long and just go home. I even thought about skipping lunch but I was starving since I didn't have any time to grab a bagel before classes started. Warren, bless him, didn't say a word about how awful I must have looked but hugged me hard after lunch, like he was concerned for me. Katy pulled me into the girls' room and let me use her concealer. Thank goodness for good friends.

I tried to work on my essay during chemistry but my brain felt like it had been fried. I barely got more than two paragraphs done, which left me tonight to finish it and type it up on top of all the other homework I had.

When I got to the lab tonight, I started to tell Warren about the essay and how it still wasn't done (I hadn't wanted to admit that to him. He's always so on top of things. I feel so stupid around him sometimes, I swear). Then I don't know what happened. Something in me snapped. One minute I was explaining about the essay and how I needed time to work on it tonight, the next I was apologizing for being such a screwup and sobbing into his chest while telling him about how hard Prescott was for me. Well, and not just Prescott. But my father being distant, missing Bex, missing my mom. . . . It was so bad I soaked his uniform sweater. I think . . . I think maybe I didn't realize how stressed I've been until I started talking about it. I don't think I knew how much I was missing my family, either. And how tired I really am. Even on good nights I'm hardly in bed by midnight, and classes start by seven thirty. At most I get six hours' sleep, if I can sleep well at all.

He held me, stroking my hair and telling me to tell him everything. Then he lifted me on top of the counter, kissed me, and started working through the problems with me in this amazing, confident, calm way. Exactly the opposite of me.

Warren: Everything is okay here, Bailey.
Don't worry about the product. I can
handle it.

Me: But . . . but you have a lot of work too.

Warren: Yes, but you have the essay to do.
That's an extra thing I don't have, since I've
been admitted to that program before. So go
ahead and work on it. Use my laptop to type
up what you have, and write the rest when
you're done. That way you're not writing
it twice. You can e-mail it to yourself and
print it in the lab in the morning. I'll give
you my calculus homework to copy, and

chemistry, too, if you haven't done it. I can't do your reading for you in English, though. If you can do it after your essay, great. If not, read it this weekend and catch up. If you're called on in class, tell her you think the stories are metaphors for sex or politics or something. That will make you sound like you know what you're doing. Works like a charm, trust me.

Me, grabbing his face and kissing him: You're wonderful, you know that? I'm a mess, but you're wonderful. Thank you.

Warren, smiling, intense gaze on me: You're not a mess, Bailey Wells. You can do this. And I'll help you.

And that's just what he did. I somehow managed to get everything done, and for the first time since break, I feel relaxed. It's late now, and I'm setting two alarms for tomorrow, just in case. And even though it was late when I went to bed and I set two alarms for myself just in case, for the first time since break, I felt relaxed.

January 19

I got my application in on time. I'm not sure the essay was the best it could be, but at least I got it done. I did decide to write about making drugs that are non-addictive in the future, and I managed to work in some info about the drug problem in the local area as well. No outside sources needed.

Warren insisted we go into Wiltshire to celebrate, and since Drew needed to make a few drops, he and Katy went with us. It turned into an excellent evening. Drew suggested we catch a movie while he was out taking care of business, so Katy and I overruled Warren to see a romantic comedy. We kept joking around that Warren had a harem, since it was like he was taking us both on a date. It totally embarrassed him, I think, but it was so fun to watch him blush and seem awkward for once. We were the only people in the theater, and so we got a little rowdy and had a popcorn fight and kept a running commentary of the movie as it played.

When we came out, Drew was waiting by his car for us, mission completed. He gestured to Warren, and Warren nodded, then the two boys went off a little ways to talk alone. Katy and I crawled into the warm car to wait, me in the back and her in shotgun.

Me: What's that about?

Katy: Probably just business. Who knows? They do this all the time.

Me: And it doesn't bother you that you're not included?

Katy, shrugging, focusing on her phone: Nah. The less I know, the better, really.

Me: But won't we all get in trouble anyway? If one of us is caught? Don't we all . . . you know, go down with the ship?

Katy, finally looking at me: Oh, you sweet, innocent child. Of course not. If Drew gets caught making drops, it's all on him. Or if you and Warren get busted in the lab one night, Drew and I don't know you. No, if you get caught, you take one for the team. Why do you think I always let Drew do the drops alone?

Me: So . . . cut and run?

Katy: Cut and run. As much as we can.

Me, squinting at her: Save yourself instead of all of us in it together? That doesn't seem very loyal.

Katy, snapping: Loyal? You don't think that's loyal, Bailey? If I got caught, I'd do everything I could to keep the rest of you from getting caught too. I'd take all the blame. You guys could go on with your lives while I rot in prison. I'd do it for all three of you, and I know Drew and Warren would do the same for me.

Me: Okay, okay. Sorry. I didn't understand. I get it now. I'd do it too. I just . . . didn't see it like that before.

Katy, softening: In this business, it's about doing the least amount of damage to ourselves that we can. You got me?

I think I got her. There is honor among thieves, so to speak. The most honorable thing you could do if you were caught would be to keep your mouth shut about everyone else and their involvement. And for some reason, it makes me feel safer. I mean, of course it's nice knowing that if one of us got caught, we wouldn't all go down. But it is also good to know that we'd all go to such lengths for each other. Again, I feel that weird sense of trust in this little group.

Of course there's the collateral to consider. Which would be used if we ever betrayed one another. But we would never do that.

Warren and Drew got back in the car, none the wiser to the conversation Katy and I had just had. Warren took my hand.

Katy: Everything okay?

Drew, smiling: More than okay. You know that thing we talked about? How we could expand? It's gonna start next week. One of our dealers has made a few connections, so there will be about five degrees separating it from us.

Katy: Excellent.

Drew: But that means Bailey and Warren will have to cook even more. Can you handle it?

Warren, squeezing my hand: We can handle it.

But . . . I'm not sure I can. I'm barely making it as it is. And I want to know more about this so-called expansion. Where are we expanding *to*? But then again, the less I know, the better (Katy's words). I think I should probably heed them. The less I know, the fewer lies I'd have to tell, and the more I can keep the distribution part of this process far, far away from me.

January 21

I have literally all my books piled up with me on the bed right now. Emily wanted to know if we could go see a movie with those passes I gave her and there's just no possible way I can. It's Sunday night, and it's my own fault because I left all of this to do until now. After the news Friday that we'd be expanding, Warren and I kicked up our production majorly yesterday, and we were there until late (luckily, no one else was, so we got in some great making out while things cooked around us), and we were at the lab most of today, too.

I apologized to Emily, saying it was bad planning/procrastination and totally my fault, and she nodded understandingly. She said the workload this semester was overwhelming, even for Prescott. We joked that the teachers are all involved in a conspiracy to drive us insane. Then she asked if Warren and I are pretty serious.

Emily: You're just spending a ton of time with him is all.

Me: You really want to know?

Emily, rolling her eyes: It's fine. I'm fine.

Me: Then yes, I think we're pretty serious.

Emily: But you're not hanging out with him tonight? He could probably help you with homework. He's smarter than anyone else here.

Me: I'm aware. But he's got his own work to do.

Emily: I'm sure he does.

I didn't really appreciate her talking to me like I don't know Warren or something. I'M his girlfriend, after all, and pretty soon he and I will have been together longer than he and Emily were. She was barely a blip on his radar. And I didn't like the knowing way she said, "I'm sure he does." She doesn't know the half of it. If she knew how he keeps up with his classes while also basically running a whole business . . .

Deep breaths, Bailey. Emily is no longer your competition. He broke up with her. And he's with you now. Relax. Okay, self. Good talk.

I just don't know why Warren seems to bring all the jealousy out of me. And really, thinking about our conversation, she could have meant everything she said innocently. It's just that I already have my hackles up with the stress and . . . yep. The jealousy. I vowed to give her the benefit of the doubt. Maybe this is more MY issue than hers.

Anyway, as we were working, Emily got a text. She glanced at it and got up, throwing her coat and boots on. She looked at me and shrugged, saying she'd be back later.

I was trying to seem calm and casual (I hope she couldn't tell that she'd gotten a rise out of me), so I didn't ask her where she was going. She can do whatever the hell she wants, as long as it's not with Warren.

January 27

I haven't written in a few days again. It's not just that I'm busy. It's that my hand actually hurts from writing as much as I have been. Warren and I are basically working from the minute classes end for the day until ten or eleven at night, then I come home and do any work I still have left, and fall asleep, usually on a book.

At least I'm not the only one. Emily's obviously been just as stressed-out. If she's here at all, she's sometimes passed out in her bed, snoring slightly. I can totally understand where she's coming from, so I just throw a blanket on her and let her sleep. We've both had to wake each other up for classes in the morning a few times now. Emily's incredibly hard to stir, so I sort of hate it. She acts like she doesn't know where she is for a while, and she always wants food first thing. Sometimes we're both so late there's no time to get breakfast, so she gets into our stash of granola bars and takes five or six for herself. I don't mind it, really. But I feel like if she's going to take a whole box of granola bars, basically, in one day, she should probably pay for the bulk of them. Whatever.

Mr. Callahan said I'd hear from Princeton in about a month, so nothing to report there yet.

In other news, I got a B on another English paper. This time about Chaucer. She said it was a good premise but not enough support with the text, and it lost its focus. I'm upset, but only at myself because she's right. The paper is a mess. I'm lucky she gave me a B, honestly.

But between that and the bad civics test, I've got to double my efforts in those two classes. I still have a chance to pull all As, if I can do phenomenally well in the next few assignments.

I'll start tomorrow. I'm just too tired tonight. I can't wait to get in bed and sleep. I feel like I could sleep for days.

January 28

Nothing really to report except to say I'm super pissed at myself. First day of trying to double my efforts in civics and English and I got home later than usual from the lab and fell asleep with my English book on my stomach.

I just can't stay awake, but if I can't stay awake longer, how can I get everything done???

January 29

Tonight I actually fell asleep in the lab. I woke up hunched over a lab table to Warren rubbing my shoulders. When I asked what time it was, Warren told me it was just after ten and that I'd been out for almost a half hour. A HALF HOUR.

Then he told me to go home and rest, that he could handle all the product tonight. And I looked at him and his bright blue eyes and sweet smile and I looked at all the books spread around me on the table and all the things we had simmering and smoking and cooking and . . . it just hit me that I'm failing everything. I'm failing school, I'm failing my friends, I'm failing Warren. I'm even failing Bex. I haven't called her for ages. I can't keep up with it all, can't hold up my end of the bargain.

All I do is disappoint, let people down, and break promises. Everything feels so out of reach and I can't remember the last time I had a break to rest. No break in sight, and only constantly disappointing everyone I care about and I . . .

I just lost it. Completely lost it. And it wasn't like I let out this big scream or sob or anything. I just sat there numb and tired and silently crying. That was the worst of it, I think. That there was no warning. The nervous breakdown sneaked up on me, and I was completely unprepared.

So was Warren. His eyes got as big as I'd ever seen them and he hugged me hard. Then he knelt in front of me, holding my hands while I cried and cried and cried.

> Me: I can't leave you to do all this alone anymore. I'm not being a good partner. Or girlfriend. Or sister or student or roommate or friend or . . . or anything right now. I just can't get it all done. All the homework and the Science Club. I thought it would get better, or I would, and it just hasn't.

> Warren, squeezing my hands: Bailey, it's okay. Everyone is struggling right now. Drew and Katy, even.

Me: What? They are? See? I don't even know that. I hardly see Katy. I haven't really seen her since before break. Just that dinner we had.

Warren: And I'm sure she misses you. But we're all really busy right now. Katy and Drew have a lot of responsibilities too, even though they don't have to work here as much. It's just hard right now. We'll get through it.

Me: What about you, Warren? I mean, you don't seem like you're tired like me. I know you're supposed to be a genius and all, but it can't be that easy for you, right? Please tell me it can't. Lie. Just for my sanity.

Warren, laughing: It's not that easy, Bailey. I promise. It's hard for me, too.

Me: But why aren't you tired?

Warren looked at me for a long moment, like he was considering his answer very carefully. Then he stood and took something out of his back pocket. He handed it to me. It was a plastic bag with small orange pills inside. They looked like candy. I stared at it. Oddly, I wasn't shocked or surprised, but I WAS curious. Scarily curious.

Warren: I AM tired all the time, Bailey. But I have a little extra help. From these.

Me: But . . . what are they? A prescription?

Warren: A mixture of amphetamines and dextroamphetamines. And yes, a prescription.

Me, knowing enough of those chemical names to understand now: Stimulants.

Warren: Adderall. I was prescribed it after Mitch died. Couldn't concentrate.

Me: And it helps keep you from falling asleep on your books at night?

Warren, nodding: And it makes me super focused and confident. Like I can do it all. And with the energy it gives me, I can.

Me, shaking my head: Why didn't you tell me before? I mean, don't you trust me?

Warren: No. Nothing like that. I guess I just hate admitting that maybe I can't do it all on my own, you know?

Me, nodding: How much do you take?

Warren: Whatever I want, really. Depends on the day and what I'm doing. I don't remember what the prescription was for. Two a day, maybe? Doesn't matter. I can always get more. It's an easy trade for what we make, and so many people around here take them.

Me: And it really helps you?

In answer Warren took my hand and folded it into his, around the bag of pills. He said they were mine, and I could try it and see if it helped. He said it was absolutely up to me and also that I could trust him.

They're sitting here next to me as I write, and I feel like I'm in a cartoon with a devil on one shoulder and an angel on the other, thinking about what I should do. Emily is fast asleep, so there's no worry about being found out. Warren told me if I want to take one, wait until tomorrow so I won't be up all night.

On one hand, it's a pill. On the other, they could obviously help me right now. I could be like Warren and actually get through the day and do the things I need to do. I could stay on top of my work and have energy. I mean, look at him. He takes them, sometimes more than he was prescribed, and he's doing so well. He's practically a model student.

Is he right? Can I trust him? Of course I can. I know that. Not only that, but he knows chemistry inside and out. If there was a real danger to these, he would have said so. Besides, he was prescribed this as medication. It's meant to be used for focus.

I tucked them under my pillow. I think I've decided. I'll see how tomorrow goes.

February 1

By third period today, I felt like I was dragging. I could feel the pills in my jumper skirt pocket. They felt heavy as lead but so did my eyelids. I kept thinking about how easy it seemed for Warren to do everything, and I raised my hand and got permission to go to the bathroom.

Inside the bathroom I slipped one pill out of the bag and into my hand. I looked at myself in the mirror, like I was asking permission of myself or something. Or maybe advice. My reflection offered neither; the Bailey who stared back at me looked exhausted and scared, terrified of failing, and barely hanging on. I wanted to help her. I turned on the water and cupped my hand, ready to toss the pill back, and the door swung open. Luckily it was Katy.

Katy: Hey. You all right? Saw you leave calc.

Me, nodding and balling up my fist around the pill: Yeah. Fine. Thanks. You okay?

Katy: What's that?

And because it's Katy, and because I feel like I need some advice from someone who isn't just a reflection, I opened my hand. Katy snatched the pill from my palm and a huge grin spread over her face.

Katy: An Addy? Bailey! Did Warren give this to you?

Me, apprehensive: Yeah. Is that a problem?

Katy, snorting: Yes it's a problem! He's been
holding out on me. Said he couldn't get me
any until next week.

Me: You take these?

Katy: Yeah. Who doesn't? Wait. Don't tell me
this is your first time. . . .

I stared at Katy dumbly. All of a sudden it was like a door
had opened into a world I hadn't been able to see before. Or
maybe it was just that *Wizard of Oz* kind of thing. . . . Suddenly
I was seeing things in color.

Katy's world, apparently, was already in Technicolor. She
was laughing, calling Warren stingy, then she asked me if I had
any extra.

In answer I pulled out the bag.

Katy, laughing harder: Mind if I join you,
then? I don't think I'm going to get through
this day without something.

Me: Sure. But . . . why does Warren get them
for you? Aren't you the contact?

Katy: I make the contacts. I don't necessarily keep them. Sometimes they like to deal with Warren directly.

Me, not sure what to make of that, so switching the subject: Are you serious, though? Everyone here does this? It's no big deal? I mean, it's not dangerous?

Katy: Hell no. I think it's how most of us survive Prescott.

So Katy took one of my (Warren's) pills out of the bag and handed it back to me. We both swallowed them at the same time and headed back to class, giggling like idiots. I felt good. A little nervous about how it might make me feel, but good.

When fourth period came around, something changed. I just felt more ALIVE. Like everything was super interesting. Even Shakespeare. I didn't feel high or anything, just energetic. Almost hyper. And very, very capable.

I'm noticing as I'm writing that it has worn off a little, but I still feel better than I have in weeks. Honestly, Warren was right. This was exactly what I needed.

February 2

Yesterday was amazing. I did well in all my classes, did my homework, and helped Warren at the lab until it was time to go home for the night. (And since we were alone in the lab, we took advantage. At least we pretty much always know ahead of time when Katy and Drew are going to stop by, so we didn't worry about getting caught.) He walked me home, and as we were walking he smiled at me and said I seemed to be having a pretty good day. I got his hint and played along. I told him I was and asked if I could take more than one. He laughed like that question was adorable or something. Then he told me not to take both at once but to spread them out. He said I'd be able to tell when it was leaving my system, and I could take another then. We talked for a long time about what it felt like, and he was so amused by how excited I was. He said he could tell it was really working for me.

I don't know why I doubted him there for a little bit. Warren really cares about me. He's not going to do anything that would hurt me.

He did tell me it would make me feel like crashing later. He said I'd feel really aware and kind of hyper still, but also tired at the same time. He told me to drink lots of water and eat something, even if I didn't feel hungry yet. He also gave me a bottle of melatonin, which he said would make me sleep even if my brain felt really active still.

He was right about all of it. As soon as my energy waned, I felt thirsty and hungry and a little grumpy. I took one of the melatonin and lay down. Emily wasn't home, thank goodness, so she wouldn't know something strange was going on. Luckily, I didn't have long to think about any of it. The melatonin kicked in, chasing out the energy left over from the Adderall, and I went to sleep. I think I slept like a baby. I woke up early and ready to do it all over again. I felt like I could take on the whole world.

February 9

So, when Drew said we were expanding, I guess it didn't really compute with everything else going on that we would also be making more money. A LOT more money. Warren and I have nearly doubled our output and . . . the money appears to have doubled as well.

I've been keeping money in an extra makeup bag I had, but now it's almost too small for that. So, naturally, the only solution is to go buy something else to put it in.

When Friday night rolled around and Drew had to make his deliveries, Katy and I caught a ride into Wiltshire with him, and of course Warren came too. We didn't have to cook tonight. We'd decided we'd take most of tomorrow to do that. Sunday, Emily and I are going to the movies, so it makes sense to get the bulk of the supply started Saturday.

Warren didn't come with me and Katy to the mall, though. He said he was going to help Drew. That worried me a little. I like thinking Warren's not directly involved like Drew, but I guess Drew needs extra help now, so this is going to be a regular thing. He told me not to worry about it. He said Drew's good at what he does and they always deliver on their promises. Essentially, they're too valuable to be hurt or ratted out. When I pressed him a little further, he told me Drew had protection taken care of.

I'm not sure what that means. Do they pay someone to be their muscle? Does Drew pack a weapon? Have I watched far too many gangster movies?

So I tried not to worry while the boys were doing business. Neither of them seemed like they'd be useful at all in a street fight (I can only write that here. They'd probably be so mad at me for thinking it, but come on, they're brainy boys who don't even play sports).

To keep myself from worrying, and also because I had more money than I knew what to do with, Katy and I went into Sephora and had them do our makeup. I ended up buying every single thing they put on my face, as well as a few other things they recommended, and something they promised would keep my hair super soft, which was more for Warren than me. Katy bought some Dior lipstick and

a French perfume I've seen Isa ogle before. Then we left
in search of purses. I picked out a really cute brown-and-
turquoise purse and matching wallet—for all my extra money.
Katy assured me the designer was worth the price, even if it
was half a week's "paycheck."

We tried on dresses for fun. I guess Prescott has a formal
(they don't dare call it prom—proms are for peasants) in the
spring, so it's months away still. Only juniors and seniors can
go. I assume Warren will ask me, if that's his type of thing. Katy
said he'd take me even if it wasn't. I asked her if she'd go with
Drew.

Katy: Why would you think that?

Me: You guys do everything else together, I
guess, so why not formal? And you flirt all the
time.

Katy: We do not.

Me: Liar. Come on. What is up with you two?

Katy, pretending to be interested in a black
sequined dress: Okay, don't tell anyone I told you

this. Even Warren, though I'm sure he knows. What's up with me and Drew? I really don't know. Sometimes he acts like he wants to be together, then he doesn't. So, it's confusing, and I feel like we're always kind of together but not, but I'd feel weird about being with anyone else. I don't know. I guess it's friends with benefits, but a little more sometimes and a little less other times.

Me, shocked: So . . . you fool around with him and stuff but you're not really together?

Katy: Oh, come on, Bailey. Don't be a prude.

Me: I'm not! I'm just surprised that it's not official. I never see him with anyone else. So what's his deal?

Katy: He's so busy, I guess. The business is his first love, you know?

Me: Yeah, but . . . Warren's busy too. He still finds time for me.

Katy: Yeah, because you're both in the lab all the time. Drew and I are constantly out making connections in different places.

Me: Yeah, okay. And you two must have done a hell of a job with this latest expansion. Warren and I can barely keep up.

Katy, grinning like the cat who caught the canary: Yep. And it's not going to slow down. The market's getting huge. And you know what? It was all my idea.

I didn't ask what market or what, exactly, her idea was. Again, there are some things I don't want to know. And also, it doesn't really matter. We're doing this safely, for people who are already addicted. It's not like Drew is pushing meth on anyone who hasn't been using already. He's not even a dealer himself, just a supplier. It is as innocent as we can possibly make it.

When I got home I put my money in my new wallet, in my new handbag, and slid it under my bed. Innocent or not, Emily doesn't need to see it and get nosy.

February 12

Yesterday was fine. Emily and I went to see a rather serious film about World War II and went to dinner afterward, and she didn't mention Warren once. But she did seem particularly restless. During the movie she kept squirming, and she rushed off after dinner. Maybe she had a lot to do as well. I ran to the lab when we were done and helped Warren all I could before I had to finish up what was left of my homework. I got it all done before midnight and actually got about six hours of sleep.

But still . . . classes were the last thing I wanted to do today. What I really wanted to do was spend all day with Warren. Preferably alone. In his bed.

It feels like break was forever ago, okay? And it's hard that we don't have that much time alone anymore.

I ended up taking another one of the Adderalls that Warren had given me. I hadn't all weekend, but I felt like maybe it was the only way to face this stupid day. It kicked in after breakfast and I felt good to go. I swear it gives me more brainpower or something. It's like it unclutters my mind and lets me focus on the important things. I don't find myself zoning out, even when Mr. Callahan is working over the sixth equation in a row, and they've all been things I could solve in my sleep.

Then in the afternoon, after classes ended, I took another

one. I was starting to feel that downward slide Warren warned me about, and I still had most of my day to go. I'm so glad I did. I had the energy to do all my homework and still stay in the lab until late. Warren was so entertained by how talkative I was, and I could tell he was also super impressed with how much I did tonight in the lab. I usually let him handle the bulk of the work so I can get my homework done, but tonight it was completely equal.

I thanked him for the pills and told him they were helping. He said they've been helping him for years. If he's been on these since middle school and he's so completely together and brilliant, it clearly doesn't have any bad side effects. I've heard pot can make you lose brain cells and be lazy, and people do that stuff all the time. Of course, Adderall is a prescription, so it must be safer anyway.

Going to turn in. Another long day ahead of me tomorrow.

February 19

It's been a while since I've written. Again. I probably should get better about this, but honestly, with everything going on, the diary my father gave me is just not a priority. Besides, Isa was probably the one who picked it out or told him to get it for me. It wouldn't surprise me if Isa still keeps a diary *insert massive eye roll here*. It's probably filled with things like "Got Greg to spend Christmas with me instead of his horrible brats!" or "Convinced Greg to send the ugly stepchildren to boarding school. It means one fewer trip to Paris this year, but c'est la vie!" But it's weird. I feel bad when I don't write. Guilty. Like I'm not holding up my end of the bargain, even though I never really made one with Dad. I guess maybe I'm hoping that one day he'll want to know what's been going on with me.

Also, I have to admit, there's something about writing down what's going on with my life that feels a bit like therapy. It kind of helps me sort out my thoughts, which seem to be scattered at best. I'm just SO busy, so tired, and I feel like I will never catch up.

Not that there's much to report at the moment. Every day is just like the last. Too much homework, not enough time with Warren, Emily is sometimes restless or complains about Warren but is mostly okay and usually absent from our room anyway, and Katy and I have been meeting in the bathroom every morning to throw back an Addy before classes. We've been out for coffee only once this week, but she's so busy too, all we can do is check in. She and Drew stop by the lab a lot, though.

And Warren. I swear, he's gotten even better over the last few days. I don't know how. Maybe it's just that I haven't had a freak-out for a while, so he feels like he can relax around me again. It's some kind of record for me or something. Whatever it is, I swear he's more awesome than ever before. I've never seen him smile so much. And he's just as anxious as I am to find some time alone together, but he's never pushy about it. I really could not have asked for a better first boyfriend.

Oh, and did I mention how beautiful his eyes are? Not lately? Ha. Okay.

Anyway, off to bed. It's 12:30 a.m. Tomorrow morning is going to be a bitch.

February 21

You know how the last time I wrote I was praising Warren for being so awesome?

Well, we had our first fight tonight. It's okay. He's still awesome and all. It's ME who's not awesome. I'm just so afraid I've let him down somehow. He seemed disappointed. It was almost like what I felt like when I'd get in trouble with Mom: not scared about the consequences so much, just afraid that she thought less of me.

It started at the lab. It was all fine. We were joking around and having a great time. We were even going over some ways we could maybe tweak our process to make it more streamlined, or at least a lot less messy. I'm not even sure how we even got on the subject from there. . . . I think I may have asked him what meth was really like. If it was like Adderall but stronger. And he asked me how much of the Adderall I'd been taking.

Me: A couple a day. I'm about out, actually. I was going to ask for more. If that's okay.

Warren: How are you out? I gave you a couple dozen pills. It's not even been a week. Are you lying?

Me, horrified: No! I'm not lying. I've just been giving some to Katy. I didn't realize she took them sometimes. So she and I have been taking a few together every day.

Warren: (cursing like I've never heard him curse before)

Me: I'm sorry. Was I not supposed to give any to her?

Warren: No, Bailey. You weren't.

Me: Okay, well, I'm sorry. I won't give her any more. I didn't realize it was a problem. She kind of implied that you knew, that everyone did it, so I didn't think it was a big deal.

Warren, snapping: Of course not. She's getting all the pills she wants. You don't have any left?

Me: No. Did you . . . did you need some? Did you give me all of yours?

Warren, sighing: No, I . . . I shouldn't have used so many. I just figured you'd still have some. And I can't get you more until next week. I can't get US more until next week.

Me: Okay. I'm really sorry. And I was going to ask how I could pay you for them, I guess? They probably cost a lot, right?

Warren: Yeah, Bailey. They cost a fucking lot.

At that point I made myself really busy with chemicals and started crying because I'd screwed up . . . just one more thing I was screwing up in a long list. And honestly, because I'd never seen Warren this angry. I'd never seen him angry, period. He's always been so patient and understanding. Now he was beyond irritable.

I wiped at my eyes and that's when he must have noticed I was crying. He immediately pulled me into his arms and kept saying, "Shhh," over and over, even though I wasn't talking. I buried my head in his chest and he stroked my hair.

> Warren: I'm sorry. I shouldn't have snapped
> at you. I shouldn't have expected you to
> know. It's just that they're not easy to get.
> Not in that kind of quantity. And I'm . . . I'm
> a little over my head right now in what I owe
> people.

> Me: Can we make more product? Exchange it
> or sell it to make up for it?

> Warren: No. I don't owe anyone money for
> drugs. That's not what I meant. I owe for
> my car. For Princeton's program. And I owe

it to my parents. They pay for everything;
I just pay them back. So finding some
extra for pills is hard, even with all we're
raking in.

Me, understanding now why everything was
so serious and important: Then take some of
what I'm making.

Warren: I couldn't . . .

Me: Come on. This is for me, too, right?
And honestly, Warren, this week . . .
having that extra energy? I finally feel like
I can handle everything. And I won't share
with Katy again. Unless she gives me a
cut too.

Warren, kissing me hard on the lips: I really
am sorry.

Me, kissing him back, but sweet and long: I
know. Me too. Everything's going to be all
right.

We ignored the chemicals simmering around us for a while and got quite lost in, um, apologizing to each other after that. As much as I don't like fighting with him, I certainly LOVE making up with him.

February 26

I was a little off today. Just . . . sluggish. Kind of short-tempered. I was even a little rude to Mr. Callahan after class when he asked me if I'd heard from Princeton yet. I don't know why. I just have this sinking feeling that it will be bad news and I don't know why he has to bug me about it. So I said something snarky like, "I'll let you know when I get my rejection letter," or something and pretty much fled the classroom before he could say anything back. The last thing I needed today was him trying to convince me that I'm good enough to get in. I don't need that kind of pity.

At least I got all my homework done, but it was at the expense of spending time in the lab, and I really could have used some more time with Warren tonight. Like, a lot more time. After the little fight we had the other night, I've wanted nothing more than to be with him and let him convince me that everything is okay. But I had to leave the lab early to do my reading in civics and English.

Emily was in a foul mood tonight too. I don't know what's going on with her and I probably should have asked, but quite frankly, I don't have the energy to invest in her right now. I'm just scraping by as it is. And if it's about Warren, I don't want to hear it anyway. So when I got in and she snarled something about "trouble in paradise" with me and Warren, I pretty much threw in my earbuds and buried myself in my civics textbook. She stayed up even later than me and I nearly screamed at her for drumming her fingers on her desk and keeping me up with her impromptu percussion solo.

Thank God I'm about to fall asleep from pure exhaustion, or it might have come to blows.

February 27

Everything seems to be fine with Warren, and he's getting more pills tonight, but something about that fight has been bugging me since it happened. And it took me until tonight to figure it out:

If he thought I'd taken all those pills, shouldn't he have been concerned about me? Not the pills?

But that's silly. I told him I'd been sharing with Katy right after that. He probably didn't even have time to worry about me. And wasn't him thinking I was lying concern for me anyway? I mean, if I'd taken those all myself and lied to him about it, of course he'd be concerned. Obviously he was just trying to make sure I was taking them properly.

. . . Right?

March 3

I went with Warren and Drew to make deliveries tonight.

Katy thought I was nuts and asked to be dropped off at a frozen yogurt place. She said she makes enough connections, she doesn't want to be seen with them too. But Warren and Drew said it would be okay, as long as I waited in the car.

I don't really know why I wanted to go. For one, Katy has been a little cold to me since I told her I was out of Adderall and that Warren didn't want me to share anymore. She said Warren was always selfish like that, which I thought was uncalled-for and completely untrue, so we haven't been talking as much as usual. I mean, really, how dare she? He's trying to help me, and she's only focused on the pills. She hasn't asked me how I'm doing at all.

But other than that, there was no good reason for my sudden desire to stick with the guys. I've been pretty happy with keeping my distance from this part. Blind eye and all that. But now that Warren is involved ... now that I know why he did this and why he works so hard ... and also, now that we are making more than we've ever made before, I want to know how it works. I want to at least understand every cog in the machine, even if it doesn't really touch mine.

We dropped Katy off (after she asked me again to be sane and come with her instead) and headed to the east end of Wiltshire.

As we drove, we literally went across some train tracks like some horrible cliché to a part of town I was completely unfamiliar with. As soon as we were on the other side, everything changed. The houses were more run-down. There were bars on the storefront windows. There were people out walking, and none of them were dressed well, like the people we saw in the mall in Wiltshire. We passed under a bridge and there were tents there.

Me: So, when you said we were expanding . . .

Drew, shaking his head: This is our territory, Bailey. All of it. Has been for a few years. The expansion was less about an area, more about attracting a new type of clientele.

I wanted to ask, but I didn't. I was beginning to think this was a mistake. I didn't know any of the people we were passing by, but I saw their faces now. Their eyes. Their hopelessness.

Warren, disgusted, turning away from the window: There's lots of heroin down here too. But, as you know, we wouldn't ever get into that scene.

Drew: No. The guys that deal it too . . .
straight-up frauds. They put all sorts of shit in
their product. Or they don't even know where
it's coming from.

Me: Fentanyl?

Warren, visibly agitated: Yeah. Fentanyl.
Whatever they can get their hands on.
(Cursing under his breath that I couldn't quite
make out.)

Drew slowed to a stop. I couldn't help but think his fancy
car stood out in this area like a sore thumb. The dome light
came on as Drew pushed open his door. I felt like it was the
only light around for blocks.

Drew: Lock the doors. Don't you dare leave.
And on the off chance that something bad
goes down, do not under any circumstances
call the cops. Drive away. Park a mile or
two from campus, leave the keys inside, and
walk back.

Warren, handing me the keys to his car: And
come back to pick up Katy with mine.

Me, staring dumbly at the keys: There's a
possibility that something bad will happen?

Drew, smiling warmly: Usually not. But
sometimes people we don't know show up.

I noticed that nowhere in this plan did they want me to
come back for them. Meaning they would either be in jail or
dead. Panic seized me, and I must have been showing it on my
face because Warren reached out for my hand and gave it a
squeeze, promising everything would be fine. Then he pecked
me on the cheek and they both climbed out of the car, taking
several duffel bags with them. I saw them disappear into a
house that was mostly dark. A light flipped on inside, but only
one. I locked the doors and waited, watching and listening.
Anxious. Time moved so slowly I thought I was going to grow
old and die in that car. But then I heard voices. Drew and
Warren were back.

Me, more relieved than I'd ever been in my
life: Everything went okay?

Drew, smiling: Yep.

Warren: I think perhaps we should up our prices.

Drew: Maybe. In a week or two. Materials are getting expensive. (He turned back to me.) Okay if we make one more stop?

I said sure, because I'd survived one, so I could surely survive another. Unlike the last place, though, we didn't stop at a house. We were outside of what looked to be an abandoned gas station. The boys told me it was the same deal as before, and left me. This time, by way of the streetlights, I got to see what went down.

I felt like I was watching a movie. Like this couldn't possibly be part of my life.

As Warren and Drew headed toward the station, a solitary man came from the other direction, shaking their hands like they were old friends. There was some talking, some laughing, then Drew pulled out what was obviously a wad of cash. I started to worry, because this seemed so public. So VISIBLE. But the man didn't hold on to the cash for long. I don't even think he counted it, just pocketed it and withdrew a couple of small bags from the inside of his coat. Drew took one, and

Warren took two. Even from this distance I could see the pale orange color inside one of them. The guys all shook hands again and then it was over and they were back in the car.

Warren slid in next to me, letting Drew play chauffeur. I looked at him questioningly, and he pulled out the bag of orange pills. We smiled. So that was it. Not that hard. And the guy had just wanted money in return, not our product.

When we crossed back over the train tracks, Drew pulled something out of his coat pocket and tossed it unceremoniously into the glove compartment. As he shut the door I caught a glimpse of a dark metal barrel and a leather grip. It was a small gun, but I had no doubt it would do the job and that Drew knew how to use it. The protection they'd mentioned before. But somehow, it didn't make me feel safer.

I curled into Warren and he wrapped himself around me. When Katy got in, she leaned over and whispered something into Drew's ear that made Drew turn back to us and ask if it was okay if we split up for the night. It meant that Katy wanted Drew to come back with her for a while. It also meant Drew and Warren's room would be unoccupied.

I put the worry out of my mind so that I could enjoy having some time alone with Warren, but now that I'm writing, I have to wonder . . . if you have to bring a gun to feel safe, do you really feel safe?

March 7

Today I saw for myself what Katy was talking about with Warren and Emily. I'd gone into the dining hall between first and second periods to grab some coffee (the dining hall coffee is rather horrible and weak, but I don't have time to get to the coffee shop until after school) and as I was walking out, I spotted them. They were deep in conversation by the English building, exactly where I needed to go. I could tell by both their expressions that the conversation wasn't pleasant.

I felt absolutely ridiculous and kind of paranoid, but I totally hid behind a tree and watched.

We have fifteen minutes between periods so we can all get to the other buildings on campus, and getting the coffee couldn't have taken me more than five, if that. Which left nearly ten whole minutes of them talking to each other. Emily's brows were furrowed and she spoke through a clenched jaw. Warren seemed impatient, shrugging and shaking his head. I think I even saw him roll his eyes once.

Then, to my horror, she stepped closer to him and took his hand. He let her take it for a moment, then dropped it, and his lips formed a forceful "No."

I was so relieved. It was like seeing that everything he and Katy had ever told me about Emily, and how Warren felt about her now, was completely true. I mean, I knew deep down he wasn't lying to me, but I guess there was a part of me . . . that scared and paranoid part, probably . . . that still thought maybe he had some feelings for her. Or, if I'm really honest with myself, he didn't feel that strongly about ME.

I figured it was time to mark my territory, so to speak, so I wandered over to them, gave Emily the brightest smile I could muster, and kissed Warren on the cheek. He shot me a grateful look and reached down for my hand. The warning bell rang, so Emily excused herself, and Warren gave me another kiss before we went into the English building.

Me: Everything okay?

Warren: Great now that you're here. Sorry about that. She seems to find the worst times to corner me.

Me: What did she want?

Warren, with a sad smile: She just wanted to remind me, again, that I'm a horrible person and everything is my fault. Don't worry about it. Coming to the lab tonight?

Me: Wouldn't miss it.

Warren, wrinkling his nose: Unfortunately
we won't be alone tonight. I think Drew and
Katy want to have a little meeting. I swear,
every time Katy has a whim to hook up with
Drew, we have to rehash everyone's roles
again. It's like they forget how to be normal
around each other.

Me: She obviously wants more and he won't
give it to her. It's sad, really.

Warren stopped walking, right in front of our classroom,
and looked at me strangely.

Warren: Is that what she told you?

Me: Yeah. Why? That's not what it's like?

Warren, laughing: Not at all. Drew's been
crazy about her for years but Katy only wants
him when it's convenient.

Me: So Katy's lying?

Warren: Katy's a master manipulator, Bailey. I know she's your friend, but she only looks out for herself. She's incredibly selfish.

It was weird that he called her that, when she'd used the same word about him last week. But I had to admit, in Katy's word against Drew's, I'd believe Drew first. Maybe I'll try talking to Katy again, though. Selfish or not, she's super fun, and I miss having her to gossip with. And we haven't even discussed the other night yet. Plus, with my only other female friend actively trying to hold my boyfriend's hand, I think I'll take the lesser of two evils, thanks.

I'm so mad at Emily I could scream. Honestly, there's no way to deal with her and maintain peace in our room. I guess I should just accept that and tell her to back the hell off my boyfriend. Or maybe I should take a kinder approach.

Ugh, Mom. I'd give anything to talk this over with you. . . .

March 8

To say that Emily and I had it out tonight would be the understatement of the year. Maybe even the century.

I got back from the lab and she was sitting at her desk,

doing her homework and tapping her fingers like she does in that way that grates on my nerves, and I don't know what it was, but I snapped. There was no way I was going to take the "kinder" approach when I'd seen her try to hold hands with my boyfriend earlier. I just couldn't take it.

I threw my bag down and just kind of unleashed. Then she accused me of spying on them and being paranoid. I told her I wasn't paranoid when I'm clearly seeing things with my own eyes. Then she fed me some bullshit about how she wasn't trying to hold hands with him, just trying to make him listen. She kept saying he was cutting her off, and I screamed that of course he was, they were no longer dating and she needed to leave him the hell alone. She yelled back that she'd leave him alone if he would leave her alone, whatever that means. Probably just trying to make me doubt Warren.

It was so bad the dorm mom came up to investigate, but luckily, Emily had already stormed off. After I apologized and the dorm mom left, I called Warren and told him what happened and warned him that Emily might come looking for him and that she seemed especially bad at the moment. He promised he knew how to handle her and told me not to worry. He thought maybe I was mad at him, but I assured him I wasn't. None of this is his fault; it's hers. She can't let him go and I think she's delusional. He told me he'd call if

Emily shows up or something, but if I don't hear from him, everything is good.

I can't do the homework that I still have to do. My nerves are completely frayed. So I took a long, hot shower, checked my phone to make sure I hadn't missed a call from Warren, then settled into bed with this diary. I am so done with today.

And just WHAT did Emily mean about Warren not leaving her alone??? I mean, she's the one who follows him around. Katy says that. Warren has implied as much. But . . .

I don't know. It totally could be my mind playing tricks on me, but sometimes I swear he ENJOYS the attention. From her, but then from me, when I get upset about it. And I don't know. I know everyone close to me says Emily's a bit on the unstable side but . . . she's never struck me as mean or vindictive. Or even a liar.

I don't know. Maybe I fought so hard with her because I'm confused and I don't know who to believe. But they both can't be right.

March 9

So Katy wasn't exactly the nicest last night in the lab. She wasn't mean; she was just kind of cold. She pretty much just reminded all of us that she and Drew take care of the selling, while Warren and I are to stick with making the product. I felt like the whole thing was meant to put us back in our place, like

172

me going with the boys the other night was crossing some kind of line. And it was definitely a reminder to Warren that he's just helping, that he's not as important as Drew.

Such a laughable thought. If they didn't have me and Warren, they'd have nothing. And Warren is the whole reason our product is the best around.

But when Katy showed up in the girls' restroom when I was about to take my first Adderall of the day, I couldn't be mad at her. Katy is who she is, and I kind of admire how strong and honest she is.

So I pulled out a pill for her and gave it to her. She looked at it, confused, and asked if my "master" was allowing me to share again.

The "master" barb stung. I mean, I was sort of following his orders, but this was a totally abnormal situation. I shrugged her off and told her I'd cover if he asked, and claim to have taken the extra one myself. Still, even for Katy, the remark was a little below the belt.

Me: Why are you so pissed at me, anyway? Because of Warren and not sharing?

Katy: No. Not really. I don't know. It's a bunch of stuff. And only some of it even involves you.

Me: Well, I'm listening.

We took our pills and I swear I started to instantly feel better. Perhaps it was just a placebo effect, but just knowing the pill was in my system now made me feel more ready for whatever Prescott or Katy threw at me. I honestly don't know what I'd do without them at this point, which is a little scary but . . . it's okay. It won't be for much longer. After that, Katy suggested we blow off class and go elsewhere. I shouldn't have missed English, but I hated thinking I was somehow not in Katy's good graces, especially with things as bad with Emily as they are. So I said yes. Moments later we were walking away from the English building and wandering in the direction of the coffee shop.

Katy: So part of it is that you and Warren are so intense. I'm jealous, I guess. Drew would never act like that with me. But also, I swear he's all you think about. It's like we haven't had girl time since break.

Me: Well . . . he kinda is all I think about. I'm sorry. I'm just so into him. I can see why Emily's so . . . irrational.

> Katy, rolling her eyes: He is hot, in a sort
> of subtle, nerdy way. And I get it. You're in
> love with him. But between you and Drew
> not paying attention to me, then Warren
> apparently not even liking me enough to
> share Addys with me, I just feel sort of . . . I
> don't know. Left out. When you went with
> them the other night . . . I was worried for
> you. And worried I'd be on the outside even
> more after that.

I think I stared at her for a full minute, mouth hanging open, because I couldn't wrap my head around the impossibly cool, glamorous Katy Ashton feeling left out or caring about what anyone else thinks, period. But I thought about it, and, as loyal as the SC is to each other, we're also super isolated. If Katy or any of us feels left out, we don't have anyone else to turn to. I suppose it's for good reason, but it means I've got to keep myself in. I regained myself and tried to say something useful.

> Me: First of all, I just wanted to see what went
> down. I won't go again. And I do think Drew
> would pay attention to you any time you
> wanted him to. Clearly. I mean, he dropped

everything for you the other night. Lastly, I
don't think Warren's not sharing because he
doesn't like you. They're just expensive and
hard to get.

Katy, snorting: No they're not. Warren gets
whatever pills he wants, any time he wants them.
Everyone wants to keep him happy because his
product is so good. Your product too, I guess.
But he won't even share his sources.

Me: Wait, pills? Like plural?

Katy: Of course. You know Warren by now.
He wouldn't touch heroin or, you know,
ACTUAL drugs. But Oxys, Percs, whatever
you want, he can get them.

I thought about the other night, how I'd seen Warren pocket
the Adderall but something else as well. Inwardly I started to
panic, thinking about what else Warren could be taking, but I
tried to be as casual as possible.

Me: Right. The other pills. Sure.

Katy: What I don't get is that he knows I
need them. And I hate begging. But I made
our contacts, damn it. I don't see why he gets
to use them but I don't. He says it muddies
the waters, whatever that means.

The Addy had taken full effect by the time we made it to
the coffee shop, and it was like Katy's voice was a buzzing bee
in my ear. I let her drone on until she seemed satisfied but I was
no longer listening. I was thinking about Warren and that other
bag of pills.

What else is he keeping from me?

March 13

I'm so upset but I don't know who to be more mad at: me, Mr.
Callahan, or Princeton.

Mr. Callahan told me after chemistry that he heard from
his friends at Princeton that I didn't get into the summer
program. Not officially. I got wait-listed. I guess that's still
good. Out of all the people that apply they take only twenty,
and twenty more go on the wait list. But that means there
were twenty people who were better than me. More, maybe.
And it means that unless someone drops out, I won't be
spending the summer with Warren.

It was the essay. I know it was. Sure, my grades slipped some for a while there, but not that much. Thanks to the Adderall, I've been keeping up okay again. But my grades from my last school and first quarter here were amazing, and Mr. Callahan would have given me a great recommendation, so the only thing it could be is the essay.

I know I didn't do that great with it. I kind of left it to the last minute. But Mr. Callahan said it was fine. Shouldn't he have known if it wasn't? And if it wasn't, shouldn't he have helped me make it better? He just nodded his head and sent it in.

I'm so mad I could scream.

I'm home now. It's lunchtime. I couldn't face anyone in Science Club yet. Especially Warren. But I'll have to tell them soon. Will they even still want me making product for them? Me, the girl who got wait-listed at Princeton?

The room is a freaking wreck. I didn't see Emily at all last night. She must have sneaked in while I was sleeping and slept late. It looks like she couldn't find something to wear, even though we have uniforms. Her clothes are everywhere. If I hadn't seen this from her a few times before I would think we were robbed.

Whatever. If I'm going to deal with another afternoon of stupid Prescott and having to tell my boyfriend I'm not as smart as he is, basically, I'm going to need another Adderall. Warren said I could take more as long as I space them out. I usually wait until after school, but I'll take another one now, and another later. I just can't deal with this on my own.

March 14

Warren can be the sweetest sometimes.

When I got to the lab last night, he took one look at my face (yeah, I'd been crying. It started after dinner while I had a moment alone in my room and I couldn't stop it) and asked Katy and Drew if they'd excuse themselves so we could talk. I told him between hiccups that I didn't get in, all panicky and hyper because of all the Adderall in my system.

He told me that he was wait-listed his first year, which made me feel infinitely better even though that was three years ago, and that I'll probably still get in anyway. He said a lot of people apply then realize they can't give up their whole summer or can't spend that much money.

I told him I feel stupid and not good enough and it makes me doubt I can even get into Harvard. Or anywhere, for that matter.

Then he did the most amazing thing. He scooped me up in his arms and set me on the counter and told me every single thing he likes about me. He told me I'm brilliant and beautiful and sexy and funny and sweet, and kissed me SO passionately in between every word he said. He made me feel like I'm all those things, if only to him, and that's really all I need. He truly does believe those things about me. The best part was that he acted like he couldn't get enough of me tonight, like he was drunk on me, like he'd do anything as long as I kept kissing him. And we totally took advantage of being alone in the lab. But I have to admit, even though I feel special every time with him, tonight was so different. I wondered briefly if that's what it felt like to be a drug, and craved and needed all the time. I found myself wanting to be HIS drug.

His only drug.

Regardless, he definitely made me feel better about myself. If Warren loves me, that's all that matters. Screw Princeton.

March 15

After the high of Warren wore off, I woke up this morning accepting Princeton's decision but faced with the cold reality of it: I won't be seeing Warren at all this summer, I'll be spending it in misery with Dad and Isa instead, and I have no one to blame but myself.

Warren was extra wonderful today. He brought me coffee and walked me to all of my classes and told me I don't have to tell Katy and Drew if I don't want to. I took three Adderall again today, because it was really hard to focus on anything while I was so depressed about not getting into the program.

By the time I got to the lab tonight, I was a mess again. Probably shouldn't have taken that extra Adderall because it seems to make me more anxious somehow when I'm upset, but at least I could get all my homework done.

Drew and Katy were just leaving, and judging by the looks on their faces and the speed with which they excused themselves, they had plans. Warren looked up from the chemicals he was stirring and shrugged, a cute smile on his lips.

Me: Well, maybe it will be more official after all?

Warren, not-so-subtly flirting: Or maybe there's just something in the air in this lab.

Me: Yeah, noxious fumes.

Warren, laughing: Are you feeling okay?

Me: Not really. I'm so sad I won't be with you over the summer. I can probably get over not getting into the program if I never get off the wait list. But I'll miss you. And I do feel stupid. And I've felt anxious all day.

Warren hugged me and I felt better, but I was also wondering about what Katy had told me the other day, about how Warren could get anything I wanted, and if he was taking more than Adderall. I was scared to just straight-up ask him; sometimes direct isn't always the best approach with him, but I thought maybe there was a chance I could lead him to telling me on his own.

Me: Does the Adderall make you feel sort of . . . jittery? Like you could have a panic attack but you never quite reach that level?

Warren: It never makes me feel anxious, but if you were already anxious . . . maybe it could do that.

Me: Huh. Well, I love being focused and having energy, but now I feel like I need something to calm me down, too. Kind of ironic, isn't it?

Warren, studying me intensely: Well . . . maybe you do need something else. Okay. Promise me you won't freak out?

Me: Uh, sure, I guess.

Warren looked at me for a long moment and then went to his overcoat, which was hanging on an old coatrack in the corner. When he came back to me, he had a bag of pills in his hand. I took them from him. At first glance I thought they were white, but they were actually just this side of yellow. One side said "10/325" on it, the other spelled out the answer to my question: PERCOCET.

> Warren: Maybe these would help you more.
> Just to relax. Probably not when you're in
> class. They sometimes make me drowsier if
> I'm already tired. But these would probably
> help you calm down when you're upset.

> Me: These are what you bought the other
> night? I saw you slip more than the Adderall
> into your pockets. (Warren nodded.) So . . .
> you take these too?

> Warren: Sometimes, yeah. When I don't
> want things to bother me. When I'm stressed
> or angry or . . . whatever. Like, if my parents

call, I'll definitely have one. It's just peaceful,
you know? Like how Addys make you feel
like you can do anything? Percs make you
feel like nothing can upset you. Takes the
sting out.

I eyed the bag of pills for what seemed like an eternity.
What he was saying they could do for me ... that sounded
exactly like what I needed. What I wanted. And he was
TELLING me. He was being honest. He'd told me he used
them completely on his own. He folded his hands around mine.

Warren: Take them, Bailey.

Me: Okay. Do you ... do you want money
for them?

Warren, with a soft laugh: No. No, not from
you, baby.

I thanked him and pocketed the bag. When I got home,
Emily was asleep. I turned her desk lamp off and slipped the bag
of pills into my purse, with all of my money.

Warren was sweet to offer them to me. It was a sweet

184

gesture, wasn't it? He knows I need to feel calm right now. He knows how anxious I've been.

He also knows how much I need them. How tempted I'd be with them.

In most cases, giving someone something they need is a good thing. But . . . but maybe in this case, it's the worst thing you could do for someone, and Warren had just done it to me. And what about his own habit? If he's doing these, what else is he doing? Could it be that there's more he's not telling me?

I took the pills out again and memorized them, planning to do some research on them later. I held them in my hands for what felt like an hour, thinking about them, about Warren, about what they meant, about how I wanted to be calm for once.

I didn't take one.

March 16

I tried not to take any Addys today because I didn't want to feel so on edge. I thought maybe that would help me feel calmer, or at least more normal.

But by the time I got to third period I realized it actually had the opposite effect. I was way more jittery than normal, and I felt like my eyes were crossing or something. I couldn't focus at all on the reading in English. Not like I just couldn't concentrate, but like my eyes wouldn't work correctly.

I felt right as rain, though, after I took one between classes and went to chemistry.

Mr. Callahan is disappointed that I didn't get selected for the Princeton program, but he said he'd talk to someone at the school and see if he could pull some strings. I asked him why I wasn't accepted, if maybe it was my essay. He said it might have been, but not for the reasons I thought. Turns out the selection committee probably gets tons of essays every year about wanting to make drugs that aren't addictive. He said the opioid epidemic is so bad around here, it's a common theme for hopeful young chemists.

> Me: I've heard this area is seeing a lot of heroin addiction.
>
> Mr. Callahan: Heroin, but prescription drugs too. The kind usually prescribed for pain treatment. Things like OxyContin and Percocet or Vicodin. Oxycodone, hydrocodone, morphine. You know. But then people get addicted and can't stop.
>
> Me, alarmed: So Percocets ARE really addictive?

Mr. Callahan: Oh, I know they are. All opioids are. Studies show it affects the body in more permanent ways than other drugs, so the body ends up craving more, and addiction happens faster.

Me: So . . . it's more addictive than something like, say, meth?

Mr. Callahan: Well, everything like that is addictive, Bailey. One isn't better than the other. Meth, for example . . . the users sometimes go through withdrawal or comedown for days. Users can hallucinate or get very depressed when they don't have a supply, which makes them need more to get rid of the feeling. So, like I said. Neither is particularly better than the other. Are you worried about someone?

I looked at him, confused as to why he would assume that. I shook my head and, luckily, was quick enough to cover.

Me: I just feel silly for thinking I had an original idea, I guess, and I realized I don't really know much about drug addiction.

Thanks for talking to me about it.

Mr. Callahan: Of course. I'll call my friend at
Princeton tomorrow. See what he says.

I thanked him and got out of there, but honestly, I couldn't stop replaying what he said over and over inside my head. Meth causes depression? Hallucinations?

And perhaps more important, considering what my boyfriend gave me last night, Percocet is highly addictive?

March 19

Well, the second fight with Warren is down in the books.

I don't quite know what happened. What I do know is that when I went to the lab tonight, it was just us, and everything was going fine. Then I guess since he told me he takes Percocet, he's super comfortable with taking them in front of me. Warren joked that he really needed to relax because the day had been such a pain in the ass, and he took a Perc out of his pocket and threw it back and panic sort of seized me. I was scared for him.

Me: You know those are really addictive.

Warren, actually rolling his eyes at me, which pissed me off to no end: They're just Percocets, Bailey. It's fine.

Me: Just like the Adderall?

Warren: I thought the Adderall was helping you.

Me: It is. But I tried not taking it, and I was a nervous wreck. Seriously. I felt weird.

Warren: Well, yeah. You have to go off slowly. It's medication. Come on. Plus, you've been sort of a mess for a while now.

Me, stunned and feeling betrayed: *I've* been a mess?

Warren: Since Christmas. At least.

Me: Well, I'm sorry I can't do all of this effortlessly like you. I'm sorry I have to study and sleep and go to classes.

Warren: Hey, this isn't my fault. I'm trying to help you. I help you study, I do most of the work in this lab, I gave you the Addys to help you focus. What else do you want from me?

Me: How many of the Percocet do you take a day, anyway?

Warren: Don't try to turn this around now. You're angry at me because this is easier for me than it is you.

Me, ignoring him: Those are opioids, you know. Addiction to those leads to heroin.

Warren, with a shocked laugh: Been on the Wikipedia page, Bailey? Suddenly you think you know everything? And do you actually think I'll get addicted to heroin after what happened to my brother? You think I'm that stupid?

Me: Well, how much do you use? I bet your brother didn't think he'd get addicted either.

That was it. I'd crossed a line. If there's one thing I've learned about Warren, it's that you can't talk about his brother that way, even if what you're saying is true. Warren's pretty blue eyes turned to ice.

> Warren: Not that it's any of your goddamn business, but I'm fine, Bailey. I don't take that many. I'm not addicted. It just helps me relax sometimes.

> Me: I don't see how it's not my business, since I love you and you love me. Isn't that what relationships are about? (He didn't say anything to that, so I went on.) So you think you could stop taking them and it would be fine?

> Warren: I know I could. Here. Take them. Take the whole damn bag.

He put on his coat and reached into the pocket, removing a bag full of yellow pills. He threw the bag at me and I barely caught them before they hit me in the chest.

> Me: You don't have to. . . . I'm sorry.

Warren: No, let me prove it to you, since you obviously don't trust me.

Me: That's not how I meant it.

Warren: Whatever, Bailey. Do me a favor and finish up here tonight. I'm done.

Me: No. Warren, don't go. I'm sorry. Please.

Warren: I'm just going home. To be sober. But if you don't trust me, ask your roommate for stalking tips. She always seems to know where to find me.

Because I was all alone, I didn't finish up work at the lab until one in the morning. When I got home, Emily was still up, and I must have looked like hell because she immediately asked if I'd fought with Warren. I couldn't help but wonder if she already knew that we had. She told me she was sorry, but she was also glad I was finally seeing this side of him.

And the thing is, she sounded genuinely worried for me, and . . . kind. I mean, if you can possibly believe that someone would want you to think of your boyfriend as a bad person and that would be kind, but it threw me for a loop. Especially since the last time we really talked was a fight.

I thanked her for her concern but swore to her that Warren treats me well, although I have to admit it was more trying to convince myself than her. I think Warren has good intentions. I think he truly wants to help me. But I can't help wondering if he's really helping me at all.

I fell asleep with my uniform still on, most of my homework undone.

March 20

Warren wasn't waiting for me before class today, although that could have been because I was so late I didn't even have time for breakfast. And honestly, I didn't have time to shower, either. Emily was just as late. She stayed up even later than I did last night. It's gross, but I was kind of lucky I was still in my uniform. I sprayed on extra perfume so I wouldn't smell like BO (or chemicals) and that was all there was time for.

But during first period, a page showed up at the door with a note asking me to come to the principal's office.

I immediately panicked, thinking perhaps someone had found out about Science Club or the Addys or even me staying the night with Warren. Then I thought maybe Mr. Callahan's call to Princeton actually did some good, and got excited.

It wasn't anything related to school, though. Good or bad. It was a giant vase of purple hyacinth. There was a card, and I opened it and read it to myself several times.

> Bailey:
>
> I was a giant asshole last night. A giant STUPID asshole. Please forgive me?
>
> Love, Warren

I tucked the card back into its holder, smiling. I asked the school secretary what I should do with the flowers and she told me to take them back to my dorm and then come back to class. So I took them to my room and I'm here now, enjoying a moment with them. They're gorgeous, and they smell so wonderful, plus I got out of most of first period. The fight was terrible but . . . maybe this is a sign that he's trying, and he does love me. At the very least, he understands how terrible it was.

March 20, later

Well, I think Warren and I are okay. He told me that his brother is just a touchy subject and he tends to get overly emotional when he's brought up. I told him I was just worried about him and that I still am, and that I sometimes feel like I don't know what's going on with him, and he promised me he would talk to me more about everything. We held each other for a long time at the lab tonight. Not really talking, which was probably the safest thing we could have done, but just leaning on each other. He asked if I liked the flowers, and I really do. They're sitting here at my desk, all cheery and bright and perfect. Mom would have loved them, I think. She liked girly things, so the purplish pink would have suited her.

I wonder if Mom would have had that superpower that some moms seem to have, that they can tell if a guy is right for their daughter or not.

The thing is, I really love Warren and I know he's got a good heart, and I think he wants the best for me. But there's something about the way we fight . . . I feel like the fight always turns on me. And I just never feel like I get the whole truth from him. Just bits and pieces of it. That's how I feel about Emily sometimes, and really the Science Club too. It makes me feel a little like I'm still on the outside of everything, which was what I wanted to avoid with joining the Science Club in the first place.

I'm probably just overthinking as usual and making myself depressed, so I'm going to go to bed and try to rest.

March 23

It turns out I'm not that far down on the waiting list for the Princeton summer program, and Mr. Callahan was able to get me bumped to the top spot, so as long as I can keep my grades up, I'm in if anyone drops out or can't go.

I feel so much better about everything right now because of that. For some reason, my whole perspective is more positive. I feel like I'm actually doing okay with all the work, school and otherwise. It's like the perfect reward for how hard I'm working, and all the hours I'm putting into everything, school and otherwise.

Well, that and the money. It keeps rolling in like it's the tide or something. I'm literally to the point where I don't know what else I really could buy. I'm not out of uniform enough to justify a huge wardrobe (plus the closet space in the Prescott dorms seriously sucks), and I can wear only so many pairs of flats. I bought a few new coats for myself and sent one to Bex as well. I wish I could have made the time to go visit and deliver it in person, but I'm way too behind with schoolwork and the lab to give up a weekend day.

Maybe it's time to start thinking of a little trip. Spring break is perfectly nestled between third and fourth quarters this year. Most likely, Dad won't want me home so he and Isa can be gross and happy together, and Bex will probably have made plans with all her new friends. But should it be only me and Warren? Or should we include Katy and Drew?

Hey, maybe a little trip together, all four of us, would push Katy and Drew together. For real.

Okay, I'll bring it up at the lab later, assuming everyone will be at the meeting tonight.

March 23, later

Tonight it was just me and Drew for a few minutes. Katy was late, as usual, and unusually, so was Warren.

It's silly, but it's hard to remember that I actually thought Drew was cuter than Warren at first. I guess I'm so into Warren, all I see when I look at Drew now is a friend. Or Katy's potential boyfriend, which is considerably more important.

> Me: How long have you and Warren been friends?

> Drew: Since Campbell, really.

> Me: So you knew him before his brother died?

> Drew, shrugging: Yeah. I only met Mitch once. I went home with Warren one weekend

because Mitch was home from college. But he was pretty messed up already. And I mean, Warren totally didn't exist.

Me: What do you mean?

Drew: His parents acted like they only had one son. It's no wonder Warren's so screwed up.

Me: You think Warren's screwed up?

Drew: Yeah, don't you? I mean, I love the guy, but he's got serious issues. I'm surprised he even told you about Mitch. Usually that's verboten. Especially with girlfriends.

Me, suddenly curious: You make it sound like he's had a lot of girlfriends. Has he? I mean, how many are we talking?

Drew, shaking his head and laughing: Nope. Huh-uh. Against the bro code. You'll have to ask him yourself. But why? Obviously it's different with you if he trusts you enough to tell you about Mitch. My advice? Don't worry about it. Digging around like that is asking for a ride on the pain train. Let it go.

Me, deciding to let it go (for now anyway): So . . . are you worried about him? I mean, do you think he's okay?

Drew: Warren's okay, Bailey. He deals with shit his own way. Seems to work for him. That's what we're all doing, right? Just trying to deal with shit in our own way.

Drew was right, I suppose. I know I'm certainly trying to deal with things in my own way, and I can hardly blame Warren or anyone else for trying to deal with them in his. I thanked Drew for the chat, and we spent a few minutes joking about teachers or a few of the ridiculous rumors around school. When Warren and Katy showed up, the lighthearted atmosphere in the room changed. Warren and Katy had obviously been fighting. But Katy, in typical Katy fashion, pulled out her lipstick and applied a fresh coat, and plastered a smile on her dark lips.

Katy: So what are we talking about?

Me: Drew was going to update us on numbers and probably insist that Warren and I increase production again. (Everyone chuckled, and the tension dissipated somewhat.) But more importantly, I wanted to ask about spring break.

Katy: Ooooh, I like this subject much better.

Me: Do we have to keep the lab open? In other words, any chance of us all getting away for the week?

Warren: I love the way my girlfriend thinks.

Me: I was thinking of somewhere secluded and warm.

Warren, pulling me to him and stealing a kiss: I REALLY like the way my girlfriend thinks.

Katy, shooting Drew a rather seductive look: I like the way she thinks too.

Drew started talking seriously about production then and what we'd have to do to be able to take time off but also keep our buyers happy. What it amounted to, realistically, was that Warren and I would have to work our asses off in the weeks leading up to it so that we could have enough of a supply to take time off. Drew and Katy said they'd pitch in, if we thought they could measure up to our standards. Warren and I exchanged a look, silently communicating that we doubted they could, but we agreed to keep an open mind. It would be worth it if we all got to go somewhere together.

Then the conversation turned to plans. Wouldn't you know, Drew's family has a time-share in the Cayman Islands?

I am just full of excellent ideas.

March 25

I just keep screwing up with Warren. It's like I can't help myself. I must be incredibly bad at being in a relationship. I mean, what's wrong with me???

First, I asked him what he and Katy were fighting about, and he kind of shrugged it off like it wasn't a big deal. Asking isn't a crime, right? Seems pretty normal in a relationship. But when he wouldn't say, I kept pressing him about it. He finally admitted that it was about two things. One, they'd fought about Adderall. Katy wanted him to get her some, and he wasn't comfortable with the idea so he told her no and she went off on him. The second was the expansion of our sales. Warren isn't very happy about having to do so much of the actual delivery and thought Katy should take over, but she refused, and they said some pretty nasty things to each other. He reiterated how selfish Katy is, saying that she's willing for everyone else to take a risk but won't take any herself.

I trusted my gut and didn't ask about the expansion, again. But for some reason, my stupid gut asked Warren if he'd been the one to give Adderall to Katy for the first time. Honestly, it's been bothering me that he's given me something that is so addictive, and so easily. And he's done it twice. It made sense in my head that maybe he'd given it to Katy, too. But when I asked, everything changed.

The look in his eyes was clearly a warning, but he did answer me. He said that it was actually Drew who'd brought out Adderall the first time. So I guess maybe it really is as common as Katy said, if even Drew does it? Everything seems so easy for him, even easier than Warren, so it makes a lot of sense.

But something was nagging at me. It was the way Warren and Katy were late, and how they seemed to truly despise each other on occasion. It reminded me too much of . . . well, of Emily and Warren.

So I asked Warren, flat out, if he and Katy had ever been a thing. And if maybe leftover feelings were why they fought.

It was just as bad as the other night, if not worse. He accused me of not trusting him. I tried to defend myself, saying I'd heard that he'd had a lot of girlfriends, and then of course it became about how I must be gathering information on him, like a spy or something. At that point I'd lost any control of the conversation and it was in a spiral. I kept trying to defend myself or tell him it wasn't that I didn't trust him, that I just wanted to understand, but it seemed like everything I said just dug me deeper into the hole I'd made for myself, so I gave up and started crying.

That's when Warren apologized and pulled me into his arms. He told me over and over that there was nothing with him and Katy and that anyone who came before me didn't matter. He said I was the only thing that mattered now. He said he just wanted me to be happy. Then he asked me if it was all right if he took a Percocet to calm himself down.

Yes. He had more of them. I don't know when he got them or if maybe he didn't give me all of them in the first place, but when I told him it was okay, he pulled one out of his pocket. His hand was shaking a little as he put it in his mouth, and I felt terrible then for even bringing any of this up. He's working just as hard as me, harder, really, and then I go and put him on edge with all of my insecurity and immaturity. I apologized to him over and over and he held me for a long time as I cried more.

He finally got me to smile by talking about spring break, and I felt like things were going to be okay.

I think the stress of everything is getting to me. And I'm just so afraid I'll lose Warren. Like, any minute some cuter/richer/smarter girl is going to take him away. He'll wake up and realize he's wasting himself on me or something. Me, the girl who can't handle Prescott academics and can't even get into Princeton's summer science program. And obviously, every girl around me could be the one who does it. Katy's so gorgeous and sophisticated, and even though she seems to be really into Drew, she'd be the obvious choice. I'd like to think I'm cuter than Emily, but that doesn't stop me from wondering where Emily goes all the time, especially when it's while I'm not with Warren.

I'm such a mess. God, it's like I cannot keep it together at all. The Adderall helps me with energy and focus, but how do I get rid of paranoia and jealousy? Do they make a drug for that?

Sadly, I'm not even sure I'm kidding about that question. If something like that was available, I'd take it in a heartbeat. I just so want things to be easier than they are. I'm so tired of things being so hard. . . .

March 26

Got the BEST compliment from Katy today. Drew and Warren had to run into town (I know, not even on a Friday, but business is booming) and so we tagged along and went shopping. Naturally, because all we can think of is being on the beach with our boyfriends (okay, whatever Drew is to her), we tried on bikinis.

Katy looked amazing in everything she tried on, because of course she did. And I tried not to think about how that meant Warren would be seeing her in a bikini but whatever. She finally chose a retro-looking suit that was like something a pinup would wear in the forties. Kind of sailory, with a bow at the chest and little sailor stripes in blue and red.

I tried on a few that were a little flattering and some that were terrible. But when I walked out of the dressing room with a gold string bikini on, Katy shrieked and said it was the one.

She walked around me like she was inspecting a racehorse to purchase or something, and proclaimed: "You lost weight!"

And I have to admit, I've never been one of those girls to obsess about the number on the scale or even the number inside of a dress, but I looked at myself tonight in the mirror and I could see hip bones, and my stomach was super flat, and I looked pretty good (for me) in the bikini.

> Me: Maybe skipping a few meals in the cafeteria is paying off.

Katy, winking: Maybe it's all the extra cardio you're getting with Warren.

Me: Ha! I wish. We never have enough time alone.

Katy: The beach will fix that. So will this bikini. He won't be able to think of anything else.

Me: You're sure this is the one? I mean, it's not like I can't afford it, but it's pretty steep for a swimsuit.

Katy: Oh, it's definitely the one. You look SO sexy in it. Plus, Warren's such a geek, he's going to think about *Star Wars* and Princess Leia, and trust me, that's a fantasy every geek boy has.

Me: You've sold me. As long as I don't have to put my hair in buns.

Katy, laughing: Nope. Not a good look. Okay, well, as long as we're shopping for vacation, I think we both need to hit up the lingerie, yes?

So Katy dragged me off to buy more things to tempt Warren with, and I admit it, it was fun and kind of hot to think about him seeing me in a pretty bra-and-panty set. I have a few cute things to wear, but nothing like what Katy talked me into buying for the trip. Warren is going to LOVE IT. I'm not sure I'd have bought it normally, but the comment about losing weight? I mean, it was a straight-up shot of self-esteem for me. Katy's not fat or anything, far from it, but she also has some curves that I don't. I have practically nothing up top, and I've always been self-conscious about that, but if I've lost weight, what I've got going for me is a flat stomach, right?

I don't have a scale in my dorm room, so I have no idea how much weight I've lost, but I did try on a pair of shorts that I wore last summer for a comparison, and I could pull a few inches of material from around my waist.

I wonder if Warren's noticed?

March 29

I called Bex today. It's been too long, and I just needed to hear her voice. I almost called Dad, too. Almost. But I wasn't ready to talk to him about spring break yet, and I figured it would come up because he's probably anxious to know what my plans are so he can make plans of his own. To be honest, I just didn't want to hear the hopefulness in his voice when he asked if I'd already made plans.

So it was just Bex I talked to. She sounds SO happy. I've always been a little jealous of her because everything comes so naturally to her. She got all the cool factor our family had to give, I think. But tonight especially, I was super jealous of her life. She's so happy. So stress free. So INNOCENT. She doesn't have to worry about all the stuff I have to worry about, like her boyfriend dumping her for someone else. Or making enough product to keep a business going and keep everyone's pockets flush. She's not worried about keeping on top of classes and getting into Ivy League schools or summer programs. And I know for sure she's not worried that all of it is going to explode one day because someone finds out something they shouldn't have.

She thanked me for all the gifts I've been sending. She said she's pretty much the most stylish girl at school when they can be out of uniform. (I'm not sure she really is. She prefers wearing sporty clothes, things I'd work out in. That's her regular style.) So I've sent her all the best brands for workout clothes, and maybe it's a trend at Campbell. I know here Katy wouldn't be caught dead in yoga pants unless she was actually doing yoga.

Bex asked me tonight where I'm getting the money. Somehow (maybe the Adderall?) I was sharp enough to come up with a fake job: I told her I'm tutoring underclassmen on the side for some extra cash, and the students here pay top dollar.

She thought it was so cool that I'm doing that and didn't ask any more questions. So, phew. I felt bad about it later, but it's so much better than telling Bex the truth. Not only do I not want her to know, she CAN'T know. Not only because I have to protect her from it but because . . . what would she think of me? What would she say? She'd be so let down, and I can't face that.

She did say she's thinking about traveling with friends for spring break, and so I told her I'm going somewhere with mine, too, and my boyfriend, and she's under strict instructions not to mention the boyfriend part to Dad.

She's actually thinking of New York, which would be amazing for her. But she said she's totally jealous of me going to the Caymans. So . . . I guess we're even. Ha.

March 30

Today was both great and terrible.

The terrible part was English class. My teacher asked me to stay after class. Warren skipped out, luckily, so he didn't see her ask and doesn't know. And I don't think I'll tell him anything. After all we've been through (really, what we've put each other through) the last few weeks, I don't want him thinking there's another thing I can't handle. Or that he's going to have to do even more to pick up my slack. So I'm just going to have to work harder.

I have a C in English. I honestly don't know how it happened.

I've done all my work, on time, and I've made sure to meet all the requirements for each assignment. But my teacher says that my essays are meandering at best and nonsensical at worst. (Whatever that means. Honestly, I thought the last two flowed pretty well. I was typing like a madwoman.) I explained that for some reason, English and I don't get along, and her reply was basically that I need to figure out how to get along with English because no school is going to take someone who can't write an entrance essay. And she wasn't even talking just Ivy Leagues.

Plus, a C at Prescott is failing. Literally. In any other school, a C would be average, right? Passable at least. Not at Prescott. You have to repeat the class if you get a C. I'm not sure if Dad and Isa know about that policy or not, but can you imagine if I had to repeat a class? All that money down the drain. My teacher says I can bring it up if I do stellar work the rest of the quarter, and I suppose I can.

The thing is, I can probably sacrifice some time on chemistry assignments and even calculus. Maybe even not do some of the work in those classes, period, because I can ace the tests no problem. So I can devote that time to English instead and . . . I'll have to ask for Katy's help. Maybe even Emily's.

When I got to the lab tonight, I smiled and laughed and pretended like everything was fine. I think it worked. Warren seemed happy too and kept his arm around me pretty much the whole time. While he and I worked, Katy booked our flights and transportation. So it's official! I'll be spending spring break with the coolest people I know, including my boyfriend, who will see me looking hot in a gold bikini. That was the single good thing about today.

I just have to survive this quarter, I just have to survive this quarter, I just have to survive this quarter . . .

March 31

So here's a small bit of good news: Prescott grades don't get sent home in the mail. They're all available online, through the student or parent portal. I assumed Dad and Isa were getting my grades at home but they're not. And they're not even logging in to see my grades or Dad would have called, angry. I can't believe I didn't realize this until now.

So they don't know I'm not doing great.

But they also haven't even been checking?

Okay, but let's look at the silver lining here and just be happy for now. Maybe by the time they think to check, my grades will be back up.

April 1

I walked into the lab tonight. I must have been pretty quiet because Warren didn't hear me. When I came in he was bent over one of our tables, and I saw him snort up white powder.

I absolutely freaked. The only time I've EVER seen anyone snort something is in movies where they're all using cocaine, using rolled-up money on a mirror. So I naturally flipped out on him. Not only for doing cocaine, but for lying to me. Keeping it from me.

And as I was freaking out, demanding to know what the hell he was doing and how long he'd been doing it and why he was keeping it from me, he grabbed my wrists hard enough to bruise.

> Warren: Bailey. Bailey! Listen to me. It's not coke. Calm down. It's not coke.

> Me: Then what the hell?

> Warren, pulling me to him: Just the Percocets, baby. Just Percocets. It's okay. I wouldn't do coke. Okay? And I wouldn't keep it from you if I was.

> Me: Wait, so if it's Percocet . . .

> Warren: I crushed it up. I just . . . needed one. Faster. It takes effect faster this way.

> Me: But isn't it more dangerous?

Warren: No, it's not going to hurt me any
more than . . .

Me: Than taking it as a pill?

Warren: Right. I'm sorry. I really am. That had
to have spooked you.

Me: I mean, I guess I thought when you told
me the other day that you could stop, and
gave me what you had . . . I thought you'd
actually stop.

Warren pulled back a little and wiped at his nose. His hand,
I noticed, was shaking again, and something about seeing him
shake like that made me realize how on edge he was. How
possibly out of control. And it broke my heart and made me all
the more worried for him. I decided not to badger him about
it, and tucked the worry down deep inside. I didn't want to be
another source of stress for him.

Warren: I can. Of course I can. I just thought
it was okay, after you told me the other night
that I could take one.

Me: Of course it's okay. I didn't mean to imply that you have to have my permission or something. I'm not Emily, right?

Warren, smiling: Right. Thanks, baby. I love you, you know that?

Me: I love you too.

We got to work after a few minutes of kissing. I could literally feel Warren relaxing into my arms, the Percocet taking effect. After that his smiles came easier. There was a little dullness in his eyes, but the sharp, panicked look was gone, so that was good. At least I think it's good. Is it really Warren, though, if the smiles come so easily?

We worked almost completely in silence for a while; the only sounds around us were those of the process, and sometimes some sweet humming coming from Warren's direction. Then he got really still, and I looked at him, thinking he needed an extra hand with what he was doing. But no, he was staring at me, smiling bigger than I'd ever seen him smile.

Warren: You are gorgeous, you know that?

Me: Stop it, you big liar.

Warren: You are!

Me: I'm nothing compared to Katy Ashford or most of the girls at this school.

Warren: You're the liar now. Katy has nothing on you. And you look especially beautiful tonight.

Me: I think that's the Percocet talking.

Warren: Nope. Just a guy in love.

Me: Well, I have lost a little weight.

Warren, sliding his arms around me: Yeah, I can feel that. But that's not it, although you look great. I really think it's because I know you have my back. You worry about me. And I know I get upset sometimes about that, but . . . I don't think I've ever had anyone worry about me like that before.

Me: I'm sure your mom—

Warren: No. Not my mom. Trust me. And
definitely not my dad.

He put his head on my shoulder, and I don't think he was
crying, but I think he was definitely trying not to. I held him
really close, just like I had the night he told me about Mitchell
dying and losing his parents, in a way.

Me: I do care about you. And I'm sorry I
sometimes let that make me into a jealous
idiot. But, Warren, are you really okay? You
are sorta worrying me tonight. Is something
wrong?

Warren, letting me hold him: Honestly, yeah.
I, um . . . well, two things. My dad actually
called. He said Mom is going to go to a
different facility and wanted to let me know.
And he wanted to make sure I wasn't coming
home for spring break. You know, the usual
"Please don't come home, we'd rather not see
you" crap.

Me, with a bitter snort: I know exactly how
that feels. What was the second thing?

Warren: Well, I have a C in English. Probably
because I don't go most of the time.

I busted out laughing, half crying with relief that someone
else (and Warren of all people!) was in the same boat as me, and
also with relief that neither thing was very serious. With what
Warren's into, with what we're ALL into, it could have been
really bad.

Confused, Warren looked at me as I laughed until I was
full-out sobbing.

Warren: Okay, now I'M worried.

Me: No. Don't be. I have a C in English too.

We both burst out laughing then, and we held each other
some more and talked about ways to pull our grades up, and
we ended up actually scheduling out time for ourselves to do
English homework together (at the expense of some making
out and possibly some time with Drew and Katy, but not at the
expense of the work in the lab).

So . . . in a weird way, this is good. I'm not alone in this. And he's going to be just as supportive to me as I'm trying to be with him. He loves me, I love him, and we will both work together to get our grades up. Everything is fine. I HAVE to believe that.

April 3

I can't believe it. It snowed again yesterday, a LOT. It's like we were all expecting spring, thinking warm thoughts (and beach vacation thoughts), and bam! Mother Nature threw us a curveball.

We went sledding again but we didn't stay long. We went pretty quickly over to the bonfire again; the boys seemed way more interested in that. Almost immediately, they went off to talk to a group of kids I only kind of know. I saw Warren hand one of the boys something, just as another boy handed Drew a wad of cash. The boys took off, going deeper into the woods, and Drew and Warren bent their heads together, talking.

I knew what it was, what had just happened. I wasn't stupid. I'd seen it go down just a few weeks ago in the Wiltshire slums, but I hadn't ever seen it at Prescott. That was new.

No one had spiked hot chocolate this time. I'm guessing no one was prepared for this snow. But Katy came prepared.

She drew a silver flask out of her coat pocket and we shared the strong-tasting stuff in it. I didn't ask how she'd acquired it. I'm getting really used to not asking questions.

Katy seemed pretty intent on asking me questions, anyway. She asked how much Adderall I'd taken that day. I honestly didn't remember. It was such a good day. I told her three, maybe. Three usually did it for me now. She told me to be careful drinking while I had Adderall in my system. She said sometimes it makes it harder to feel the alcohol so it's easy to have too much. I noted that but took her flask every time she offered it anyway. She perked up when Drew looked like he was coming in our direction, but he was only going to talk to someone close by us. Katy nearly deflated.

Me: You've got it bad.

Katy: Hello, Pot, I'm Kettle.

Me: Shuddup. So why don't you let it be more with him? I think he wants it. For sure.

Katy: No. I can't.

Me: Why? Is he not good enough for you?

Katy, snickering: No, darling. I'm not good
enough for him. Just like Warren isn't good
enough for you.

Me: Why would you say that? Warren's good
enough for me. Why don't you like him?
Honestly?

Katy: Oh, I adore Warren. When he's not
being an asshole. But you're far sweeter
than him. Nicer. Probably even smarter. But
Warren has to have everything just so, doesn't
he? His way. That way he can always be
ahead of every situation. Always a step ahead.
Always in control.

Me: I don't think he's controlling. Meticulous,
maybe. Precise and methodical, more like.

Katy: Those things too. You know it was his
idea to film collateral.

I didn't know that. I'd assumed it was Drew who thought to
do that, and I honestly hadn't thought about the collateral since

just about the day we filmed it. Most likely because it wasn't ever something I'd have to think about again. I trusted them. They trusted me. At least, that had been the premise.

I looked over at Warren. He was smiling, and I think he must have said something funny because the people around him laughed. He seemed calm, happy, even animated, and I had to wonder sardonically what chemical I had to thank for that.

I don't remember how I got home, but apparently I set my alarm. I got up when it went off, called myself in sick for the day, and went back to sleep. I mean, at this point, what does it matter?

April 5

The shine has definitely worn off the winter, literally and figuratively. Any snow we have left has turned into gray slush all around campus, and I'm now tired of wearing my boots instead of my cute flats. Now it seems like we're all sick of winter and ready for spring. Or moreover, spring break.

I've refused to ask Warren to do more in the lab or to ask for time away so that I can study more. Now that I know he's failing too, it doesn't seem right to ask. We have been working on English together a bit, not as much as I'd really like. He's almost exactly like I am, with having a better head for numbers than words, but it still comes relatively easy for him, and he's incredibly good at bullshitting his way through essays. I'm not, so I feel like I need more practice.

So what I've been doing is staying up later these past few days. Sometimes it's one or two in the morning by the time I finally fall into bed. But I think I'm doing all the assignments a lot better than I was.

Truth be told, it's hard for me to fall asleep anyway. I feel so amped up at night, and thirsty like Warren warned I'd be. I know it's the effects of the Adderall, but if I don't take it, I'm super unfocused and I just CAN'T be unfocused right now. Besides, when I don't take it I turn into the Incredible Hulk or something. Just super irritable and completely restless. Either that or all I want to do is sleep.

I guess I should be honest in my diary, because where else can I be really honest, right? Most nights when I can't sleep, I swear those Percocets are calling to me from inside my purse, under my bed, like something trapped inside of Russian nesting dolls. I haven't taken one, but I want to. I want to know if I could sleep better or fall asleep faster. Hell, even if it just made me calmer and more chill like Warren seems to be about everything, I'd take that too. There is nothing worse than being completely on edge at two in the morning, not being able to sleep, teeth chattering, and tossing and turning.

Emily hasn't noticed, that I can tell. She's either not here or she's fast asleep when I get home. She's never awake when I come in late from the lab. And the lab . . . we're keeping up with production, but we're tragically behind right now on making any extra for spring break. But we HAVE to. We just do. We have to go to the beach and relax and not worry about anything for a week. I swear, if we don't go, the stress is literally going to kill me.

Mr. Callahan was not impressed that I missed chemistry yesterday. He says he wants to be able to say, with absolute certainty, that I'm a good candidate for the science program if his friends at Princeton call with an opening. All I could do was apologize and tell him it won't happen again, but let's be honest here: I'd do that whole night over again every night if I could. It was absolutely amazing to hang with everyone in the woods, and I have to say, everyone at Prescott treats Katy and Drew like the king and queen, and me and Warren since we're with them. I think Warren would be really popular if he wasn't so aloof. It's almost like he chooses to be a mystery to the rest of the school. I will say this: People seem to trust him. The jocks weren't the only ones who approached Warren the other night. I remember that, even if the rest of the evening got a little hazy after the tenth time I swigged from Katy's flask.

Katy said she was the one who put me to bed and told me to drink some water and to take ibuprofen, NOT aspirin or Tylenol. Thank goodness I have friends who know what they're doing.

Anyway, nothing interesting to report, I guess. Still struggling, still tired, still extremely happy that we're going to the beach, still extremely in love with Warren. And the beat goes on . . .

April 6

I feel incredibly bad for even writing this, but it wasn't until I got to civics and put today's date at the top of my quiz that I realized: Today's the anniversary of my mom's death. It was this day, two years ago, that Mom and I went out to shop and she never came home.

I took the quiz but I couldn't tell you a thing that was on it. I'm not even sure I could tell you if it was multiple choice or fill in the blank. Then when I turned it in, I asked if I could go to the restroom. I sat in the girls' room for the next two periods, perched on a toilet, crying as quietly as I could. I was already so on edge that I didn't want to take an Adderall, but I also knew it was the only prayer I had of getting through a whole day of classes. So I took two. Some days I'm so thankful that Warren gives me these pills. I'm a complete mess without them anymore, and there's no way I'd be doing even half as good in my classes if I didn't have them. Maybe when I'm home over the summer, if my dad is willing to listen, I can tell him how unfocused I am at school, and he'd take me to the doctor and they'd prescribe them for me and then it would be legit, and I wouldn't even have to get them from Warren anymore.

Anyway, I got through the day but it was all a blur. I seriously felt like Mom was there today for some reason, just this presence next to me as I went through the motions. Or maybe it wasn't her presence I noticed so much today but the lack of it.

God, what would she think of me? Of what I'm doing? Of any of it?

Would I have been able to tell her how I'm struggling and stressed? Would I be able to tell her how in love with Warren I am? Or that he was my first? Could we have had that conversation? The truth is, I miss it even if we couldn't have. If I'd been afraid to approach her about sex and birth control and my first time, that would have been okay, because she would still BE HERE.

I went home after classes and instead of lying on my bed, jittery and nervous, I went to sleep. I think all the crying exhausted me. . . . At the very least I was exhausted by trying to keep myself together all day.

I slept until eight, way past time when I'm usually at the lab. When I woke up, there were texts from Warren asking where I was and if I was okay, and one from Katy, too, asking me what was up. I threw on my coat and went to the lab, still in my uniform.

Warren stopped everything he was doing when he saw me and pulled me into his arms.

> Warren: You've been crying. What happened?

> Me: Oh. I'd meant to fix my makeup. It's nothing. It's . . . Today's the day Mom died. The anniversary of it. And I couldn't keep my shit together. And I went home after school and slept until . . . well, until ten minutes ago.

> Warren, looking alarmed: That's nearly five hours, Bailey.

> Me: I know. And I'm so sorry. I should have been here. I was just so tired.

> Warren, pulling me to him again: No, don't apologize. I'm sure today has been really hard for you. I'm sorry. Why didn't you tell me? I could have helped. You could have stayed in bed.

Me: You're already doing too much. And I don't know why I didn't tell you. I mean, honestly, I didn't even realize myself until it was practically lunchtime. What's wrong with me that I didn't realize?

Warren: Nothing, baby. Nothing is wrong with you. You've got a lot on your plate is all. And maybe . . . maybe it's kind of a good sign? I've done it, with Mitch, I mean. I remember halfway through the day. Maybe it means you're healing.

Me: Maybe. I don't know. It doesn't feel like I am. Not today, anyway.

Warren: Go on home, Bailey. You need to rest.

Me: But . . .

Warren, cutting me off with a kiss: Go home. Sleep. Cry. Do whatever you need to do. I'll stay here and get this done.

I looked at him, realizing I'd wanted him to tell me he was going with me, so that he could hold me and let me fall apart. But of course work needed to be done at the lab. We couldn't both have the night off. Of course he couldn't come.

But couldn't he? Just for a while? Wasn't I more important than making this batch perfect or being on schedule or the money we'd get from it? So I decided to suggest it.

Me: You could come with me.

Warren, smiling gently: I think you need your rest, Bailey. That would be better for you than anything else right now. Take a Percocet. It will help.

The suggestion, from him, made me mad. He wants to fix me with pills, like I need fixing instead of support. I'd be easier to deal with to him on a drug.

Me, shaking my head: No. I know you can take them without getting addicted, I'm just not going to take that risk.

Warren: Okay, I understand. They just always help me.

228

Back in my room, Emily isn't here, so it's just me alone. All I can do is think. About Mom. How much I miss her, how much I want her to be here and see how I'm growing up, how much I need her love and support and her smile. And I can't stop hearing the sound of metal hitting metal. I feel so lonely. I'm trying to convince myself that Warren is right. I need rest and it was smart of him to stay at the lab. But it wasn't what I'd wanted from him. I'd wanted him to comfort me. I'd wanted him to come back with me and listen to me talk about Mom or just hold me or sit in silence even. And if I'm honest, I wanted him to show me that I'm more important than our next batch of product.

Now all I want is to fall asleep, get some rest, and stop thinking.

So I'm going to take a Percocet. Just one. Just one can't hurt me, right? And it might help, just tonight. Maybe it will do all that Warren promised it could.

April 7

I woke up this morning feeling rested. I slept, without waking up, for a solid seven hours. I didn't think about Mom. I didn't think about Warren. I didn't dream once. Instead, I woke up this morning and felt peaceful and ready for the day. It felt amazing.

Too amazing. Which is why I reached under the bed, pulled out the rest of the pills, and went into the restroom with the intent of flushing them all. But when I held them over the water . . . I just couldn't. I kept thinking about how good it had felt to sleep and not feel stressed. So I put them back in their hiding spot. I won't take them unless I really need them, but I think I should keep them around . . . just in case.

April 8

Shit. I am the worst sister in the world. Add that to the ever-growing list of my failures.

Not only did I forget the anniversary of Mom's death, I didn't call Bex.

When I did remember, and called two days late tonight, Bex was crying when I picked up the phone. I told her how sorry I was. I even explained that I'd been so exhausted with crying myself that I had fallen asleep for most of the day, and Bex swore it was all right but I could tell how hurt she was that I hadn't called.

We had a long talk after that. She told me how wonderful everything is at Campbell, but that she sometimes feels guilty for thinking everything is wonderful without Mom. I lied and told her I feel the same way about how happy I am at Prescott. I think it made her feel better, even if it kind of threw my unhappiness into stark relief. Then we spent the next hour or so sharing memories of Mom. I was super late to the lab, and didn't get most of my homework done, but it was worth it. I got to be there for Bex, better late than never, and I got to talk about Mom for a while.

But this does go on the list. I have to be better about checking in with Bex. Apparently that's another thing Dad dropped the ball on. I have to do everything now, I guess.

April 10

Mr. Callahan asked me to stay after class today, and I thought for sure he was going to "have a chat" with me about skipping class the other day again, but it wasn't that at all. It wasn't Princeton, either, though. It was bad news.

He asked me if I remembered our conversation the other day, about my essay, and of course I did. Then he set a newspaper in front of me before he went on talking. I glanced at the headline, which read, "Meth Addiction on the Rise in Highland County." I don't think I caught much of what he was saying, because I was thinking about just that headline and what it meant.

> Mr. Callahan: So not to make you feel bad or anything, but this is why your essay probably didn't seem groundbreaking to the admissions committee at Princeton. Addiction is bad

everywhere, even Wiltshire. Wiltshire has
been a small, safe town since it was founded,
but now . . . now drugs are taking over.
And not just heroin. I mean, we had some
incidences of crack addiction and trafficking
in the eighties, but nothing like this. People
are ruining their lives. So, you see, everything
is equally bad. And these meth addicts,
some of them get so tweaked out when they
go through withdrawal, crime rates are up
because of it.

Me, scanning the article: It says meth use is
up eighty percent. Eighty percent?

Mr. Callahan: I know. Again, I'm sorry, but
this is probably why the admissions team
wasn't as impressed as they could have been.
I'm sure almost every kid applying has a
similar desire. At this point, hardly anyone is
untouched. Doesn't matter your background,
your class, your school.

Me: School? You think it's happening at
school?

Mr. Callahan: You would know better than I would, I suppose. It's not like the students here ever tell us teachers anything.

Me, nervous: You're not like the rest of the teachers, though. But . . . where do you think it's coming from?

Mr. Callahan: The meth? Could be anywhere, Bailey. That's the thing about that drug. It's not like heroin, which isn't produced here, so you can trace a route. Meth can be made in basements, garages, trailers. . . . And there's not much stopping anyone from producing it, and it's relatively easy to make, as long as you can get your hands on the ingredients. But I'm sure the police are working on tracing it.

Me: How do you know so much about it? I'm sorry, that was personal. And I didn't mean to imply anything.

Mr. Callahan, smiling gently: It's okay, Bailey. I know so much because my brother was an addict.

Me: Was?

Mr. Callahan: Was. He's okay now. Sober for five years. He actually goes around to schools and helps with drug resistance programs in the area.

Me, not knowing why I'm telling him, but telling him anyway: You know Warren Clark's brother was an addict.

Mr. Callahan: I'd heard that. I'm glad you two seem to be getting along well. You could be good influences on each other.

I blushed at that, and Mr. Callahan sent me to my next class with an excuse for being late. He also let me keep the paper, which I read during downtime in English. The rise in meth addiction is concentrated in Wiltshire proper, in the east end. Police reports of dealers and drug use, statistics on the rise of crime, everything was included in the article. One of the addresses listed was for a street name I recognized as the street where our first drop had been, the night I'd gone with Drew and Warren.

But it isn't because of us. It couldn't be. I know how much of the stuff we make every week, how much goes out into the town, and how much we added on in recent weeks. It was a lot, but there is no way it could account for all this. There are other people out there making this stuff, and like Warren said, there is no way their product is as high quality and safe as ours. So our customers are probably not the people committing crimes. And we didn't create the problem. Obviously the market is there, or the Science Club wouldn't have gotten involved at all. Again, these people are going to do it; we're just trying to make it safer. That's all.

Only that doesn't quite add up, and I can't quite convince myself of it.

After English, I threw the newspaper away. I tore it into pieces first.

April 11

I seem to be doing all right in my classes, for now. Even English, although I'm not sure at all that I'll be able to get my grade up before the quarter ends.

Emily and I had been getting along well too, or at least better. We seemed to have reached an understanding about Warren, or perhaps the understanding was just that we wouldn't talk about him much. But yesterday she saw me looking up information about the Cayman Islands on my laptop and asked what that was about. I told her I'm going with Warren over break. I may have purposely left out that Katy and Drew are going too, but quite frankly, I don't care. It's like the second she notices something about Warren, she has to mark her territory or something. Yes, I know, Emily. You were his before. I just want to scream at her sometimes, "He doesn't want you anymore! He dumped you! HE GOT RID OF YOU!" But I can't bring myself to do it, no matter how good it would feel. Mostly because she acts like such a sad puppy most of the time about him and I can certainly understand how losing Warren would hurt so much. But I swear, Emily gets me so close to that edge sometimes. And it probably didn't help that she brought this up when I had layered two Adderall so that I could be sure to stay up late and work on English after I got done at the lab.

So I told her we're going, and that creepy switch flipped, and it was Obsessed Emily again.

Emily: For the whole week?

Me: Yes. The whole week.

Emily: Sounds boring.

Me: Trust me, we will not be bored.

Emily, snorting: I guess not. But I'm surprised
he wants to go anywhere.

Me: What do you mean?

Emily: Just that he doesn't seem to like
leaving Prescott much if he can help it.
Obviously. He stayed over Christmas break,
didn't he? He can't be away for long.

I understood immediately what she was implying and . . . I
felt stupid. Stupid for not realizing that Emily would possibly
know about Warren's extracurricular activities or his drug use
or anything else for that matter. That she perhaps knows, that
perhaps Warren had told her, made my temper (and jealousy)
flare and I lost the cool I always tried to maintain around her.

Me, snapping: Perhaps he just never wanted
to go anywhere with YOU.

At that Emily blanched, but after the initial shock of what
I said to her wore off, she nodded and looked like she totally
accepted my words.

Emily: You're probably right. Maybe it was just me. Maybe he would have taken one of the other girls always sniffing around him. I mean, he's taking you.

Me, ignoring her jibe momentarily: What other girls?

Emily, sincerely: Come on, Bailey. Think he's the type of guy to be faithful? Even if he's not cheating, he's all too happy to let you think he could, right? He plants all these little seeds of doubt on purpose.

Me: No. You're wrong.

Emily: He pushes you away or gets incredibly angry at you for questioning anything he does, right? So it makes you feel like he could easily drop you. And you don't want to even bring up anything anymore, so it's like he trains you to keep your mouth shut. So when you suspect he wants someone else, like Katy—

Me: Katy? You've got to be kidding me.

Emily, rolling her eyes: Come on. Do you
think all that fighting and stuff is actually
because they hate each other? They need to
get a room more than any people I know.

Me: But Katy's into Drew.

Emily: Uh-huh. And I bet she's hoping that
will just tear Warren up inside.

I don't think she's right about that. She may even be trying to
make me paranoid. Warren loves ME, I know he does. He tells
me so and he cares about me. He comforts me and listens to me.
Okay, maybe he didn't on the anniversary of Mom's death, but
he was doing what he thought was right. And maybe he doesn't
listen to my concerns about him and the pills but . . . Warren has
some issues. He's just working through them the only way he can.

Me, trying to feel confident: Warren loves me.

Emily, rather gently: I'm sure he says he
does. Mostly after a fight, right? Or when he

needs something from you? Or he's trying to
get out of being blamed for something?

We got quiet for a while, and in the silence my head
was spinning with what she was saying, trying to find
arguments against it, and even for it. But nothing was clear
to me. I believed him when he said he loved me. I still do.
At least I think I do. I decided to try to shift the focus of the
conversation.

> Me: I think maybe he just doesn't know how
> to really be with someone. He was so hurt by
> his parents and his brother and everything.

> Emily: What are you talking about?

> Me: Oh, he didn't tell you? Never mind, then.

It felt spiteful to say that to her, but it got the job done.
Now she knows Warren shared something with me that he
hadn't with her. At least I had the upper hand back in our
conversation.

> Emily: No, what did he tell you?

Me: It's not my story to tell. Forget I said anything.

We went back to doing our homework, and I felt vindicated. I was the only one Warren had told about his brother. The other girls didn't really matter, then, did they? He felt more for me, he knew he could share more with me. I win, I win, I win.

And maybe . . . maybe if she doesn't know about that, she doesn't know about anything else, either. Maybe I mistook what her words meant.

Me: You do know where Warren gets all his money, right?

Emily hesitated, or maybe she'd gotten back into her homework enough that it took her a while to answer.

Emily: Of course. I know he's on scholarship and everything like me, but his grandparents are loaded, so it's kind of an illusion that he's poor. He likes to play up the "woe is me" scholarship student thing. He probably thinks it adds to the intrigue or something.

I didn't know what to make of her answer or the hesitation. But something tells me Emily knows more than she let on.

And this isn't the first time someone has said something to me about Warren having a lot of girls around. I mean, Drew's said as much. Now Emily. They can't possibly both be lying, right? And why would Drew have any reason to make me feel like I can't trust Warren? Emily, sure, but not Drew.

I don't know how to ask Warren about it and not sound like I'm accusing him. And if I'm being honest, even asking him as gently as possible will make him angry. I guess it's in the past, right? And I shouldn't worry about the past. Unless it's a pattern for him . . .

God, I have no idea who to trust. I'd give anything to talk this through with Mom.

April 12

Warren found me before lunch yesterday and pulled me into an empty classroom. It was thrilling, not going to lie. But he wasn't there to steal a kiss. He asked me if I could make sure that Katy wouldn't go to the lab that night.

I jokingly asked if it was because he was desperate for some time alone with me, but my laughter sounded so fake and tinny. At the mention of Katy's name, all I could think about was what Emily had said about her and Warren.

Warren didn't notice my thoughts were elsewhere and told me he had ideas about the product that he wanted to try. I promised I'd do my best to keep her away, even though I was nervous about what he was up to. I haven't mentioned the news article to anyone in the Club yet, and honestly, I was feeling guilty enough about what we're doing. If he wanted to make the product stronger or something, I don't know if I could handle it.

At lunch I brought up that I'd heard Drew talking about a movie Katy wanted to see, and the two of them made plans to go see it, leaving Warren and me tons of time in the lab alone.

When I got there, he was already inside, in his coat and goggles. Something was brewing, but the smell was a little . . . off. Not in a bad way. Just different from what I'm used to. Sharper, somehow.

Me: So what's going on?

Warren, turning to me with a huge grin:
I think I've figured out how we can make
something better.

Me: Better? Like better meth or something
different?

Warren: Better meth. Essentially. Purer.
Stronger.

Warren pulled out a notebook, an old spiral-bound thing that had seen better days. He flipped it open to where his scratchy handwriting revealed some touch-ups to the formulas we always use.

I took the notebook and studied what he'd written, and although I understood the formulas, I paid more attention to how quickly he'd written it, considering how sloppy and pointed his letters and numbers were. He'd obviously been hit by a flash of inspiration.

Me: So . . . basically we'd use more of the catalytic ingredients?

Warren: I think so. I think we'll be able to make it faster, and I think it will leave more of the actual high-inducing ingredients more pure.

Me: So it will cause a stronger high?

Warren, shaking his head: No. I mean, yes. It would. But they wouldn't need to use as much of it either. What do you think?

Me: I think we should try it. But how will we
know if it works?

Warren, with a shrug: I'll be guinea pig. Or
Drew. We've done it before. We can handle it.

Me: Okay. I trust you. I didn't know you
wanted to change anything. I mean, I'm all
about it, I just thought we were doing fine.

Warren: We are. But . . . there's always a better
way, Bailey. And I'm always looking for it.

I had a feeling it wasn't just making the product that
he was talking about. Was he always looking for better in
everything? Like, a girlfriend? Emily's and Drew's words
creeped back into my head, and I knew I had to know. Perhaps
if I wasn't direct about it . . .

Me: Can I ask you something? (His
pretty eyes clouded over, but he nodded.)
We're . . . we're safe, right? I mean, you
and me. I shouldn't get tested or anything,
right?

Warren, his eyes now dark: Are you asking me
if I have an STD?

Me: I realize it's a little late to be asking, and
I know we take precautions but . . . I mean, do
you know for sure you're clean?

Warren: Let me guess. Emily told you I
sleep around? Probably insinuated that I'm
cheating, too, didn't she?

Me: She didn't insinuate that, but yes, she did
say you had a past. And she hasn't been the
only one to say something like that.

Warren set his jaw, and for one frightening moment I
thought he was going to yell. What he actually did was far
worse. He cleared his throat and looked at me evenly, and his
voice was smooth and emotionless when he spoke.

Warren: And you believe I'd put you in
danger? You believe Emily?

Me: No . . . I . . . maybe. I mean, you've kept
things from me before.

Warren: When?

Me, scrambling to think of examples: You said you wouldn't take any more Percs, but you did.

Warren, raising his voice: You told me I could, Bailey!

Me: Okay, well, you didn't tell me about the Percocets when you bought them.

Warren: Come on. Surely you've learned by now that the less you know, the safer it is for you. I'm just trying to protect you. Everything I've done is to protect you.

Me: And the Adderall? Giving it to me?

Warren: Has it helped you or not?

It has. It has helped me. On the surface. But now I can't sleep. And now I'm not just thin, I can actually feel my hip bones against my clothing every time I move. And now I can't NOT take it.

Me: And you sell to people here? At Prescott?

Warren, with a frustrated groan: Fine. You
want to know it all? Here. Here's my phone.
Read my texts. Memorize my schedule.
Follow me around. Know everything.

He took his phone out of his back pocket and tossed it
toward me with a little more strength than one could say was
friendly. I held it in my hands. The screen was lit, waiting for a
passcode to be typed in. I stared at it for a moment, then flicked
it off and tossed it back (gently) to Warren.

Me: I don't want it. I'm sorry. Emily got into
my head. That's all. Warren, I'm sorry.

Warren: You don't trust me.

I wanted to ask how I'm supposed to trust him when it feels
like everything is a secret, but he would just argue with me again.
And . . . in truth, he's right. He has an answer for everything. The
less I know, the safer I am, and he understands that.

Me: I'm sorry. I didn't understand. I love you.

Warren: I'm sorry too.

I was stunned to hear him say it back, and the shock of it made me realize how often he doesn't say it at all. Then there was a moment when I thought maybe he would reach for me or at least seem open to me touching him. But neither of those things happened. And, I realized, he hadn't told me he loves me back. We just stared at each other, my blood cold, his eyes tired.

> Warren: I'm, uh. I'm going to go, but I'll leave that notebook here.

> Me, nodding: I'll finish up a batch and then see what I can do with the formula. Warren, please don't be mad at me.

> Warren: I'm not. I'm just . . . tired. I'll see you tomorrow.

He left, and I stayed at the lab until 1 a.m., trying to follow Warren's new instructions perfectly, so that he'll be pleased. Even if I would dare try it myself, I wouldn't know anything about what I'm supposed to feel like, so I'll leave it up to the boys, but I hope it's good. That would make Warren right about his theory and prove that I know what I'm doing with this and can be trusted to do it alone.

Emily wasn't home when I got here, which was weird, but I'm grateful. I think I probably would have taken all of my emotions out on her. I didn't fall asleep until it was nearly morning, but I wouldn't let myself take a Percocet, either, so that's at least good. I can do something right.

April 12, later

I didn't see Warren this morning, which means he is definitely still angry, or at least that's how I have to take it. My stomach twisted into a knot that stayed all day. Between second and third, Katy and I met in the bathroom. I wanted so badly to ask about Warren, to either confirm or deny what Emily said, but I let it go. I can't keep doing this to myself and to Warren. I can't keep letting Emily inside my head; I can't keep getting inside my own head like this.

And besides, the thing is, even if Katy wants Warren, she also clearly wants Drew more. I just have to have a little faith that Warren and I are more solid than that and that he truly loves me enough to turn down someone like Katy Ashford.

I did tell Katy about the fight, though, and she hugged

me and touched up my makeup out of her bag. Then I shared some Adderall with her. That's about the only thing that got me through the day. Warren was in English but came in late, so I didn't get to talk to him. When the bell rang, he was already out the door.

I went to the lab tonight, fully expecting that Warren wouldn't even come there, and I was right. When I got into the basement, Drew was there, suited up in coat and goggles.

Me, sighing: He's really that mad?

Drew, with a shrug: He'll get over it.

Me: What do I do?

Drew: Help me with this batch. It's been a while since I've had to do this. And Warren . . . Give him time. He gets in his little moods and there's no talking to him. But I've never seen him so affected by a girl, so you've got that going for you.

Although my heart leaped at that, I don't know if "affected" is necessarily a positive thing.

On the other hand, maybe I'm just reading into Drew's words too much, just like I'm probably reading into everything else too much.

> Drew, gesturing toward Warren's notebook:
> What is this?

> Me: Warren adjusted the formula. He thinks
> we can make it purer and more potent.

> Drew: That's good. That's really good. We
> could probably make less of it and sell it for
> more. Did he try it?

> Me: No. I made it last night, according to his
> instructions. He said he'd test it.

> Drew: I'll do it.

> Me, concerned: Okay, well. You won't need
> much, if Warren's right. And . . . I mean, I
> made it by myself, so . . .

> Drew: Bailey, for fuck's sake, do you doubt
> everything you do?

I drew in a breath sharply. It wasn't just that Drew had never spoken to me like that before, it was the question itself. And I knew the answer: Yes. Yes, I do doubt everything I do. It's not just Mom dying or Warren's games that have me so off, it's Prescott, not feeling like I'm on top of things for once in my life. And joining Science Club. I don't know who I am anymore. That is the reality of it. And if I don't know who I am, how can I trust myself?

I felt like a scolded child, so I merely nodded, then I opened one of our storage units and took out the batch I'd made. It was clearly marked so I would know, and so would Drew or Katy, that it was different. It looked different too. Slightly more cloudy than the other batches Warren and I had made. I wasn't sure if that was a good thing or not. Usually I thought our finished product looked almost pretty, like crystal or glass. This looked more like shards of table salt.

Drew studied it, then, without a word, went to his coat and withdrew a glass pipe with a bulb on the end.

It occurred to me that I'd never actually seen anyone use what I'd been making for months, and I was suddenly seized with the urge to run out of the lab. I couldn't explain it; I just knew that if I saw it, saw what it did to people, I could never go back from that. I could never NOT know again.

While I was freaking out, Drew was oblivious, doing the drug like it was second nature. I watched as he loaded the pipe (um, is "loaded" the right word? I don't even know) and flicked a lighter underneath the bulb. Pure white smoke drifted, tranquil, around the bulb, and after a passing moment Drew inhaled it.

When he breathed out, I stared at him, looking for some sign of being high on meth. Like maybe it would change everything about him.

A slow, languid smile spread across his mouth.

> Drew: Oh, Bailey. You . . . Warren . . .
> whoever . . . round of applause.

> Me, heart leaping: Really?

> Drew, taking another hit: Really. This is going
> to make us bank. Rich, Bailey.

> Me, smiling: I thought we were.

> Drew: No, this is next-level rich. I gotta call Katy.

> Me: Oh. Um, can I ask you something about
> Katy?

He nodded. There is something so casual and unassuming about Drew that I feel okay asking him anything. Even this.

Me: Have she and Warren ever . . . you know,
liked each other?

Drew let out a burst of laughter and smoke. The smell hit
me then. It was like what I was used to smelling while making
it, but burnt. God, people put this crap in their bodies?

Drew: Hell no. I know. It sometimes seems
like it's sexual tension, but believe me, no.
Never. Not even when we were kids.

Me: Thank you. I feel stupid for asking. Emily
said Katy was into him.

Drew: You've got to stop believing that girl.
She's a damn mess.

Me: Apparently. And I need to start believing
Warren more.

Drew, nodding, slightly nervous and with
quicker movements than usual: Warren is
the only person I'd take a bullet for, Bailey.
He'd do the same for me. And I know he'd

do the same for you. He's hard to put up with sometimes. He's kind of an asshole. But you have to trust him. He sees the long game like we can't, you know?

I'm not sure I do know, but his words made me feel better. Drew and I finished up a batch (he was surprisingly knowledgeable about the process, even if he was sometimes too hyper and scattered to really help), and I went home, finished my homework, and even had a nice conversation with Emily about normal things.

I think I need to apologize to Warren. I'll find him first thing in the morning and do just that.

Warren and I are going to be okay. And I actually feel sleepy at a normal time (for the first time in what feels like months!!!), so hopefully that means I can finally get some rest.

April 13

I didn't have to find Warren this morning. He found me. He was waiting for me with coffee in hand, and if he hadn't had a sad, droopy smile on his face, I would have thought it was the same as every other morning since we started dating. He handed me the coffee and asked if we could talk, and I was suddenly seized by panic that this was it: This was the day he was going to dump me.

I agreed, and he started heading toward the exit. I grabbed his hand and stopped him, and he didn't pull his hand away. So that was a good sign. I told him I couldn't miss English. He promised to get me back before then.

So we went out, he still held my hand, and we sipped our coffees in silence for a moment. I was the one to break the silence.

> Me: I'm sorry. I can't tell you how sorry I am, really. But I think I realize now how much everyone else is getting in my head, and I shouldn't let them. I need to listen to you and trust you.

> Warren: No, I'm not sure you should. And I should be the sorry one here, Bailey.

With those words, I got truly scared. He must have noticed, so he pulled me to a bench outside the math building, uncaring that the very teachers marking us absent would be able to see us from the window. He held me close to him. The air was chilly and slightly damp, like the fog from the morning hadn't quite cleared.

He started by thanking me for doing so much work in the lab to help him, even though I've been stressed out about school.

Then he confessed that he feels like his life is a mess right now. It broke my heart to hear him say it but . . . honestly, it was also such a relief. On so many levels. I wanted to know that he could see that he wasn't doing well, and I have to admit, a huge part of me wanted to feel a little less alone in my messy life.

> Warren: Things have been awful with my
> dad lately and . . . I should have told you that.
> You let me in about your mom, and for some
> reason I have a hard time letting anyone
> else in about my family's issues. I shouldn't.
> Especially with you.

> Me: How can I help?

> Warren: You can't. I mean, not with my family.
> It's all too messed up. There's nothing anyone can
> do about that. I try to . . . I try to ignore all the
> shit and bury myself in the work or the money
> or you, sometimes. (He squeezed my hand hard.)
> And I try to bury it with other things.

> Me: Percocets.

Warren: Sometimes. Sometimes other things.

Me, panicking: Not . . . please don't tell me . . .

Warren: No, not heroin. I wouldn't stomp on my brother's grave that way. But . . .

Me: How much? How often? What else?

Warren, rubbing his forehead: I don't know. I honestly don't know. Anything I can get my hands on. Anytime.

My heart ached for him so much then. The desire to medicate himself is only a desire to heal, to fix, just the completely wrong way to go about it.

Me: What can we do? Can I . . . take you somewhere? Rehab?

Warren: No. I can't. My family can't know. It would destroy them all over again. It's okay. I can deal with it.

Me: But . . . but you're around it all the time, Warren. Because of what we do. (I was suddenly seized with an idea. A way to make everything better. Perhaps the ONLY way.) Can we . . . can we stop? Just quit? Tell Drew and Katy to find other chemists?

Warren: I can't do that, either. I need the money. I need them.

I thought about what Drew had said about taking a bullet for Warren, and I realized the feeling is mutual. And whatever animosity he and Katy have for each other, we are still a team, a family, and he knows he can rely on her.

Me: Okay, then what can we do? What can I do?

Warren: I don't know. . . . Do you think you could just . . . let me be?

Me: You're asking me to leave you alone? Do you . . . do you want to break up with me?

Warren: Oh, no! No, baby. That's not what
I meant at all. I mean, can things just be
normal again? Back to being happy and not
questioning everything?

Me: You want me to pretend this isn't
happening? That you're not taking pills just to
get through the day?

Warren, with a slow nod: Yes. At least for a
while. Just . . . just let me get to the summer,
you know? Then I can figure it out. And I can
be away from here and at Princeton.

How on earth can I just pretend that everything is okay? I
can't help but think it's the last thing he needs, but I was scared
to push him. I'm afraid of losing him but, honestly, more afraid
of how he'd react. His anger is intense, plus it might trigger him
into using more pills. So I told him I could try. That was the best
I could do.

He walked me back in time for second period. I should have
felt good, but I didn't. Not at all. Then when Katy and I met up
in the bathroom and I swallowed down two Adderall, I told her
everything. She didn't act surprised about his apology or about

his admission that he's using pills regularly, more than Percocets. What she did act surprised about was that this was the first time he and I had talked about it.

Did everyone know? Everyone but me?

I asked Katy what to do. What WE could do, as his friends and partners. She shook her head and laughed, and maybe she didn't mean it to be cold but it felt so icy I nearly started crying.

She said he is the smartest person she knows, that he can play all of us like violins. I asked her to explain what that meant.

> Katy: He got you to apologize, didn't he? And he got some sympathy. And he got you to say that you'll leave him alone about it.

> Me: That's not what he was doing. He's hurting, Katy. And he just doesn't know how to stop hurting.

> Katy: I don't doubt he hurts, Bailey. The problem is he makes everyone around him hurt too. See you at the lab tonight.

It's one in the morning and I'm still not sure how to interpret her words or the whole conversation in general. And I still feel unsettled about the talk with Warren. Even more than I was before.

I just don't know what to do. All I know is I can't give up on him. What kind of person would I be if I did?

April 17

After school today I didn't go with Katy to get coffee, and I put off doing homework or going to the lab, and headed to Mr. Callahan's classroom. I'm not sure why I wanted to talk to him. Maybe it was just that he seems so . . . adult. Wise, even. Warm, at least, unlike how most of my friends are at the moment. He was still there, sitting at his desk grading what looked like freshmen-level homework. He was delighted to see me. He asked me how things are going, and I told him that things aren't that great, if I was being honest. He gestured to a seat in the first row, and I sat.

I chose my words carefully, and of course I didn't tell him anything that would get me into trouble. But I did tell him that my grades are abysmal, at least to my standards (and sometimes to Prescott's standards as well), and that I feel that my friends here are confusing. I told him about the problems I'd been having in my relationships with Emily and Katy, and I also told him about Warren. I said it feels like Warren is such a big part of my life, and it's affecting everything else.

I could tell he was glad I confided in him. He said he'd been worried since I stopped coming in after school to do extra chemistry but he knew how hard Prescott could be. He also, sort of awkwardly, told me that first love can be intense and often confusing. He said he imagined Warren could be extra intense. I asked if he knew anything about Warren's family, and to my surprise, he did.

> Mr. Callahan: We were told. The staff, I mean.
> There are certain things in a student's file
> that are essential to teaching them ... things
> like learning disabilities or perhaps a mental
> disorder. But there are also cases like Warren's,
> when something in a student's personal
> history needs to be known, because the
> student ... well, the student was changed so
> much by it. It helps us teach that student, to
> get through to them. It's not salacious gossip,
> I want you to understand that.
>
> Me: I didn't think so. When you say
> "changed" ...

Mr. Callahan: Well, I didn't know Warren as a child, but I have good friends at Campbell. Warren's parents are not exactly warm people. But when his brother was found dead . . . it was in all the papers locally, and the family was really under the microscope, considering their standing in the community. And if his parents were distant before that, they were downright neglectful afterward. Warren's mother took precedence. I can imagine that a boy like that, who believes he's not good enough to get his parents' attention . . . well, I imagine that his brother's death and his parents disappearing almost completely just proved that to him.

Me: He always seems sure of himself, though.

Mr. Callahan, looking at me with a gentle but probing expression: Does he really?

Me: I don't know. And I don't know how to help him.

Mr. Callahan: I wish I had an answer for you. I have a feeling that your loyalty and empathy for him have done more for him than most people in his life have, but it's probably also hard to trust that or accept it. Maybe he even wants to refuse it sometimes, because he may not think himself deserving. But . . .

Me: But?

Mr. Callahan: I hope you're not giving so much of yourself that you're giving up who you are.

Me: I'm not sure I know what you mean.

Mr. Callahan: I mean, Prescott's coursework is substantial, but you're extremely intelligent, Bailey. You shouldn't be having this kind of trouble with it, if you don't mind me speaking frankly with you. There's quite a difference between not being able to handle the work and just not doing it. And I hope

you don't give up on Emily. It sounds like
she could really use a friend right now.

At that point I could only nod to him because I was unable
to speak in the face of the harsh truths he was telling me. I
looked down to hide the tears in my eyes and my gaze landed
on a newspaper on his desk. The headline read, "Toddler Found
in the Cold." There was a picture underneath the headline of a
small, run-down house.

Tears forgotten, I turned the paper so I could see it better.

Mr. Callahan: Yes, terrible thing. Luckily the
boy will be all right. He'll be in foster care,
maybe until he's of age, but he'll live.

Me, scanning the article: What happened?

Mr. Callahan: Neighbors saw a little boy, a
two-year-old, out in the cold and rain the
other night in Frenchtown. Know where that
is? (I shook my head.) It's a trailer park in
the east end of Wiltshire. He was wearing
only a diaper, no clothes, walking in the
road. A kind soul took him in and called the

police. Turns out his parents were so high on meth they didn't even realize he was missing.

Me, heart galloping a syncopated beat: So he got out in the street?

Mr. Callahan: Could have been seriously hurt. Or taken. Or could have frozen to death. The temperatures were in the freezing range that night.

Me: How could his parents not even realize?

Mr. Callahan: When you're that high, I don't think you even know where YOU are, let alone a small child. But thank God, he's been placed in a home where he'll be safe and cared for.

Me: I don't understand how . . . how someone could let themselves get that way. That they'd not notice their kid was gone. That they'd thinking getting high is more important than their kid.

Mr. Callahan: That's how addiction works,
unfortunately. Addicts often can't think about
anything but their next fix.

For a moment I thought about Warren and the pills he
takes. And I thought about myself and the Adderall.

But I could stop taking that, couldn't I? I don't NEED it.
But I'm craving it. I'll start to want it whenever I feel my energy
fading. Or when I feel like I can't focus. Or when I have a lot of
work to do. But wanting isn't the same thing as needing.

. . . Is it?

I asked Mr. Callahan if I could have the newspaper and
he let me take it. Then he told me I could always talk to him.
About anything. I thanked him and went home.

I have to head to the lab in a few minutes, but I'm nowhere
near done with homework. Every time I try, I look at the picture
of the little house where the toddler lived with his parents. Even
if I hadn't read it or Mr. Callahan hadn't told me, I would have
known it was east-side Wiltshire.

I tucked the paper inside my purse, with the Percocets.

April 18

Drew was at the lab last night, as was Katy, and when I got
there they had my particular batch of the product out and were

in deep conversation. Apparently, Drew had filled Katy in, because when she saw me, she threw her arms around me and squealed. That was when Warren walked in.

Drew then told Warren about how he'd tried some of the batch I'd made, how it made him feel, and that I'd followed his instructions perfectly. Warren smiled, gave me a proud nod, and took out some of the new product for himself.

Drew didn't even need to be asked. He just got out his pipe and handed it over to Warren. I did my best, I think, to not look completely panicked. After all, he'd basically admitted to me that he is an addict but also that he can handle himself. Still . . . he doesn't need THIS addiction. He doesn't need to become the type of person who would let a child wander out into the winter cold without clothes and not even realize it. Will he one day do that to me? Metaphorically? Will I become just another distraction from the next high, something he'd rather forget?

But at least if I looked anxious, maybe my friends thought it was because I was worried I hadn't done a good enough job. I watched Warren heat the pipe with a lighter, watched him draw the poisonous fumes into his lungs. I wish I could say he looked awkward doing it. Or maybe that he had no clue what he was doing, or that he coughed and sputtered and rejected the drug with his body and his voice. But of course, he looked used to this. He looked as practiced and sure as he could be.

After a minute or two, long enough for the high to set in completely, a smile spread Warren's mouth wide. He started describing what he was feeling, his voice a little tighter and rougher than I was used to. There was something different about his pretty eyes, too. Less warm, more sharp. He talked to Drew and Katy, mostly, and avoided looking at me much, and honestly, that was just fine with me. I wasn't sure what to make of this new Warren, like he was more a stranger now. It wasn't just the change in his demeanor that bothered me, the obvious shift in his motor skills or the intensity of him with the high, it was something else. I watched him talk to our friends, trying to figure out what it was, exactly, that bothered me so much, and it hit me like a freight train: This was the most satisfied I'd ever seen him. I can't put into words how much that hurt, how much it felt like a betrayal that he needed a high and craved a high more than he did me, but there was no denying that it seemed in that moment he finally had what he'd been longing for.

And it made me realize that maybe . . . maybe I'll never be that important to him. Maybe nothing can be as important as a high to him.

He told us the new version of the product is stronger. He already felt like he'd used a lot more than normal, even though that was the amount he would usually use. He talked about a sort of euphoria, a powerful feeling, like he could do anything. It was like Adderall times ten, if what he was saying was correct. He felt like he could run for miles without stopping. He felt like he didn't need to eat ever again. He felt like he could ace tests, write books, recall every fact known to man. It was that kind of invincible. But of course he was talking about nothing, really. Rambling on too fast and gesturing more animatedly than I'd ever seen him. He was truly enjoying the high, and the sad part was, I wasn't surprised in the slightest.

Drew agreed with him, and then they got to work. All of them except me. Katy started talking about her contacts, how to basically pitch the new version to everyone. Drew started talking logistics with Warren: how much of what ingredient and where they could get it, how much it would take up front to manufacture this version on a larger scale, and also where we could cut back since we were using less of some of the ingredients. Then, of course, they all talked about how much to charge.

It was more than I'd ever heard them talk about prices. So far, I knew only what came to me each week. How much I could stick into my pocket when Drew distributed payment. I'd never known anything about what we were selling it for versus how much money it actually took to produce.

The markup for our labor, logistical planning, and artistry was around 400 percent.

I felt tears form in my eyes and closed them so that they wouldn't fall.

Not only were we giving addicts the means to forget about their children in the cold; we were charging them through the nose for it.

I listened to the group make plans and work out numbers. I nodded along at appropriate times. I answered questions or gave my thoughts when asked my opinion. I even laughed when they talked about how if they started selling this now, we'd have extra money to blow while we are at Drew's beach house, when I really felt like puking on their shoes I was so disgusted. But in truth, I wasn't really listening. I was obsessively going over things in my head, getting my mental files in order: how I'd joined, how the Club worked, the collateral, Warren's addiction, my own (I think I have to put that name on it now) addiction, the consequences of leaving the group, how alone I'd be, what trouble I might get in, what I might possibly lose, how I'd survive without Warren. And as I turned those things over and over in my head like some sort of nightmarish carousel, one thing became crystal clear—I had to get out of the Club. It was the only right thing to do. And I had to do it without ruining my life.

As I'm writing tonight, I'm still thinking it through. Every scenario I've come up with, from simply telling the group I'm leaving and promising to never say a word to anyone, to going full-out nuclear on them and turning myself and everyone else in, means that life will never be the same. I might be going to jail. Or they are. Or more people will end up addicted.

One thing is for damn sure: If I get out, I'll lose them. All of them. Even Warren.

Maybe especially Warren. He is the one who will feel most betrayed, because if anything gets out about the Club, his own drug use is going to come out, and the ripple effect will go through his family. And I know Warren. There won't be any understanding or forgiveness for this. I'll be dead to him.

Another thing is certain as well: If I CAN get out of this without much collateral damage, without ever telling another soul and the group letting me go without a fight, I will no longer be able to get Adderall. The thought alone makes me nauseated and shaky. If I'm going to do this, I'm going to have to stop taking it first.

I can do it, I think. I can stop. Maybe I can even get Katy and Warren to stop with me. Maybe I can convince them it's for the good of the Science Club.

Maybe there is no chance in hell.

April 19

Of all things, my father called today.

I was so startled to see his number pop up on my phone that I sounded weird when I said hello and he immediately asked if I was okay. I told him I was. What else am I going to say? "No, Dad. I'm not. I think I'm addicted to Adderall and my boyfriend is addicted to way more than that, and oh, by the way, I'm totally in the drug business now. Cool, huh?"

I shared more than I ever meant to with Mr. Callahan, so let's just leave it at that, okay?

I asked how he was, and he said he was doing really well. He said Isa's had a pretty lengthy and intense case, so he's been on his own in the evenings more than he'd like. I could hear the sadness in his voice. The loneliness. And I felt for him, as much as I don't love Isa. Loneliness for any reason sucks. I've felt incredibly lonely in a room full of people before. I felt lonely last night at the lab, being the only person who seemed to see a problem in what we are doing.

He asked if I'd be home for break, and there was some hopefulness in his voice. That was more shocking than him calling me. Then I immediately felt like crap for saying I'd be elsewhere. Dad had obviously talked to Bex. He knew of her plans to go to New York, and I wondered how often they

275

talked. Then, as if I wasn't shocked enough, he apologized for not calling on the anniversary of Mom's death. He APOLOGIZED.

> Dad: I'm really sorry, Bail. I wish I had a better excuse. I just couldn't pull myself together that day.

> Me: You mean . . . you were upset?

> Dad: Yeah. I think things have happened so fast for me, with Isa, I mean . . . I'm not sure I really had time to properly grieve for your mother. Not the way I needed to.

I didn't know what to say to that. Part of me wanted to yell and say that of course he hadn't grieved properly; he'd barely grieved at all. I also wanted to say terrible things about Isa and how she just distracted him from pain or something, but none of that makes real sense when I think about it. Of course she distracted him, but he obviously cares about her too. Most of all, though, I wanted to tell him how he'd left me all alone and moved on from Mom when I needed him most.

But I didn't say anything like that.

Me: Well, I'm not sure I've been coping in the healthiest ways, either.

Dad: What do you mean? Are you okay?

Me: I'm fine, Dad. Just . . . angry.

Dad: At me?

Me, swallowing hard: At you, yeah. I guess I felt like it was too soon for Isa. It felt disrespectful to Mom. But I'm mad at everything, Dad. Mad that she's gone. Mad at all the good things I do because she can't see them. Mad at all the bad things I do because she's not here to help. I don't know.

I have no idea if it was simply because he asked, and asked so sincerely that I truly thought maybe he wanted to know, or if with everything going on it felt good to unload something on him, but for whatever reason, I was honest. And yeah, it DID feel good to finally say it. Maybe we can understand each other a little better now. At the very least, there's not such a wall between us.

Dad, after a moment of silence: I'm really sorry, Bailey. I should be doing more. And I hope you understand about Isa. . . . She's not a replacement.

Me: I know. I understand, Dad. It's just weird to see you happy, I guess? I feel like you should still be angry like me. And sad.

Dad: I'm both of those things, Bailey. Every day. Every day I miss your mother. Is school really going all right? Have you made friends?

Me, trying to sound happy: Yeah. Friends, and a boyfriend.

Dad: Bex may have mentioned that, but don't get angry at her; she only told me because I was worried about how you were adjusting.

Me: I can't ever be mad at Bex, Dad. You know that.

Dad: So who is he?

I told Dad a little about Warren and about my friends. All the good stuff, none of the bad. I also told him I'm not doing as well as I want in my classes, and he confessed to me that he'd never been good at schoolwork and was impressed and proud that I was even in Prescott considering my genes. The conversation sputtered out, and Dad excused himself, saying he needed to get dinner on the table by the time Isa was home. He told me he knew I could handle Prescott and knew I'd get into Harvard or wherever I wanted to go. I didn't tell him about the wait list for the Princeton program. No need to disappoint him with that. If I actually get in, then I can tell him I applied.

When I hung up the phone I felt both better and worse, and bereft of a friendly voice. I considered calling Bex to give her a gentle teasing about not being able to keep a secret, but decided to let it rest.

It's almost eight o'clock, and I have a few more things to do for tomorrow's classes, but I don't feel like being alone. I need Warren. I need to know that he cares too. So I'll head to the lab and keep him company while I finish my homework, and if he really needs a hand, I can help too. It's okay. I can keep doing this. I have to, I think, until I have a better plan.

April 20

Although last night went okay at the lab (Warren mostly kept us talking as I did my homework, and even when I had to jump in and help him a bit, he kept my mind off what we were actually doing enough that I didn't have to think about it much), I just couldn't face it tonight. I wanted to be around Warren, even though I . . . I think I'm sure we can't go on like this. But I wanted to be with him tonight and kiss him and feel some of that heat. Just to feel normal. Maybe to distract me. But in the end, the image of the cold, abandoned toddler won out. I just couldn't bring myself to go through another four or five hours of pretending I was just fine with destroying lives. But I did go to the lab. I had another idea.

Warren was there, looking gorgeous in his blue cashmere sweater, his hair slightly mussed. I could tell by his eyes, though, that he'd had a lot of Percocets. Weird how I couldn't see that before. Now it's so obvious.

I asked him for his car keys. He cocked his head at me in question. I somehow, miraculously, came up with an excuse that would mean he wouldn't want to come along.

> Me: It's Bex. She needs some, um, girl help.
> She's really upset that some of the girls in her

grade already have real bras, so I'm going to
take her to get something pretty. Shouldn't
take more than a few hours. Unless you need
me here?

Warren, pulling a face: No, by all means, help
Bex with girl problems. And I'd prefer to
never think of your little sister and bras in the
same context ever again. You know how to
drive it, right?

Me, laughing: Thanks. And yes. I promise I'll
drive as carefully as possible and I won't let
Bex eat anything inside it.

Warren handed me the keys and reminded me where it was
parked. Then he reached for my hand and I let him take it.

Warren: Are you really okay? You've been kind
of weird these last few days.

Me: Weird?

Warren: Distant.

Me: Oh. I'm worried about you and trying
to control my worry for you, I guess. Trying
to leave you alone. But it's not easy, Warren.
I really care about you, and seeing you high
or not completely in control of the situation
scares me. You're high now, right? What if you
blow yourself up?

Warren, eyes flashing with anger before they
softened: You're right. I am. But I'm used to
this, Bailey. I'm okay. Don't worry. We'll get
through this. You love me, right? That's really
all that matters.

He kissed me sweetly, and my heart ached. For him. For US. The truth was that maybe loving each other isn't all that matters. Not when we're hurting others. Not when he really needs help, and I do too. Not when we're in so deep that we might all end up in prison. Some things are bigger than even love can handle.

I promised I'd be back soon and left.

His car was in a student parking lot next to the senior boys' dorms. I'd never paid attention to the exact make and model before, but tonight before I got in, I circled around it once. It was a relatively new BMW. Not exactly inconspicuous for his favorite hobbies but something with a lot of speed. I felt the power in it as I hit the gas the first time and shifted it into gear.

At a stoplight close to the center of Wiltshire, I took the folded-up newspaper out of my purse. The article about the toddler didn't mention an actual address, but based on Mr. Callahan's words about it and the trail we took the night I was with Drew and Warren, I could figure out a general area. Frenchtown, they'd called it. A trailer park. I drove over the bridge and Wiltshire changed over instantly from affluent and clean to poor and dingy. Fires were lit in what looked like a homeless camp.

I slowed to a stop across the street from that first house where Drew and Warren had left me in the car to go inside and work their deals. There was a lot of activity. I could see several silhouettes in the weak window lights. But nobody came outside, and no one stopped and went in, either. I took the car out of park and turned on the street closest to the house, following its backside half a block. The house seemed to go on forever, like over the years, people had haphazardly thrown a new house together behind it, then another behind that one. It was clearly broken up into quite a few apartments, with several mailboxes at each oddly placed entrance. All the houses around it were the same, even if they weren't as big. These were all apartments, not well kept, and I had to wonder what these people paid to live there. Probably some slumlord fleecing them for every penny.

At the next stop sign, I took a minute to get my bearings and look around. I didn't have to look far. One more block and there was a crumbling brick wall with a sign on it that, in its heyday, would have looked nice. Now it was missing a few letters and slightly crooked. It read: FRENCHTOWN CIRCLE. The trailer park.

I drove forward slowly. It didn't take me long to find the house I wanted to see. A little white thing that looked barely big enough for one person, let alone a family. I glanced from my newspaper to it, then back again. It was a match. Like before, I pulled to a stop across the street from it and turned off my lights. There were people inside. I could see someone's head through the front window, the closely shaved head of a man. The TV was on. Some show about cops, of all things. A woman walked through the room and sat by the man, her head on his shoulder.

So these were the parents of the toddler, sitting there like their world wasn't over, like their child wasn't at someone else's house because they couldn't get it together to take care of him themselves. These were the people I was cooking drugs for. The people I was enabling. The people I was making sicker. The parents I'D distracted from their son.

I glanced down the street. It was a flat street, but it was dark and muddy. Farther down the road was a tree line and, beyond that, if I had the map right in my head, the river. If the child hadn't been carried off by some devious stranger or hit by a car before that tree line, he might have gone in there and not been found in time. He might have even made it to the river. He wouldn't have meant to fall in, or maybe he would have wanted to play in the water, not understanding the insidious current beneath the surface.

I looked away from the tree line and wiped tears from my eyes. Back inside the trailer, smoke was rising in small, opaque tufts. The man moved, and the reflection of the TV caught the glass bulb just right. I started shaking from pure rage. I wanted to burst into that house and scream at them. Instead, I put Warren's beautiful car in drive and pulled away, still shaking violently. I shook all the way home.

But it's two in the morning now. I think I'm going to take a Percocet to calm myself down and knock myself out. And I think I'm finally understanding that I'm not mad at the parents of the toddler.

I'm mad at myself.

April 21

I went into the lab last night with one mission only: to convince Warren to stop. Stop it all.

The whole walk there, I felt like I was going to throw up, I was so nervous. Conversations not even half as important as this had ended badly, with him lashing out in anger or shutting me out, and there were about a billion ways talking to him could go wrong. Not the least of which was him thinking I was being disloyal to the Club and what kind of consequences that could have. The collateral was majorly on my mind.

He greeted me with a passionate kiss and I could tell he was really excited about something, and that made my heart sink and my stomach twist into a knot. I could also tell it was Adderall in his system, not Percocet. He told me, proudly, that he'd gotten the new recipe down to an art. He promised it would change our workflow a lot, but for the better.

I let him show me every change he'd made in every step of the process, only vaguely noting how it would change the product and cut down on time and some of our more expensive ingredients. He was so proud. Even a week ago I would have been proud too. Now all I felt was sick. I asked him if we could talk for a minute and watched a parade of emotions cross his face (anger, suspicion, curiosity, resentment) before he said we could.

> Me: I read the other night about a mother
> and father who were so high they hadn't

noticed that their baby was wandering around in the freezing cold for almost an hour.

Warren: Heroin?

Me: Meth. And here, Warren. In Wiltshire.

Warren: Let me guess. East side? Perhaps even Hodgkins Park? Or Frenchtown?

Me: Frenchtown.

Warren, shaking his head: That's terrible. It probably happens more than we know.

Me: But doesn't it bother you?

Warren: Of course. It's sad.

Me: Warren, it's more than sad. And it's our fault.

Warren, with a slight laugh: No, Bailey. It's not our fault. These people . . . they'd sell their souls

for another hit. You know that. They practically
do. My brother would have sold my mother
into a trafficking ring to get more heroin. He
was out of his mind. Addicts are the most
selfish people on the planet, trust me.

Me, before I could stop myself: And what
does that make you?

The light in Warren's eyes went out, then his gaze became
a cold, black stare. Fear shot through me, but I shoved it aside,
more determined than scared. He HAD to see. He HAD to
understand.

Warren squeezed his eyes shut. I watched as he balled up his
fist, raised it, and sent it down with a crack on the lab table. A
glass beaker fell on its side.

Warren: What does it make YOU, Bailey?
We can't help anybody. All we can do is keep
them safe.

Me: You keep saying that, but that's not all we
can do, Warren. We can take ourselves out of
the equation.

Warren: You want to stop making.

Me: I want us to stop being responsible for children being left out in the cold and people being too addicted to care about their lives! And I want you to stop taking pills. I want ME to stop taking pills.

Warren: Have you tried? (I shook my head no. I hadn't tried yet. It was part of my plan, but I couldn't convince myself, every day between second and third periods and every day after school or whenever, that I didn't HAVE to take them. That I didn't need them. Warren snorted at me.) If you tried, you'd know.

Me: I can. I will.

Warren: And how many Percocets do you have left?

Me: I've only taken a few. I'm fine.

Warren: But what did it feel like?

Me: Good. I mean, I got calm. Sleepy. I slept.

Warren: You need the sleep. It does feel good, doesn't it? But you know you can stop.

Me: Yes.

Warren: I know I can too. So what's the harm?

Me: It isn't right. None of this is right. You should feel worse about this. You lost a brother to this, Warren. How do you not feel anything?

Warren pulled me into his arms then, his body pressing heavily against mine. His weight and warmth felt so reassuring because he wanted me close, but also because it felt human. He was human, not like a soulless, unfeeling robot.

Warren: No, Bailey, the problem is I feel too much. Isn't it? I feel too much for my parents. For Mitch. For you. Even Drew

and Katy. I'm not abandoning them. Are
you? Are you going to? Are you going to
abandon me?

Me: No! No. I just want you to come with me.

Warren: No, just don't go. Don't go in the first
place. It will be fine. We'll get through this
year and we can stop everything. Okay? Just
like I promised.

He kissed me before I could give him an answer, and I
kissed him back, letting that be my answer because I couldn't
seem to find my voice. What I wanted to say and couldn't was
that I didn't think we'd get through the year, not this way. And I
didn't think it would all be fine. But I don't know how to stop or
stop him or get out. I don't know how to get off this ride I'm on,
but I certainly don't want to make anything worse. I'm trapped.
All I can do is walk a tightrope right now of getting by and
trying to do the least harm I can, to anyone.

So I let him kiss me until we were both so wrapped up in
each other that everything else faded away.

I have to admit I don't remember much else about last
night. When he took out some Percs to calm himself down, he

offered me some as well, and I took them. Every single one he offered. Not because I wanted it or even needed to, but because I needed to do something with him. To show him I was with him. To feel that connection. I do know that Warren and I held each other for a long time and that he did cry on my shoulder, shaking as he asked me over and over again not to leave him, and I promised I wouldn't. I remember him walking me home and stopping me outside my dorm's gate, where he held my wrists in his hands hard and told me he wouldn't speak a word to Drew or Katy about me wanting out, since I'd promised I'd stay in.

And I remember yanking my hands away and that his voice hadn't sounded reassuring. It sounded like a threat.

April 24

The last thing I needed today was Emily being Scary Emily.

I woke her up because she was clearly going to sleep through class, and she seriously growled at me like some kind of animal. She looked like hell, and honestly, it was the first time I'd really looked at her in a while. Her eyes seemed sunken in, rimmed in purple, almost like bruises, and her face looked gaunt. When she rolled out of bed, fumbling around for the pieces of her uniform, I could see that she'd lost a lot of weight too. Maybe Prescott was taking its toll on everyone this year.

Me: Wow, did the AV club have a party last night or what?

Emily, with a sneer: Did your snobby friends have one? You were home later than me.

Me: I had a lot of work to do. Are you okay?

Emily: I'm fine. God. What time is it?

Me: Ten till. We've got to get to class. And you're welcome, for waking you up.

Emily: Just consider us even. Do we have any water?

I took a bottled water out of the package we kept under our window and tossed it to her.

Emily: Thanks. How's the Prince of Darkness?

Me: He's fine.

I'd be damned if I would ever tell her he was anything but fine. Or that we weren't doing well. Or anything else for that matter. Though sometimes she acts like she's a friend, when it comes to Warren she is 100 percent enemy. Briefly, a flash of last night appeared behind my eyes . . . Warren offering me pills, telling me to stay, me being so out of it that I barely remembered a thing. I looked down at my wrists and noticed bruising, in almost a complete circle around each.

Enemies. Sometimes they're the last person you'd expect. Sometimes they're people you really care about but you find yourself on opposite sides.

> Emily: Glad to hear. I'm sure all his money makes it easy.

> Me: I'm not with him because of the money.

> Emily: Not you. I'm sure it makes it easy for HIM. He can buy himself another toy and not think about it anymore.

> Me: Go talk to him about it. I'm sure that's what you'll do anyway.

I felt no more obligation to her and left our room, headed toward my first class. Warren was outside the building, waiting with coffee, and I swear his whole body somehow softened when we made eye contact. I pulled down my sleeves, not wanting him to see the marks he'd left. He wrapped his arms around me and I felt relief. He thanked me for talking things through with him last night, as if I'd helped him make up his mind, which was almost laughable because it was clear it had already been made up. The addiction decided that for him, and I'm beginning to think it's going to decide everything for him. But not for me. I just need to figure it out.

I was so stressed thinking about it that I took my first Addy of the day before first period even started.

April 25

When Katy walked into the bathroom today and bummed an Addy, she grabbed my hand and spun me around. Even though she looked completely flawless and like she'd had a solid nine hours of sleep, she complimented ME. She told me it was totally showing how much weight I was losing (not that I was fat before, she clarified) and said I looked like a model now.

She went on, joking about how maybe it was me being in love with Warren that was making me glow from within, and I don't know, something about talking with her while she was all bright and happy made me think it would be a good time to bring up the Club.

Me: Hey, can we talk?

Katy, applying more lipstick: Isn't that what
we're doing?

Me: I mean seriously, though. Something's
really bothering me.

Katy: Of course, sweetie. That's why we're
friends, isn't it?

I told Katy as gently but matter-of-factly as I could about
the articles I had seen in the local paper, about how I was
worried we'd be caught but even more worried that we were
contributing to the skyrocketing addiction around Wiltshire.

Katy: Well, what did you expect?

Me: I don't know. I guess I didn't realize
we'd be making so much. Or that we'd be
impacting people like this.

Katy, rolling her eyes: I know Warren talked
to you about this when you joined. Users are

going to use, Bailey. What sets us apart is that
we are safe about it. And smarter, really.

Me: Safe or not, we're still putting it out
there. We're the ones making it available and
turning a profit on it.

Katy: Better us than anyone else.

Me: So you don't care?

Katy: Of course I do.

She cares. At least she said so. And this is Katy, right?
Fabulous Katy, who has been there so much for me this year
and who is fierce and loyal and ambitious but also good. She
IS good. But she's also THE Katy Ashton, fierce and loyal
and ambitious, and perhaps all of those things to a fault,
who might see me as a complete traitor and has the power to
destroy me.

But still. It's Katy. I just can't believe she wouldn't listen to
reason. That she wouldn't see the truth.

Me, taking a shaking breath: Then we should stop.

Katy took a step backward from me, like I'd struck her. Some underclassman girl came in and used the bathroom. Katy and I stood there silently until the girl had finished and vacated the bathroom.

Katy, whispering: You want out?

Me: No. I promised Warren I'd stay in. But . . .
I thought that maybe if you wanted to stop too,
we could all agree to it, so Warren would as well.

Katy, eyes steely: I don't want out. But if you
do, if you want to leave us, and betray us to
anyone, you know what happens.

The collateral. I promised Katy I wouldn't say a word.

Me: I don't want out. Unless we all do. I'm
just . . . worried. And I think we're probably
going to get discovered.

Katy: And you're bailing before that happens.

Me: No. It's not like that.

Katy: Sure it's not. Are you going to rat? (I didn't answer, and Katy grabbed my wrist, right where the bruises were that Warren had left. When I squeaked at the pain, a flash of a smile perked up Katy's mouth, then was gone. She squeezed my wrist harder.) You can't tell a soul, Bailey. You know that.

Me: I'm not. I promise. I don't want to leave. I'm sorry, I'm just scared.

Katy, letting go of my wrist and patting it softly, like an apology: We all get scared, sweetie. It's okay. But sometimes a reminder of the consequences can keep that fear in check. Know what I mean?

I knew exactly what she meant: I needed to shut up, or they were going to make me, and their way of making me would destroy my life. I would go to jail, I would never get into Harvard, I might not be able to even graduate from high school. And the pain I'd put Dad and Bex through . . .

So Warren won't budge and Katy not only doesn't want out,

she's ready to let me take the fall. I don't know who else I can trust. I feel even more trapped than before.

I have a thought, though, and it's either the smartest or the dumbest idea that I've ever had in my life. I have this diary. Maybe it wouldn't count for much to the police, but if they WOULD use the collateral, at least I have my own record of events.

I can't believe I'm thinking like this. Just a few weeks ago I would have done anything for them. Now all I can think about is how to get away and possibly how to make sure they'll go down with me if they frame me.

April 26

I was catching up on homework when there was a knock at the door. Emily and I exchanged a look of confusion, then I got up to answer it. It was Katy. She said there was going to be an emergency meeting and I needed to come with her now. I shut my books and left with her, heart beating a frantic, uneven rhythm in my rib cage.

We walked across campus to the lab without speaking a word. When we got there, the boys were already there, sitting on stools. There were two empty ones in front of them. Katy and I sat on them.

Drew spoke first.

Drew: Bailey, Katy told me about the conversation you had with her recently. About wanting out. It's understandable. I think we've all had moments where we've been scared, and we've thought about leaving the group. But then I brought it up to Warren, and he admitted he'd had nearly the same conversation with you a few days ago.

Me: No. I don't want out. I told Warren that.

Drew: I don't think we need to waste time arguing about whether you do or not. We have two people here who can attest to you saying as much. So let's talk about what happens next.

Me: But there is a reason to argue. I told Warren and Katy that I'd stay until summer. That I'd keep working and I wouldn't tell a soul.

Drew, looking more like a parent running out of patience than a friend: Bailey. You've

expressed interest in leaving to two people
in this group, and you told them that
individually, while also trying to persuade
them to leave with you.

Me: Well, I mean, of course. Warren is my
boyfriend. Katy's my best friend. I trust
them. I wanted to talk about what I was
worried about. And I'm worried about them,
too. And you.

Katy: And what if I wasn't your best friend?
Or Warren wasn't a boyfriend? Would you run
to someone else, someone outside the club, to
get advice?

Me: No. Of course not. I know the rules.

They continued grilling me for what felt like hours, asking
me about Mr. Callahan, how close we are, and how much I'd
told him about any of the Club, its actions, OR its members. I
didn't fare well under the pressure, because some of what they
were insinuating was partially true, at least without context. I
WAS close to Mr. Callahan, we had discussed drugs (generically

speaking) and especially meth, and we'd even discussed Warren. I'm sure the guilt was all over my face, even if I didn't feel what I'd done was wrong.

I ended up reiterating my stance that police are really cracking down and we need to lay low for a while, maybe stop making until we are sure we won't be caught. Maybe even until after summer. They stared at me, all of them with expressions that oscillated between embarrassment and flat-out anger.

Drew: You sound like a coward, Bailey.

Me: It's not cowardly to want to be sure that we don't get into any trouble.

Warren: The only way we get into trouble is if someone talks. Someone like you.

Me: No. I won't talk.

Katy: You say that now, but what happens when there's some pressure on you?

Me: I'll be fine.

> Warren: Bailey. You're not fine. You're about
> ready to crack just because of Prescott's
> classes. Your grades are bad, you've said so
> yourself. You barely sleep. You have a hard
> time keeping up with the lab work. I mean,
> you're barely keeping it together.

He was being extremely unfair. He knew how hard I was trying. He also knew that I knew he was struggling too. That he was so stressed and his emotions so unmanageable that he was self-medicating just to get by.

> Me: What do I do? What do I do to prove to
> you that I'm in, that you can trust me? I mean,
> I gave you collateral. I've promised I won't talk
> and I will keep doing this. What can I do to
> convince you?

Again the three of them exchanged a look.

> Drew, clearing his throat: I don't think that
> we can be convinced, Bailey. You've already
> betrayed us, really, by trying to break us apart.

Me: I swear that wasn't what I was doing. I
just needed to talk things out. Please. What
can I do?

Drew looked to Warren, then away, and I knew something
bad was coming.

Warren: We think perhaps it's best if you take
some time and think about this. Think about
what you really want and what it means to be
part of this group. Alone.

The boys again exchanged a look. Katy didn't even raise her
eyes and kept them glued to her polished nails. And it was then
that I understood.

Me: No. No. Please. We were all supposed to
go together. It was supposed to be our trip,
our reward for all the hard work we've done.
And I was part of that hard work.

Katy: We're not sure we're comfortable with
you being there at the moment.

Me: But . . .

Warren: Our buyers want the new version of
the product. In two weeks. Obviously I won't
be able to help get the batch ready. But if you
decide you really want to stay in, and that
you can handle it, you could prove it to us by
making this batch.

It was so unfair. So cold. I'd worked just as hard as them.
Harder, sometimes. And here I was, ultimately just trying to
protect them, even if they couldn't see it. It felt like a huge
betrayal. They are shutting me out and I know it's just because
they are in denial or in too deep to want to hear what I'm
saying. Now it's clear: I'm totally alone in this.

Me: I don't know why you're doing this.
I don't understand. I was just worried for
you. You're my friends. I didn't want any of
us to get in trouble. I haven't betrayed you
at all. In fact, it's the opposite. I'm trying
to help.

And then . . .

Drew: Your method of "helping" is going to
land us all in prison. If you can't shut up and
get it together, the collateral goes out.

Katy said nothing. Neither did Drew. No one could meet
my eyes, like they couldn't stand to look at me. Voice shaking, I
appealed to the one person in the room who might care enough
to be sympathetic.

Me: Warren? You know I can be trusted,
right?

Warren raised his gaze to mine. His pretty eyes were dull,
filled with disappointment and, I think, disgust. He gave a short
shake of his head.

Warren: I don't think so, Bailey.

They left me in the lab, crying and stunned, with no one to
turn to.

I took a Percocet to help me sleep, but I'm truthfully so
exhausted I probably didn't need it. I'm sitting here writing,
still in shock. If I don't keep my head down and do what they
say, my life will be ruined. I'm so angry and so . . . I don't know.

Is there a word that's worse than devastated? Even Warren wouldn't speak up for me. How could he? After all I've done for him, after all we've been through and the things he's said to me. How could he say he loves me and then just talk like that to them about me? And THEY'RE concerned about betrayal? What do they think this is?

I've got to get out. At this point, maybe all I can do is do the things that will cause the least amount of problems for me: stay here, make the next batch, keep my mouth shut, do as I'm told. Then once it's summer I can be home and beg Dad to let me go back to my old school. Maybe I can disappear and never see any of the Science Club again.

May 4

I've been aimless for days. And utterly alone. They left Sunday, but even before that . . . I just sort of wandered in and out of classes, went to the lab, did what was expected of me. I wish I could say I tried to talk to them, tried again to get them to understand or change their minds about the trip, but I didn't. I can't decide if I'm cowardly or just too tired. Maybe I'm just done caring.

Warren talked to me. He kissed me too but gave up when I was unresponsive. It's weird. It's like I'm not even really angry now. I just feel empty. He told me not to be upset, that when they got back and the new batch was done, everything would be okay again. He told me it was just business and not to take it personally. But how can I not? It WAS personal.

And I can't stop thinking about how Warren didn't defend me. He didn't tell them how hard I'd been working. And he had no defense for not defending me, other than telling me this was for the best. How could it be for the best to spend a week apart when we could have been on a warm beach together?

And . . . HOW COULD HE DO THIS TO ME? To someone he loves? Or maybe . . . maybe that's just it, isn't it? Or he does love me but not nearly as much as he loves himself or his money or pills.

And Katy. She didn't defend me either, and she knew the stress I'd been under. She'd been helping herself to my Addys for weeks, for Pete's sake. But apparently all that meant nothing.

I considered calling Dad and telling him I was going to come home for break, and maybe going home and staying home. That would show them. The more I thought about it, though, the more I realized that wouldn't fix anything. My grades would still be abysmal and I'd have no chance of pulling them up, not to mention I really wouldn't have any friends. I didn't keep in touch with my old friends at all, so I'd be alone there, too.

Added to that, I didn't want to have to tell my dad that I wasn't going on the trip. I have to hang on to what little pride I have left, and besides, he'd ask so many questions. Also, there's no way I want to go home and be a third wheel with him and Isa. That would make everything so, so much worse.

I thought about calling Bex, too. But I didn't want to worry her and I really didn't want her to invite me to New York with her friends out of pity or something. Talk about pathetic, having to hang out with your little sister's friends over break.

So I am alone.

Plus I have to make the batch of new product. And I knew I was going to and that I have to do a perfect job. I've already made it once before and I'm certain I can do it again. I need to show them I'm serious, I'm in this, and I'm not going to let them down, because I need to buy time. I need to figure out how to get out of this without landing myself in jail. And if I'm honest, I need time to wean myself off pills, too. Needing them means needing Warren, and I still need both.

Warren did come to say good-bye, so that's something. He pulled me into his arms and apologized over and over, and told me he hoped I would understand. If not today, then sometime in the future. How the hell will I ever understand what he's done to me? I loved him. I DO love him, even if I know I won't ever mean as much to him as money or a quick high. I've only ever wanted to help him, to make sure he was okay. In exchange he's given me what? Pills? Paranoia? He certainly hasn't given me any reason to believe he wouldn't let me take the fall for everything if he felt like he was in trouble.

And he can talk all he wants and try to make it sound like no big deal, that he's leaving without me, but it's a punishment, I know it is. It's like when my mom and dad used to make me sit in a corner and "think about what I've done." It's not even about the thinking. They want it to sink in just how miserable they could make me. And I know that somewhere on Drew's hard drive is the video he took, the collateral I gave them, and he's just itching to use it, should I step out of line and narc on them.

To top all of this off, report cards came out for third semester. As in chemistry and precalc, naturally. A B- in civics and Spanish. C- in English. C MINUS.

I'm failing English, officially. I have an appointment with my guidance counselor for tomorrow, and I expect that she will tell me I have to retake English over the summer. I mean, she scheduled me during a student break . . . the news can't be good.

English aside, Bs have never been a thing for me before. Never. I feel like I'm failing those, too. The teachers say my work is sloppy, careless, thoughtless. That I'm not thinking critically enough, writing well enough, whatever. I don't know how. I feel fine about my assignments and tests when I turn them in. I feel like I've focused so well during my classes, even when I'm tired or stressed or worried about Warren. The Adderall really helps with that. But maybe it's all an illusion. Maybe the Adderall only makes me feel that way, but that's not the reality. Obviously they don't think my work is up to par.

I'm scared. Harvard doesn't exactly take B-average students. They certainly don't take students who can't write a coherent essay. I don't know what I'm going to do. Prescott was supposed to improve my chances, but I think it's done the opposite. I can't keep up. Even when I try my hardest. And it's not just the schoolwork; I'm obviously failing at everything. I disappointed my friends; I let my business partners down. Even my own boyfriend would rather go on vacation without me.

And ugh, Emily is staying over break too, and she seemed too distracted to even notice that I'm not in the Cayman Islands. Honestly, she's been a wreck. I don't know. Maybe my nerves are so shot they're rubbing off on her. She seems jittery and stressed. She won't stop moving when she's in our room. She's either bouncing her leg while she's reading or tapping her pencil or her fingers on the desk. And even when she's asleep she's restless. I think she tosses and turns all night long, and it keeps me up too, even when I take a Percocet.

And I don't even want to admit how many of those I've taken this week. I know I shouldn't, but I can't convince myself to care when I'm finally, FINALLY falling asleep. Everything seems so peaceful, like none of this stuff matters.

The Science Club is probably on a beautiful white, sandy beach, staring at a gorgeous blue ocean. The kind where you can't even tell when it ends and the sky begins. Probably drinking piña coladas and laughing and not missing me at all. And Warren is probably massaging sunscreen on Katy's shoulders and back, seeing her curvy body in a revealing bikini. She's probably trailing a hand lightly down his chest and speaking in double entendres that make him blush and plant all sorts of ideas in his head.

I sort of hate them right now. I hate everyone. I hate me, too.

May 6

I was right. Kind of. I will have to retake English, maybe. IF I can't keep my grade above a C the last semester. And honestly, since I thought my work was okay and it obviously wasn't, I can't see how I'll keep my grade higher than a C next semester. I don't even understand what I'm doing so wrong. There's a snowball's chance in hell that I'll be able to pull it off, especially if I'm going to keep up the workload in the lab like I promised.

At least it will be summer class. Which is good. That way I'm not held back an entire year. But it also means there's no way I could go to Princeton's summer program, even if I get in.

So, you know, I HAVE to keep this grade up, but I probably can't, so I'm probably not going to Princeton.

My anxiety is out of control. I don't want to keep taking Percocets and end up like Warren, but the Adderall isn't cutting it anymore. I have much bigger problems now, but what can I do? Go to a therapist and tell her I'm stressed out because I'm afraid I'm going to get caught making highly illegal drugs?

I think I need to be honest here: I can't talk about this with anyone, so no one can help me.

I'm completely alone.

May 7

I've spent eight days in a row by myself, save only for Emily, who has tried to be kind, even, but I'm so irritable I can't even deal with her voice. Besides, she's so annoyingly restless I find myself staying in the lab even longer just so it doesn't rub off on me. I sometimes eat some cereal in the dining hall in the morning and maybe get a piece of pizza or some mac and cheese sometime in the afternoon. But other than that, I don't eat. I think I'm losing more weight, but that could just be my imagination.

I do some extra work for English in the hopes that I might be able to salvage my grades (and the entire course of my life, while I'm at it), then I go to the lab.

It's weird keeping it running all by myself while everyone is gone. It's lonely and it's very, very quiet. If the Club truly wanted me to think about what I've done and what it means to be part of their group, well, I've had nothing but time. Mark came by to grab his money, which Drew had left for him in a drawer, and I nearly begged him to stay and keep me company.

But the work isn't hard. The instructions are clear, and Warren is nothing if not precise, so it's no trouble. I've looked at his notes and worked the equations out myself just to see if I could. Everything is sound; Warren truly knows what he's doing. Maybe he can find the cure to help addicts, once he stops making drugs for them and all.

I stay until late, make sure everything is off that should be, and lock up. It's usually midnight or after before I'm back in my dorm room and back in bed. Emily's usually there sleeping restlessly, but once she wasn't, and I couldn't bring myself to care. I'm just grateful we're not fighting and she hasn't said anything about not going with Warren.

Warren and the rest will be back tomorrow. The batch is nearly done. If it passes muster, maybe I can regain the Club's trust so maybe they won't be watching me so closely. After all the thinking I've done this week, I know for sure: There's only one way to keep going. They're not going to just let me out of this. They're too afraid I'll narc. And what else or WHO else do I have at this point? I have nothing. So I'll do what it takes to stay in. It's the only way I can get through this year. Then . . . then I'll be able to get out somehow. I'll vanish. I just need to make it through for right now.

I will just have to keep my head down, keep those blinders on, and not think about what happens after our product leaves our little lab. Or who it affects.

It's better this way. For everyone.

May 8

Warren is back.

He came by, knocking on my bedroom door. When I opened it up, I didn't really know what to do. Part of me wanted to shut the door in his face and shut him out of my life forever. But there was another part of me that just wanted things to be okay. I wanted him to hug me like everything was going to be all right. And . . . I guess old habits die hard. I wanted his approval. I wanted him to let me back in and accept me. I've held him up on that pedestal for so long, and I've felt so low and beneath him . . . and I know he's part of the reason I've felt so low . . . but I was just so tired. So tired and so desperate to have SOMEONE. I'm so tired of not having someone. Mom, Dad, Bex . . . all my old friends and now my new. Something about seeing Warren made me cling to that last bit of hope I had that maybe things could change. That maybe I'm not alone.

In the end, Warren made the first move and pulled me into his arms.

> Warren: God, Bailey. I've missed you so much.
> It's so good to see you. I'm so, SO sorry.

It was probably a lie, but I let myself believe it. Maybe holding on to the fantasy of how things could be would get me through the end of the year. Emily was there and saw the whole exchange. She shot him a particularly grouchy look, which he shrugged off, then asked me if we could go to dinner.

> Me: Are you sure? I mean, are you allowed to?
> Is this okay?

> Warren: Of course! All of this . . . It's not
> about us. You understand that, right? This
> wasn't about you and me. This was about trust.

Trust. Yes. Trust is a funny thing. He thinks I can't be trusted because I talked about wanting to stop the Club. While he's the one who didn't defend me and didn't have my back. And now I need him and the rest of the Club to trust me again so I can get out.

I threw on a sweater and went with him. We got in his car and drove into Wiltshire, saying nothing to each other most of the way there. But he did put his hand on my knee when he wasn't shifting gears. His touch was somehow both reassuring and sad at the same time. He was wearing a short-sleeved shirt, and his skin was a deep golden tan. When he pulled to a stop in front of one of the best restaurants in town, he looked over at me, smiling. Neither of us was in any hurry to go in, though. I noticed Warren wasn't fidgety, nor were his movements sluggish. He was as sober as could be, and I silently thanked my luck that we could talk without any chemicals . . . assisting. Or getting in the way.

He confessed that he made a reservation at the restaurant, thinking I'd probably turn him down. I almost laughed. How could I turn him down? If I broke up with him right now, he and Drew and Katy would probably panic and threaten me with the collateral. Or worse, just hand it over to the police. It was easier to just smile and act like there wasn't any reason for him to think I wouldn't come with him.

I asked him about the beach, and he talked about how high and drunk he was the whole time. He said nothing about how pretty the water was, how the sun felt, or what it was like with the sand between his toes. Instead he told me he'd found a good combination of pills that let him sleep through Katy and Drew fighting, which apparently they did the whole time, and bragged a little about not having any hangovers because of yet another concoction of pills.

Maybe I should have been concerned, but I certainly was not surprised. Besides, that kind of conversation always led to a fight, and I couldn't afford a fight with him now. Head down, blinders on.

We got really quiet, both of us, and I looked at Warren, but he wasn't looking at me. He was staring straight ahead. It was starting to rain a little, and the mournful patter of raindrops on the roof was the only sound for a moment or two. Then Warren spoke.

> Warren: Bailey, I can't tell you how sorry
> I am. I wanted so badly to just have a nice
> week with you, relaxing and fun and sexy.
> I've wanted so much more for us, and for
> you. I wish we were just normal, you know?
> Just normal kids. No Science Club. No
> demanding Prescott classes. No worrying
> about colleges or summer programs that are
> incredibly hard to get into. And no . . . no
> family problems or pills or . . . anything else.
> Just you and me.

319

He wasn't crying, exactly, but he had his eyes so tightly shut that no tears could have fallen, which might have been precisely his goal. It struck me again just how similar Warren and I are, how abandoned we both feel, and my heart broke for him all over again, but I couldn't let myself lean into him or even put a hand on his to comfort him. As bad as I felt for him, as much as I felt he was telling me the actual truth this time, I also couldn't let myself soften toward him when he'd so coldly and easily told the Club that I shouldn't be trusted. I leaned against the car door, away from him, instead, and did my best to tell him what he wanted to hear even if my body language was saying something else entirely.

> Me: We aren't normal, though. And we can't be.
> But we're not alone, are we? We have each other.
>
> Warren: We do? We do. I just . . . I wasn't
> sure. I thought when we left without you, that
> maybe that was it. You'd decide it wasn't worth
> it. That I wasn't worth it. And you wouldn't
> want anything to do with me when I got back.
>
> Me: I was really upset. Really angry. I won't
> lie to you about that. And I still think it was
> unfair.

Warren: It was. I've made mistakes too, but Drew and Katy were never that harsh on me. Hell, Drew and Katy have made mistakes themselves. I tried to tell them they were overreacting, but they wouldn't listen to me.

Me, heart skipping: So . . . it was them?

Warren: Oh, baby. Of course it was. I wanted to just forgive you and let it all go and let you come along with us. They wouldn't let up, though.

Me: But . . . but . . . you didn't defend me.

Warren, taking my hands in his: Baby, I defended you all I could. By the time we talked to you about it, though, I couldn't do anything. They'd already made up their minds. Arguing with them then would have probably just made it worse. But I tried, I really did. I hope you're not angry with me.

Me, honest: No. I'm not angry. I've had a lot of time to think, which is what Katy and

Drew wanted. And I understand why what
I did made everyone freak out. I won't do it
again. I want back in. I want everything to be
our normal again.

Warren: It will be, soon. And if you made this new batch
correctly, you'll prove it to them. So . . . we're good? We're okay?

Me, forcing words and a smile: Of course. I
love you.

Warren: I love you. And I'm so glad to be
back here with you. Honestly, I couldn't stop
thinking about you the whole time I was gone.
Everything would have been so much better
with you there.

Although that was nice to hear, I was thinking about his
explanations. Plausible or not, none of it meant he couldn't
have fought for me more. And he'd left me, thinking that might
possibly mean I'd break up with him. There were alternatives.
He could have stayed with me. But clearly, the Club was still
more important to him than I was.

We went into the restaurant then, and I let him treat me to

lobster. And since it was the last night of break and the dorm parents weren't too inspired to make the rounds religiously, I went back to his room with him since Drew was spending the night at his parents' house. I wish I could explain it. Maybe I should have just gone back to my room alone but . . . it felt good to be wanted. And maybe I just wanted to feel normal for a while.

Maybe I just wanted to feel anything at all.

May 11

It's Friday night and I'm not sure what we did tonight was the best idea.

The Science Club had to let our, um, investors try the new product because of course they were skeptical, and they weren't going to give us a penny without making sure it was good. Drew was going, naturally, with Warren as the extra male muscle, I guess. And Katy insisted on going too, because she's the contact maker and she wanted to make sure her people were satisfied. As for me, well, I couldn't NOT go. I didn't want to be left out of one more thing, to be honest. Plus, I was the one who actually made the new version of the product. I had to see for myself.

We loaded up Drew's car, and a few minutes later we were in Wiltshire's east side, in front of a house I recognized from that initial trip with the boys, and then seeing it when I went to find the trailer park. Drew turned to me and Katy in the back before we got out.

> Drew: Let me and Warren do the talking. I
> know they're yours, Katy, but they're used to
> us now. We deal with them every week. And
> let me do all the negotiating. The money is
> MY thing. If they have any questions about
> the product, though, Bailey and Warren
> should answer. And dumb it down, okay? They
> don't need to know our formula, just that it's
> safe. Capisce?

Warren laughed. He was especially mellow tonight, so if I had to guess, I'd say Percocets. Snorted. Or perhaps something even stronger. I didn't even acknowledge it. I think I'm slowly starting to realize that he'll never stop. It reminded me that I need to talk to him about something for my nerves. I want that kind of mellow, and at this point, it can't hurt. Just one more thing I have to stop.

> Me: Drew, what if they don't like it?

Drew, shrugging: Then we go back to the old formula and keep our rates the same for a while so they forget about it.

Me: Yeah, but . . . what about me?

Katy, glaring: You'd better hope to hell it's good.

Me: I followed Warren's instructions exactly! I'm sure it will be.

Katy: You follow a recipe okay. Instructions, like keeping your mouth shut, seem to be different.

Me: I haven't talked to anyone but you guys since. Well, Emily, because I had to. But I swear, not another word to anyone.

Drew: Yeah. We'll see. We do appreciate you making this batch, though. It was nice not to have to worry about anything for a few days.

Me: So . . . I'm in? We're good?

Warren, now serious: Yes. We're good. (Katy
and Drew looked at him. He looked at me.)
We ARE good. C'mon, guys. She's learned.
And it's my fault if they don't like this batch,
not hers. It was my idea.

Finally, FINALLY, he defended me. I should have been
happy about that, perhaps, but I was just tired. All I could do
was give him a weak smile.

So we went inside the house, Warren carrying a plastic bag
in the pocket of his overcoat. I'm not sure what I expected when
I got inside. Perhaps an old-fashioned mob movie scene . . . guys
polishing guns and cooking marinara while smoking cigars and
talking business. Or maybe something like out of a true crime
show, with high people and drug paraphernalia everywhere.
Neither of those things awaited us inside.

The house wasn't exactly clean; it looked really run-down,
with yellow walls and stained carpet and secondhand furniture,
but there were only three people inside the house that I could
see. All three of them seemed so young and all three of them
were sober from what I could tell. They were also surprisingly
clean-cut and wearing clothes that, though not up to Prescott

standards and trends, were clearly of a style and brand they loved. An expensive brand.

Katy and I hung back, letting the boys do the work. She and I didn't talk. We didn't look at each other. I hadn't seen Katy much this week, probably because she knew exactly how to avoid me, but something told me it wasn't all because she was angry with me, either. Even when I saw her and she didn't realize I was there, she was distracted, angry, and very irritable. I know Warren said she and Drew fought a lot, but I had to wonder if she'd fought with Warren, too. I knew he was her source, and if she'd gone without during their vacation, Warren would have been to blame. And honestly, it felt like something Warren would do . . . deny her, maybe for revenge for not letting me come. Maybe just because he wanted to remind her who was really in charge. But the way Katy was acting . . . so on edge . . . well, I know that feeling acutely now. I feel it every time I don't have an Addy in my system.

The three men didn't introduce themselves but they definitely wanted confirmation that I wasn't a snitch. Katy snorted, and Drew shot her a murderous glare before telling the men that I could absolutely be trusted and, as a matter of fact, I was the "head chef," so to speak, for this particular batch. Then the three guys really got down to business, taking the bag from Warren and proceeding to get high from the crystals I'd created.

It took a few minutes, and the three men exchanged looks between them before one of them said, "This is some really good shit," and the rest echoed that exact phrase.

I breathed out a breath I hadn't realized I'd been holding, and Katy grabbed my hand, anger forgotten, squealing with delight. Warren came over and kissed me and whispered how amazing I was and how we'd done it, we'd done THIS together, and we were perfect together, and he loved me, which made my stomach turn.

Of course. For this he loves me. What would he have done if the product hadn't been perfect? Would they all have turned their backs on me or sold me out?

While this was happening, Drew started negotiations for price on the new product. By the time we left, he'd secured significant raises for all of us, with the promise that our product was going to be even more famous now. On the way home, Katy proposed we celebrate in Drew and Warren's room, so that's where we went. We finished our planning with a bottle of champagne Drew had been "saving for a special occasion." Drew did some quick math and we realized exactly how much more we were going to be making per week, and we toasted. Then Katy brought up that we could also push this product to our newest expansion, and I agreed it was a good idea, even though I still wasn't clear where exactly we'd expanded to. Then Katy and I fell asleep in Drew and Warren's beds, respectively, and had to sneak out at dawn. Honestly, it was nice to feel like she liked me again. Being on Katy Ashton's bad side feels absolutely terrible.

I DO think I can keep doing this until the summer. I think this will work. Warren will be at Princeton, so we can't cook, and I won't be able to get my pills. I can stop taking them then, and then the plan is to fade away. Not come back after summer. They'd have to be okay with that, right? If I didn't come back? What could they do? At the very least, it might even be worth my while to keep working on the product. Maybe I can make it even safer and assuage some of my guilt. And hey, if I fail out of Prescott, at least I'll have a backup career waiting for me. Ha, I'm hilarious.

May 14

I haven't written for a few days. I've just been so busy and I've been trying so hard to get my life back on track, in every department.

First, I've been working a lot on English. I was allowed to work on some extra credit, so I did all of that and maybe I can pull up my grade some. Mr. Callahan has actually put me in touch with one of the professors from Princeton that's in charge of the summer program. He thinks that maybe if I can make a personal connection and show this prof how much I want in and what I'm capable of, he might bend some rules and get me into the program this summer anyway.

Second, Warren has been extra sweet this past week. We haven't fought at all. He's super proud of the way I've made the product lately, so maybe it's that, that the business is going well. I often wonder, though, if he's being so nice because he feels guilty. I even told him about my anxiety, and he promised he'd get me something to help. I don't think I'll take whatever he gets me, but I suppose it's just his way of trying to help. In the meantime, he got me more Percocets. He got me more Adderall, too, and even though I had decided to cut back, it seems to help me focus on schoolwork, which I really need right now. Like Warren, I can just keep on keeping on until summer. I think that once I push through that shaky, irritable feeling, I should be fine after a couple of days. I won't ever have to take it again. I didn't tell him about how many Percocets I took over break, or anytime, really. It's not like I'm lying. I just don't want him thinking I'm a hypocrite for asking him to stop.

Third, Katy has been incredible this week. She really has. She's been so happy about the new product and getting it out to everyone that she's been the same fun Katy she was when we first started hanging out. She even promised a shopping trip this weekend. After all, we'll be making a bit more money this week, if everything goes according to plan. We're thinking Saturday. Clearly, as long as I do what the Club wants and keep my mouth shut, they'll act like they like me.

Last, there haven't been any new developments in newspaper coverage of the drug problem in Wiltshire. I heard some of my classmates talking about it in passing, but they all agreed that heroin is a bigger problem. Around here, they said, it's almost easier to get heroin than meth, and it's not like people die from meth like Warren's brother did from heroin. You're not going to find a meth addict dead with a needle in his arm. So I've been able to let it go, keep my mouth shut, and do my work.

The only thing that hasn't gone well this week is Emily. I walked in the other day and she demanded to know where Warren was, and we got into a huge argument. She was super aggressive, almost hyper or panicked. She reminded me of a hummingbird or something, the way she was pacing the room, back and forth, quick and with sharp movements. It actually reminded me of the way Warren and Drew were when they tried our meth, but I realized there was no way she was on meth of all things. Ridiculous. Emily seems pretty straitlaced, really. Not exactly a Goody Two-shoes, but nowhere near the Science Club. It was probably my own paranoia that made me even think it.

She was driving me so nuts I finally told her Warren was with Drew in their dorm and she left. I think it would have bothered me more if she'd tried to hide that she was going to him, but I knew exactly where she was headed. I texted Warren to warn him, and he told me later that he cut her off right before she tried to get in the dorm and talked her down from this particular episode. I told him it wasn't his responsibility to do that for her, but he said he felt bad for her and felt obligated because before him, she wasn't so bad. He said he felt terrible for being the one to cause her to spiral.

I had to wonder about that, why he would have been the cause. It was one thing for Emily to imply it, and another for Warren himself to say something.

Things almost felt "normal" with the SC this week. I must be doing an okay job of seeming normal myself.

May 18

Oh my God. Just got back from the lab, where Drew handed out our "paychecks." I can't even believe it. Not only are we selling the product for more, while our ingredient costs are down, we are selling more product itself. Word definitely got out that we have something of better quality, which doesn't take as much for a high. It's worrisome; that's going to make it easier for the police to track us down, not to mention maybe even make more addicts. But like everything else right now, I'm shoving those feelings aside so I can finally get out of this.

Warren is going to be here in ten minutes to take me

to dinner at a swanky place in the country. . . . He said it's somewhere his dad used to take his mother for anniversaries. I hope he won't be uncomfortable there because of that family history. Anything that reminds him of his parents usually is upsetting to him. But this seems like a good memory, and I won't lie, I want to try this chocolate dessert he was raving about. I've gained some of my appetite back.

Speaking of, Katy and I are going to breakfast tomorrow morning. (She's thinking IHOP or even a Waffle House. "Slumming it," she says. I just shook my head. Those are normal breakfast places for me and my family. At least they were before Isa.) Then we're off to shop. She reminded me that I need a dress for the formal, not that Warren has asked or I've even thought about it.

If I'm being honest, getting dressed up to go out in public and act like everything is great with me and Warren, or just ME, is the last thing I want to do.

May 18, later!

Okay, just writing to say that Warren has now officially asked me to the formal. He did it tonight at the restaurant. It was like a marriage proposal. He literally got down on one knee and asked, and he had a bracelet for me in a pretty turquoise box. The bracelet was gorgeous. White gold, with his birthstone, a sapphire, in a very delicate filigree link. I put it on, since at that point everyone in the restaurant was watching, but I took it off immediately when I got home. It feels so . . . permanent. And public, maybe? Like this is a symbol to everyone that I'm Warren's. Really, the whole "proposal" felt like it was just for show. At least it was for me, and I have to wonder if it was for him, too. A way to show everyone what an upstanding guy he is.

Katy texted while we were at dinner. It seems the boys had planned it: Drew asked Katy as well.

So tomorrow we'll get our dresses, and I'll smile and laugh with her and act like I'm so, so happy that Warren Clark is taking me to formal, and I'm the luckiest girl alive to be in their group and have all this money.

May 19

Oh God. Oh God oh God oh God.

I don't know what to do. I can't . . . I can't even think. I'm trapped in a nightmare.

I came home from shopping with Katy, and Emily was in her bed, taking a nap. Or I thought she was. But then I realized that she was in a weird position. I turned her over and her lips were blue. HER LIPS WERE BLUE.

I screamed for help down the hallway. I screamed for the dorm mom. Then I called 911. I don't even remember what the person on the phone said to me. I think she got my address and asked if Emily had a pulse. I couldn't find one. Oh my God, I couldn't find a pulse. The woman on the phone made me keep talking to her until the paramedics arrived, and my dorm mom came in and was trying to do CPR for a while, but it wasn't working. Other girls were gathered in the hallway, whispering and scared. I just sat by Emily, my whole body shaking, hoping to feel a pulse.

The paramedics arrived and put her on a stretcher. I couldn't stand, I was shaking so badly. When they laid her down . . . it was like she didn't have any bones. Her arms hung down . . .

Lifeless. She was lifeless.

I think she's dead.

I wanted to go to the hospital with her but everyone told me to stay there. To go back in my room and wait. So that's where I am. I'm all alone, sitting on Emily's bed. I haven't heard from anyone yet. I don't know what caused this and I have no idea if she . . . if she made it or not.

I didn't tell Warren. I didn't want to hear him talk about Emily negatively, not now. And also . . . I can't explain it, but my gut was telling me to keep this from him for now.

I have buried myself in blankets and I'm going to stay here until I stop shaking or until I warm up or until someone comes to talk to me. I don't know what else to do. I'm just so, so cold. . . .

May 19, later

About two hours later someone knocked on my door. It was a woman and a man, both police officers in uniform. They flashed their badges to me and wanted to know if I could answer a few questions for them.

I told them yes, even though at that point I was close to throwing up or passing out from fear. What were POLICE here for? What was going on?

They came in, standing awkwardly in the neutral space between my and Emily's desks. It was the woman cop who talked to me most. They asked for my name and age, and I could barely remember. I asked them if Emily was okay.

> Cop: They're working on her at the hospital
> right now, but that's why we wanted to talk
> to you.
>
> Me: Okay. Sure.
>
> Cop: So can you tell us what happened?

I told them all I could remember, that I'd returned home from shopping with a friend and thought nothing of Emily sleeping until I realized she looked weird. Then I called 911.

Cop: Are you and your roommate close?

Me: Um, not really, I guess. We're only kind of friends. Sometimes we didn't get along too well. She had, um, dated my boyfriend last year so there was a bit of jealousy and tension sometimes.

Cop: Are you aware of any mental health issues such as depression? Anxiety?

Me: Emily is kind of off sometimes. I don't know how to describe it. Like sometimes she gets really angry and upset but other times she's completely happy and fun to be around.

Cop, scribbling on a pad of paper: And how would you describe her mood lately?

Me, shrugging: She seemed better than usual, I guess. I don't know. She's not home much.

Cop: Where is she when she's not here?

Me, feeling suddenly guilty: I'm not sure, honestly. I assumed she was with her friends or the AV club. She was really into movies. IS. Sorry. She IS really into movies.

Cop: How often would you say she's gone, and for how long?

Me, suddenly feeling chilly: I don't know. I'm sorry. I've been so busy myself that I haven't really kept up with her. She seems to be gone a lot in the evenings. She gets back later than me and sleeps later. I sometimes have to wake her up so she doesn't miss class.

Cop: And when you wake her up, how does she seem? Moody and confused? Or lucid and calm?

Me: Very moody. Sometimes like she doesn't know where she is. She's always pretty mean when I get her up. She's a heavy sleeper. She usually just barks at me to get her water and leave her alone.

Cop: How often do you have to wake her?

Me, shrugging: Once or twice a week.

Cop: Do you have any reason to believe that
Emily may have been under the influence of
illegal drugs?

Me, my heart dropping into my stomach:
What? No. Emily was a good student. IS a
good student. I don't think she ever missed
school unless she was sick.

But as I was giving the cop my answer, things started
locking together in my brain like pieces of a jigsaw puzzle. Her
near-instant switch of moods, her restlessness, irritability, odd
hours, lack of a social life here at Prescott . . .

Her always wanting to know where Warren is. How she
seemed to find him out of the blue, usually where they could be
alone. Her exaggerated need to see him. Her angry accusations
that he's basically the devil incarnate.

Just be careful. He'll get you hooked, she'd said.

My whole world shrank down to the realization:

It was Warren. Warren gave her meth. Warren probably got

her started on drugs, just like he gave me the Adderall, then the Percocets. He probably told her how much he cared about her, swore that it was okay, she wouldn't get addicted . . . they would help . . . and maybe, when he broke things off and no longer gave her Adderall for free, maybe she started using meth. And where else would she have gotten that? The ex-boyfriend that was still playing her every emotion and vulnerability like a violin, naturally.

Panic seized me; bile rushed up my esophagus. I tried hard to focus on the policewoman.

Me: You think Emily was on drugs?

Cop: We have reason to believe so, and that's the reason for her medical condition.

Me, thinking of Warren's brother: Like an overdose? Heroin?

The cops looked at each other, then back at me, communicating something silently. The cop who wasn't talking to me walked slowly around my dorm room.

Cop: No. Not heroin.

Quiet Cop: Hey, Gina. Look at this.

The cop named Gina nodded and walked over to where he was, and I could see they were holding a small plastic bag in their hands, which the male cop had pulled from behind Emily's desk. They shook out something from the bag and it landed in Gina's palm. I knew instantly what it was.

I knew instantly because I'd made it.

I flexed every muscle in my body to keep myself from vomiting, and tried to steady my breathing, hoping the cops wouldn't see how panicked I was. This couldn't be happening. Meth didn't hurt people like this. It made them hallucinate, maybe. Made them addicted and they committed crimes, but it didn't make people's lips turn blue.

Cop, to me: Is this yours?

Me: No.

Cop: Do you know what it is?

(I shook my head, afraid to speak in case they could tell I was lying.)

Cop to the other cop: Call the chief. We're
definitely going to need some help from
narcotics. (Turning back to me.) Ma'am, we
need to hold this room for search. You can
either consent to a search of the room or we'll
need to obtain a search warrant. Either way
you'll need to be removed and detained during
its duration.

Me, thinking quickly: Oh, um, you can
search. It's fine. Could I take some books and
my purse? I need to do homework, and I'll
probably get something to eat while I'm out.

The cops looked at each other, then the woman nodded.

Cop: Normally we wouldn't, but if you give
us consent to search now, we can oblige, since
you're cooperating so well. Give us about an
hour? And here's my card. If you can think of
anything that may help us, please call. Anytime.

Me: I will. Thanks. Is Emily okay? Is she
going to make it?

Cop, patting me on the shoulder: She's in a
coma right now. And I don't know. I'm sorry.

I quickly grabbed my purse (with all my money and my pills
tucked safely inside) and a few books, including this diary, then left
as quickly as I could. Outside the building, I headed around the
corner, waiting only until I was out of sight to lean up against the
wall and let myself fall apart. I cried and cried, until the nausea hit,
then I vomited too. I don't know how long I stood there, hidden by
the sophomore girls dorm, crying and vomiting bile. Long enough
that I was truly dehydrated, but I was, remarkably, starting to think
more clearly. Then I headed to the coffee shop, forced myself to
drink some herbal tea, and sat down to write and think.

I don't know what to do, but I do know one thing: I have to
tell the club.

May 20

It's Sunday. Really early in the morning. I can't sleep. Not even
the Percocet helped. The headmaster called. He said there's been
no change in Emily's condition and her parents have arrived.
He told me to please come forward with any information I may
have about Emily. It felt . . . accusatory.

But I've had some time to pull myself together. To think.
And here's what I've decided:

I have to get out of the Science Club. Somehow. I can't wait until school is over anymore. I don't have that much time.

The Club may or may not be responsible for Emily. As the articles in the paper said, meth is really common around here. And I know we have competitors locally. There's a small chance that it wasn't us. Until I talk to Warren, there's no reason to believe definitively that Emily had the meth I'd made.

I won't tell anyone here about the Club, not even Mr. Callahan. I certainly will not tell the police. If I do, the Club will just give the police my collateral, which is a video in which I take the blame for everything and confess to blackmailing the rest of the Club into working for me. I'll go to prison; they'll get off scot-free. If we're going down, we're all going down together. That was our whole philosophy. That's what they tried to teach me.

But . . . I think I need to tell my dad. Or maybe just Isa? She could help me, legally, if it comes to that. And I've heard for a long time about how she's the best. She could help. It's a terrifying thought, but I don't know where else to turn.

I'm going to try to sleep some more. Then I'm going to call my dad. Warren's been texting, but I don't know what to say yet. I need a plan on my own before I can talk to him. I need . . . well, I need someone I can trust helping me right now and I'm afraid Warren would only look out for himself. Apparently the rumors haven't spread too far. Prescott staff must have threatened my dorm mates to remain silent.

I'll have to talk to Warren soon. Very soon. But first . . . I'm calling home.

May 22

I told my father about Emily, and then about Science Club. Everything. About how they approached me, how I was fascinated by them and felt so amazing being part of their group, how I'm in love with Warren, what I do know about the group and their business actions, and what I've purposely avoided knowing, even how much money I've been making. I told him about the collateral, too. At some point, probably when he realized just how deep in trouble I was, he put me on speaker, and I could hear Isa humming as she took in the facts.

I didn't tell them about the Adderall or Percocets. I didn't tell them about my abysmal grades.

I'm completely surprised that my father revealed only a small amount of disappointment and frustration with me, and instead jumped into action alongside Isa, who was in full-blown lawyer mode by the time I finished my story. It makes my heart kind of break all over again, for even doubting that Dad was on my side and for thinking such awful things about Isa.

Isa: Do you think your group has been selling to students at Prescott?

Me: I don't know. . . . We expanded recently, but I don't know where or to whom. I . . . I once saw Warren make a deal with some students, but I'm not sure it was for meth.

Isa: Good. It really is best that you don't know much. Katy was right about that. But you need to distance yourself from them. All of them.

Me, heart sinking: Even Warren?

Isa, sighing loudly: I think maybe especially Warren. But if you care about them, you need to make sure they're not selling to anyone on campus, and you need to try to make them see reason. They've got to stop selling, period.

Me, near tears: I tried. No one wants to drop out. It's like they see it as betrayal.

Isa: You can only try, Bailey. But try, and then get away, you understand? This could really impact your future. And do what you can to remove any evidence that you were in that lab.

Me: So . . . lie? I mean, what about the collateral? Even if I don't tell the police about them, they could use that to frame me.

Isa: I could get around that in court. I think. It's coercion at the very least. But if you have any documentation that would prove otherwise . . . that would be extremely helpful.

Me, remembering my idea about this diary: What about my diary? I've written about everything. Real names. I know it was probably stupid because it implicates me, but . . .

Isa: No. If they do try to blame you for this, that would be a good tool to fight it. But . . .

we have to keep it out of the hands of the police. For right now, we wait and see. If it's meth that put Emily in a coma, they might try to trace it, but with the way things are in Wiltshire, it would be hard to trace back to one source. Emily could say who she got it from, though, and if it's anyone from your group, we'd better pray they take the fall, as they so HONORABLY swore they'd do. But let's not panic. Let's wait and see.

Me: Okay. Thank you, Isa. And Dad. I'm so . . . so sorry.

There's a pause, then only Isa answers.

Isa: I know. We are too, Bailey. I'll . . . I'll tell your father.

Me: Wait. Where is he? I thought he was listening.

Isa: He was. I think he went outside. You know how he gets when he needs to cry. He

can't stand anyone else to see it. We were actually talking last night about how bad we feel about not being there for you this year, like we should have been.

Me, stunned: . . . What?

Isa: Your dad and I. We should have been more supportive. We know you're still grieving for your mother, and with switching to a new school, a difficult school at that . . . we should have called more. Visited. I'm really sorry, Bailey. There's no excuse. Your father is sorry too. More than I can tell you.

Me, trying to make my voice neutral: It's okay. Really. You two are really happy together, and I'm glad for that. I'm glad Dad has you, and you need some newlywed time. I understand.

I told her that, but the truth was I didn't really understand at all. I HAD felt unsupported, unloved, even. I'd wanted so badly for my father to call, to check in, just to talk.

I've been so lost without Mom, and all the changes recently left me even more unmoored, if possible. The Science Club and Warren especially had helped fill the void. Until they hadn't.

My dad got back on the phone and told me he loves me and thanked me for coming to him and Isa about it. They promised to do all they could to help. I was so overwhelmed with gratitude that I sobbed out my good-byes.

But as soon as I hung up the phone, the hope drained out of me. Isa had sounded so worried, like even she might have trouble in court with this. And Emily's bed is still empty and mussed, from how she left it. There is still no word on her. What if she never comes back?

What if what I made is the reason why? How am I ever going to forgive myself?

May 23

Emily is gone. She's . . . dead.

May 23, later

I am . . . I'm going to try to write this down but . . . I just don't know how. I don't know how to say any of this. It doesn't feel real. I keep thinking I'm going to wake up and it's all going to be some horrible dream from stress or the Adderall or . . .

something. I can't even feel the pen in my hands, but I've got to try.

During first period, our headmaster got on the intercom and informed us that Emily had passed away.

Metallic ringing filled my ears. I left class. I went to the restroom and vomited. I nearly went to sleep with my head propped up on the toilet seat, I don't know why. Exhaustion? Emotional overload? Maybe my body was just trying to shut itself down so I wouldn't feel anymore.

When I came out, the headmaster and the school counselor, the one who had informed me I was dangerously close to going to summer school, were waiting. They spoke to me like I was a fragile thing, telling me that they were very sorry and that I could talk to a professional counselor on staff. They told me her parents would come by to get her things. They told me the funeral would be in two days. I think they said other things, but I don't remember. I nearly collapsed. I realized I've barely eaten since brunch with Katy four days ago. They also told me that if I knew anything at all that could help Prescott or the police, to please say something. Then I asked. I asked what had killed her.

Drugs, my headmaster said. He said that, unfortunately, the doctors could tell Emily had been using for a while but that for some reason, the last dose she had was different, and it sent her into cardiac arrest. By the time she got to the hospital, her brain had been cut off from oxygen for too long.

For some reason, the last dose she had was different.

Different because Warren and I had changed the formula. We'd made it stronger. We'd made it, like he said, more effective.

We killed Emily.

May 23, even later

The headmaster and counselor offered to walk me home, but I promised them I would be all right and that I could use the time alone. But I didn't go home. Home was the last place I wanted to go, to see Emily's empty bed and know I was the reason it was empty. And what if her parents came to get her things while I was there? How could I face them? How could I even be in the same room with them? So I went to the lab like a coward. I sat on a stool and looked at Warren's formula and for the first time realized . . . we'd nearly doubled the toxicity of it. Sure, meth was all poison, but what we'd done . . . if Emily had built up a tolerance to our previous recipe, then tried the same amount with this . . .

As I was sitting there, horrified, the rest of the Science Club came in, tiptoeing, almost like they didn't want me to notice. I looked up and caught Katy's eye.

Katy: How are you doing, sweetie?

Me: How do you think?

Drew: We're really sorry for your loss, Bailey.

Me: MY loss? She was OUR loss. Ours. Her friends'. Prescott's. God, her parents' loss.

Warren, almost angrily: Yes. It's sad, but this is what happens when you let addiction get the better of you. Just like my brother.

I noticed that he wasn't anywhere close to me. That he hadn't hugged me or even taken my hand. He felt light-years away.

Me: But it wasn't like your brother, Warren. It wasn't anything like that. Sure, she chose to do drugs. Got addicted. But she had no way of knowing that we'd made something far more toxic than she was used to.

Drew: Wait. What?

Me: Yeah. Emily died because our new formula was too strong. She didn't know to use less.

Katy, shaking her head: No. They can't prove that. They couldn't possibly know that.

Me: I know that. Warren does too. (I threw the notebook with his formulas in it like a frisbee to him. He caught it but didn't look down at the pages.) We need to track down every bit of this that we sold so more people don't die.

Katy: No. No way. That's pretty much admitting that it's us. EXPOSING us.

Me: Maybe we need to be exposed!

Warren: God, Bailey. Don't be stupid. We'll lie low for a while, go back to making the old formula. Maybe stop selling around campus.

Me: That's another thing. No one told me we were selling to Prescott kids. Was that your expanded market?

Katy: You didn't want to know. You never asked. I'm just doing my job. My job is to get buyers.

Me: Something like that, you should have told me.

Katy: I didn't tell you so I could protect you!

Me: And how's that working out? My roommate is dead. They found our meth in my room. What do you think the next step is going to be? They'll trace it. It'll come back to us.

Warren: Oh, Bailey. Don't be stupid. It's not like our fingerprints are on it or something. No one's going to talk.

Me: Yeah? Want to bet your future on that? Have we given all the dealers enough money not to squeal? What about our friend Mark?

Warren, rolling his eyes: Don't be dramatic. It was one incident. Compared to what's going on, police will hardly be bothered.

Me: One incident? Is that how you think of Emily's death? An incident?

Warren, biting: Yes. An incident. An unfortunate accident because she made a stupid mistake. She always made stupid mistakes. Completely led by emotions.

Me: Yes, and you knew that about her, but you kept selling to her anyway, didn't you? Was it just the money or did you like having that power over her? Did you love how she'd come running to you, needing a hit, begging for one? You love to see people at their lowest, don't you? Makes you feel better about yourself.

Warren, emotionless: Going to blame me for your own stupid mistakes too, Bailey? You think I don't do the math? I know exactly how many Adderall you need to get through the day without the shakes.

For one terrible moment, I thought I was actually going to kill him. The urge to run at him and wrap my fingers around his neck and squeeze . . . for what he'd done to me, for what he'd done to Emily, and probably Katy and Drew and who knows who else. . . . That urge was so strong I actually pictured myself doing it like some sort of fever dream. But I didn't. I had too much blood on my hands already. I took a deep breath.

> Me: Our whole goal, in your words, was
> to make our product safe for addicts who
> were going to do this anyway. (I pointed to
> the notebook in his hands.) You made it
> lethal.

> Warren, unfazed: WE. WE made it lethal.
> You saw the formula and you said nothing.
> Either you understood and you didn't care,
> or you are terrible at chemistry. I've seen
> your work, Bailey. I know you're not. And
> now your roommate is dead. But it's no
> more my fault than it is yours. We didn't
> force her to use.

> Me: . . . But you did get her into it, didn't you?
> You gave her that first hit.

Warren's eyes widened, like he was stunned that I figured that out, but somehow I'd known it since I found Emily with her lips blue. I'd known Warren was involved.

> Me: You dated her. Don't you feel anything at
> all? Sadness? Guilt? Don't any of you?

Drew and Katy looked away from me, but Warren kept his eyes on mine. Steely.

> Me: And what about me? Did you ever
> actually love me? Or was I just another Emily
> to you? And we were just so easy to control,
> weren't we? Once you got us hooked on pills,
> we needed you. Desperately. We couldn't leave
> you. Couldn't give you up.

He didn't answer. Honestly, his silence was answer enough. I picked up a glass beaker off the nearest table and threw it on the floor. Everyone flinched as it shattered, and the sound pushed me onward, like it was the auditory equivalent of my own heartbreak. I reached for another beaker, and another. I don't know how many I smashed before Drew grabbed me from behind, holding me in a violent hug so I couldn't use my arms. I screamed in frustration and kicked until I landed one, my heel meeting his shin with a painful-sounding thump. He let me go and I turned around, facing all of them, tears blinding me to their horrifyingly blank faces.

> Me: This has to stop. We have to turn ourselves in. Emily's parents deserve to know why their daughter is dead.

> Katy: You know what happens if you talk, Bailey.

> Me: Maybe you should consider what happens if you don't.

I ran out of the lab. No one tried to follow me, either to try to convince me to stay in the group or to shut me up. If it was the first, they didn't want me; the latter, they think I'm too cowardly to actually turn myself in. Or maybe it's both.

But I'm not too cowardly. I'm done with them and their lying. I'm done with Warren, too. If it weren't for him I wouldn't have lost sight of the important things. I would have noticed Emily's decline. I would have noticed my own. But then he would just say it was my own choices that did this, wouldn't he? He had nothing to do with it. I was the one who took the Adderall when he offered, knowing I was too tired to get all my work done. I was the one who joined the Club, even though they all knew I had no other friends. I was the one who didn't know enough, even after they all swore it was best for me not to know. I was the one who took the Percocets when he offered, knowing that I was depressed about my mother.

Mom. God, I miss my mom. And I've missed my dad so much, and now I won't see him for a long time. I know what will happen now. I'll call up the cop, the nice lady one. I'll tell her everything. And if the Science Club tries to use that collateral against me, it's okay. Because I'm going to give that cop this.

My diary. Maybe it won't count for anything. Maybe I'll still take the fall. But if they corroborate the events in it, find some evidence that I haven't lied in these pages, maybe . . . just maybe, it will clear my name.

So that's what I'm going to do. I'm going to call that cop.

I'm in my room now. Emily's room. I wish I'd been a better friend to her. I wish I'd listened to her warnings. I wish I'd just listened to her. Maybe then I would have understood that the girl who seemed so bitter and jealous sometimes was a product of Warren Clark.

I am probably going to prison. I will never do the Princeton program, never go to Harvard. I may never graduate from high school.

I guess Warren is right, though, even if he is partly to blame as well. This is all because of what I did, choices I made. My heart hurts so bad, almost as bad as when Mom died. I've done so much the last couple of years, hoping to make her proud if she can see me from Heaven, if Heaven exists. Now I know that if she's looking down at me, she must be so disappointed.

I need to calm down. I can't think when I'm hurting this bad. I'll calm down, then I'll call the cop. Maybe a Percocet won't hurt. How could it hurt now? Soon enough I won't be able to take them anyway.

I took one. It looked so small in my hand. Such a tiny thing to help me face such a huge problem. Emily is gone. Forever. It's my fault. And these pills are so damned small. They can't change that. But another can't hurt. I know I've built up a tolerance. That's what addicts do, and I'm an addict, aren't I? That's why I get shaky without pills. That's why I've lost all this weight. Just a few more. Just to stop from feeling so much. Then I'll call the cop. She seemed so nice. Maybe it won't be so bad. Something about her smile kind of reminded me of Mom.

It's not that many. They're so small. I'll just finish the bottle and it will all be okay.

Wiltshire Gazette

May 25

Just days after Prescott Academy was left reeling from the drug-related death of one of their students, the academy is again facing the loss of another promising young life.

A seventeen-year-old girl, a junior at the academy, was found dead in her dorm room yesterday after a brief search by campus security when the young woman failed to attend classes that day. She was the roommate of the other teen who died unexpectedly this week. Though the first death remains a mystery—crystal meth was found in her system but has yet to be directly tied to her heart failure, according to the county coroner—the newest death was likely caused by drugs. According to the police report, the seventeen-year-old girl was found holding a handful of Percocets that were not prescribed.

Headmaster William Stevens issued a formal statement calling on all students to come forward with information about drugs and drug use on campus and asking that space and privacy be granted to the grieving students at this time.

Headmaster Stevens also went on record earlier today to say that there has never been a drug problem at the prestigious boarding school before, but that this year, in particular, the community of Wiltshire and the surrounding areas have been hit hard. The headmaster stated that he expects the students of Prescott to rise above the temptations of peer pressure and believes that the school provides plenty of support and care for the student body. He added that counselors and therapists will be on hand for the next week so that students can work through their grief.

A Prescott student who wished to remain anonymous said that the headmaster's view of the drug use at Prescott is naive at best and willfully ignorant at worst. He said the pressure the school places on students to excel in every subject and task often leads the students there to turn to chemical stimulants keep their heads above water academically.

Though there are no leads as of yet as to how the drugs are finding their way onto school grounds, Detective Gina Eisley of the Wiltshire Police Department believes several pieces of evidence found at the scene could lead to answers the shaken school community so desperately needs. In a small press conference this morning on the stairs of city hall, Detective Eisley revealed that one item, a leather-bound book believed to be the journal of the most recently deceased junior girl, was being analyzed by the narcotics department for any information it could provide.

The Wiltshire Police Department urges anyone with information on the deaths of the two Prescott students to call their tip hotline at 555-6384.

July 4

~~Dear Diary,~~

That's ridiculous. Who writes "Dear Diary" in a diary? I mean, who writes in a diary at all? Shouldn't I be blogging?

This is lame.

July 5

Okay, so this isn't going to be a diary. It's a journal. I guess that's the same thing, but "journal" sounds less like I'm riding a tricycle or something.

Yesterday was my birthday. I turned 16.

It's so weird sharing a birthday with your country. Always fireworks: never for you. Mom always plans an actual birthday dinner—usually the Saturday night after July 4th so that I can have a day where we celebrate just for me. It's fun, kinda like having two birthdays in the same week.

We're not big July 4th celebrators . . . celebrators? Celebrants? People. Whatever—we're not big on July 4th. Usually in the afternoon we have friends from school over and walk down to the beach to play volleyball. There are lots of nets at the beach just down the hill, then we haul ourselves back up the canyon to our house for a cookout in the evening. My brother, Cam, invites his friends from the varsity soccer team. Mom gets my favorite cake (the one with the berries in it).

After we gorge on grilled meat and birthday cake, we all crowd
onto the balcony outside my parents' bedroom and watch the
fireworks down the coast. You can see the display at the pier
really well, and the ones in the cities just up the coast shoot off
too. Last year Cam (nobody calls him Cameron except Mom)
climbed onto the roof from the front porch so he could get
a better view, but Mom freaked and said, CAMERON! Get.
Down. This. Instant. Mom's big on safety.

I got a lot of cool presents yesterday. Mom got me the
swimsuit I tried on at the mall last week. It's a really cute two-
piece with boy shorts, and this fun, twisty top. Dad's present
to me was that he's taking me to get my license this week. I've
been practicing with him in the parking lot near his office at
the college. He gave me a coupon for one "Full Day with Dad."
On the back it says, "Good for one driving test at the DMV,
followed by a celebratory meal at the restaurant of holder's
choosing, and a $100 shopping spree/gift card to store of
choice."

He made it himself out of red construction paper and drew
this funny little stick figure on the front. It's supposed to be him.
He draws curly hair on the sides of the round head so the little
man is bald on top like he is. The coupon is sort of cheesy, but so
is my dad. I think it's funny. And cute.

Cam got me this journal. We've been going to this yoga

class together, and the teacher is this woman named Marty with bright eyes who talks about her birds a lot. She told us to get a journal and spend a few minutes each day writing down our thoughts and feelings.

I just looked back at everything I've written, and it's mainly thoughts. Not very many feelings. I'm not sure how I feel right now. I mean, I guess I feel fine? Happy?

No, just fine. I feel fine.

I also feel like people who have birds are sort of weird.

July 6

It's funny that Cam bought me this journal. It's one of those things I would never have bought for myself but secretly wanted. I don't know how he knows that stuff. I guess that's what older brothers are supposed to do: read your mind. I mean, who actually goes out and tries the stuff that their yoga teacher says to do outside of class?

Cam got way into yoga last summer when he had a crush on this exchange student from England named Briony—like Brian with a y. (Really? Who names their kid that?) Anyway, she wouldn't give Cam the time of day, so when he found out that she went to this yoga class, he started going to the same one. He bought a mat and this little bag to carry it in and just happened to show up in her class like, Oh my God! Wow!

What a coincidence. Briony never went out with him. I didn't even know she'd gone back to London until I was teasing him about how he should be glad Briony didn't do something like synchronized swimming. He was like, Briony moved back to London right after school got out.

I asked him why he was still going to yoga, and he said he really liked it. And he said I should come.

I'm not sure why I did, really. I guess I was just bored last summer. But now we go to yoga together. It's this really great studio a block off the Promenade, and they run it on donations. You just pay what you can or what you think the class is worth. I didn't think I'd like it at first. It was hard, and I got sweaty and slipped on my mat and couldn't do any of the poses. But I sorta like spending time with Cam.

Who am I writing that to? It's not like anyone is reading this but me. This is exactly how it feels when Grams asks me to pray over dinner. I feel like I'm saying all this stuff that is bouncing back at me off the ceiling and landing in the spinach salad.

Cam probably didn't have to read my mind about wanting a journal at all. He's really smart. His early acceptance letter to this great college up north came last week. He's going to be a biochem major, which just makes me want to lie down on the floor and curl up in a ball. He's a brainiac. And on top of it he's nice and enthusiastic—which has a tendency to be dangerous.

Last semester Mom was always telling me to ask Cam for help with my geometry homework. I did, but instead of telling me what to do, Cam always talks and talks and talks. It's like he knows so much about stuff and likes math so much that he has to say it all instead of just the answer.

I stopped asking questions. It sort of annoyed me. Just did it myself, and didn't really understand it. I got a C in geometry. You'd have thought I'd flown a plane into a building. (That's bad to say, I guess. I mean, I know people died and everything, but it was a really long time ago.)

Dad came unglued. He's the chairman of the music department at the college where he works. He made me sign up for tutoring this summer with a student that his friend in the math department recommended. Our session starts in a few minutes. I was relieved when Nathan showed up the first time. I was afraid I'd get stuck with some weird math girl.

Nathan is a freshman. He's from Nebraska and has brown hair that's cut short. He works out a lot, and he wears these polo shirts with sleeves that are tight right around his biceps. I just stare at his arms a lot instead of listening when he's trying to help me find the answer.

I wish somebody would just tell me the answer.

Nathan's here. Gotta go.

Later . . .

OMG.

I TOTALLY JUST INVITED NATHAN TO MY
BIRTHDAY DINNER.

OMG OMG OMG OMG

And

He

Said

YES!

This is totally crazy. I can't believe I actually said the words
out loud. I didn't mean to. We were just sitting at the dining room
table and he was talking about the hypotenuse of a right angle,
and while he was looking at the protractor he was using to draw
lines, I was staring at the lines of his jaw and noticed that they
were almost a right angle, and the hypotenuse of the right angle
of his jaw was this line in his cheek with a dimple in the middle
that he gets when he smiles, and then I heard myself saying,
You should come to my birthday dinner on Saturday, and then
I realized that Mom was looking RIGHT AT ME like my hair
was on fire, and I realized that I'd just invited an 18-year-old over
for dinner in FRONT OF MY MOTHER. OMG. I just wanted
to CRAWL UNDER THE TABLE.

But he stopped with his pencil stuck into the protractor and looked up, and then glanced over at Mom like he was looking to see if she'd heard, and she smiled at him, sort of weakly. I guess he took that to mean that it was okay with her 'cause he looked me right in the eye and said, Sure. That'd be fun. Now look at this triangle.

I tried to look at the triangle for the rest of the half hour, but I have no idea what he was saying. When he left, I walked him to the door, and Mom said, Nathan, come by around 7:30. He said, Sure thing, and you can call me Nate. He waved at me before he got in his pickup truck and said, See you this weekend. Then, he drove away. Just like that.

I went running back up to my bedroom and buried my head in my pillow and did one of those silent screams where you just breathe out really hard, but with no sound; it's sort of a soft roar, but the excitement on the inside of me made it feel like my head would explode.

I could hear my heart pounding in my ears, and I took a couple of deep breaths and then I remembered what Marty said in yoga this morning about trying to meditate and how to focus on the breath, so I sat down on the floor and crossed my legs like Marty does in front of class, and I closed my eyes and took really deep breaths and tried not to think about Nate. I could do it for about 5 breaths at a time, but then I'd see that line with the dimple in it behind my eyelids, and then the rest of his right-angle jaw would appear and I'd see a triangle fill in the space on his face.

I mean, it's really no big deal. My dad is two years older than my mom. Nate's only 18, and I'm 16, and it's not like he would be robbing the cradle or anything.

I think I really like him.

OMG I CAN'T BELIEVE THAT NATE IS COMING TO DINNER ON SATURDAY.

July 8

I was just standing in my mirror trying on a couple of different options for tonight. I passed my driver's test and got my license yesterday (YAY! OMG. Finally!), then Dad and I went shopping on the Promenade. I'm a really good bargain shopper. Cam worked at the Gap last summer and taught me to never EVER pay full-price for anything 'cause they just mark it down every two weeks. Primary, secondary, clearance. Primary, secondary, clearance. Every week on Tuesday night the markdowns would come through from the home office, and we'd all run around with those price-tag guns the next morning, marking down tops that some poor dope had paid $20 more for 12 hours ago. So, anyway, I got a lot of great stuff. Even Dad was surprised with how many items I got for $100. Well, then I splurged a little and added $40 from my savings to get these supercute sandals that I'd been wanting.

Anyway, I have all this stuff to try on, and I felt myself doing that thing I do where I put on, like, 12 different outfits and stand there and pick every single one of them apart, and I end up standing in front of the mirror in my underwear with this pile of really cute clothes with the tags still on them lying on the floor. I had just put on the second skirt I bought and could tell I was about to find something wrong with it, and then I just stopped, looked at myself, and thought: Don't be that girl.

I just don't want to be that chick who is always staring at herself in the mirror whining about how she looks and having a meltdown in the fitting room. I mean, I'm not a model or anything, but I think I look okay. I have already showered and straightened my hair. It's not frizzy or even curly really—just has some waves, and when you live this close to the waves it can get wavy. (God. Stupid joke.) Whatever, I stepped away from the mirror and saw my journal sitting on my desk, and I thought I'd write about it. I mean, this is a feeling. I'm not sure what kinds of feelings I'm supposed to be writing about in here, but maybe this is what crazy Marty the bird lady was talking about.

I'm SO EXCITED about Nate coming over and I want to look really hot, but the excitement also feels like nervousness, like I'm going to barf or something. Mom is downstairs putting a marinade on some shrimp that she's going to have Dad grill, and the smell when I walked through the kitchen made me feel like I was going to hurl up my toenails—and I LOVE shrimp.

I know I look good in this skirt. Dad told me it looked "far out" when I came out of the dressing room to check it out in the mirror. He said this in his I'm-being-a-little-too-loud-so-the-other-people-present-will-hear-me-and-think-I'm-hilarious-when-really-I'm-just-torturing-my-daughter voice. I told him to please be quiet and offer his opinions only regarding possible escape routes in the case of a fire, or a random stampede of wild bison. In all other matters, I respectfully asked him to please refrain from speaking to me until we had reached the cash wrap.

I looked in the mirror again just now. This skirt totally works.

Weird how excited and scared feel like the same thing.

July 8—11:30 p.m.

I shoulda known.

I shoulda known when he walked up the front steps with flowers and handed them to Mom.

But he brought me a card with a joke about having pi on my birthday instead of cake (guh-rooooan) and it had a $25 gift card for iTunes in it. Which was cool and so sweet of him, but he just signed his name. Shoulda known when he didn't write anything personal. Just "Happy B-Day! Nate."

But he was really funny and sweet at dinner. He sat across from me and told us all this hilarious story about when he was growing up in Nebraska and he and his brother raised sheep for the county fair. (Yes. Apparently people still raise animals and take them to fairs where they win ribbons and titles and scholarships. Thank you, CHARLOTTE'S WEB.)

One morning he and his brother went out to scoop food out of these big 25-pound sacks of feed for the sheep, and there was a mouse in one of the bags that ran up his little brother's jacket sleeve. He was telling us about how he thought his brother had been possessed by a demon because he kept screaming and shaking his arms and beating at his chest and running around in a circle while the mouse wriggled around inside his shirt. We were all crying, we were laughing so hard, and Cam almost inhaled a bite of shrimp, which sent him on a coughing fit that made the rest of us laugh even harder.

He jumped up and helped me clear the table when Mom asked who wanted dessert. When Mom told him he didn't need to do that, he smiled at me and said, Oh yes, ma'am, I do. My mama'd fly in from Grand Island and smack me if I didn't.

When we were in the kitchen, I started rinsing plates and he loaded them into the dishwasher like he lived here. We were laughing and joking around and no one mentioned geometry.

He was so easy to talk to, easy to be near. I didn't feel nervous even once. I couldn't help but wonder what it would feel like if we were married and this was our house and we were loading the dishwasher together. That's probably stupid, but it made me feel hopeful inside, like maybe something like that was possible.

When Nate bent over to put the final plate in the dishwasher, a necklace fell out of his shirt. It had a tiny key on it, and I was about to ask him where he got it, but Mom came into the kitchen to get some coffee mugs and the French press. Nate tucked the necklace back into his polo before I could ask him about it, but I shoulda known.

There's a long porch on the back of our house that looks over the bottom of the canyon out to the water. We ate dessert out there. Dad lit the candles in the big lanterns on the table outside. Cam sat next to Nate and they talked soccer. The flicker made their skin glow like they were on the beach at sunset. Nate looked all sun-kissed and happy. I felt a foot nudge mine just for a second under the table and my heart started racing. I was glad that it was just the candles outside in the dark 'cause I started to blush like crazy. I thought maybe Nate had touched my foot, and I kept sliding mine a little bit closer toward him under the table, but his foot never touched mine again.

It was almost 10 when he pulled out his phone and checked it, then said, Whoa. I gotta go.

I felt really bummed all of a sudden, and then silly. What was I hoping? That he'd stay and walk me down to the beach? He stood up and shook my dad's hand, then gave Cam one of those weird hugs that guys give each other where they grab hands like they're gonna shake and then lean in and hug with their arms caught in between them. He kissed my mom on the cheek and told her what a good cook she was.

Then he looked right at me and said, Will you walk me to my truck?

I got so many butterflies in my stomach, I thought they might start flying out of my ears. I said SURE, and realized that nobody had really heard him ask that because Mom was pouring more wine and Dad was pouring more coffee and Cam was texting somebody. So I slipped into the house and out the front door.

He'd parked on the street, and when he got to the door of his pickup, he leaned against it and looked up at the sky and said, Huh.

I said, What?

He told me that in Nebraska at this time of night you could see lots of stars. I followed his gaze up to the sky, but I knew there wouldn't be any stars. Out here, the sky just glows this weird purply color even on the darkest night here. It's the light pollution bouncing off of the marine layer, I said. It's what happens at night when 8 million people get jammed up against the ocean. I turned around and stood next to him with my back up against the truck.

He said it was funny how you always hear about all the stars in Los Angeles, but at night in Nebraska, it's like the sky is covered with diamonds. Then he looked over at me, and I don't know what happened, but I just knew that I had to feel his lips on mine. So I leaned in and kissed him.

Nate jumped like I'd shot him with a taser. He said, WHOA, what are you doing? OMG! I was SO EMBARRASSED I couldn't even LOOK at him. It was like we were having this PERFECT night, and then BLAM-O: I broke the spell. I was blushing and stammering and then I felt the tears come to my eyes, and I didn't wait. I just sprinted back across the street toward the house. I was not going to let him see me cry.

As my foot hit the curb on the other side of the street, he said WAIT!

There was something in the way he said it that made me turn around. And then he shook his head and smacked his forehead, and he walked over to me, and just looked at me. He pushed my hair over my shoulder and said, No. I'm sorry.

He told me that I had come along two years too late. And that I was beautiful. And that he has a girlfriend.